The Crash

Kate Furnivall is the author of thirteen novels, including *Child of the Ruins, The Russian Concubine* and *The Liberation*. Her books have been translated into more than twenty languages and have been on the Sunday Times and New York Times bestseller lists. Kate lives in Devon.

The Crash

Kate Furnivall

HODDER &
STOUGHTON

First published in Great Britain in 2024 by Hodder & Stoughton Limited
An Hachette UK company

1

Copyright © Kate Furnivall 2024

A CIP catalogue record for this title is available from the British Library

Hardback ISBN 978 1 399 71362 7
Trade Paperback ISBN 978 1 399 71364 1
ebook ISBN 978 1 399 71363 4

Typeset in Fournier MT Std by Manipal Technologies Limited

Printed and bound in Great Britain by Clays Ltd, Elcograf S.p.A.

Hodder & Stoughton policy is to use papers that are natural, renewable
and recyclable products and made from wood grown in sustainable forests.
The logging and manufacturing processes are expected to conform
to the environmental regulations of the country of origin.

Hodder & Stoughton Limited
Carmelite House
50 Victoria Embankment
London EC4Y 0DZ

www.hodder.co.uk

For April and for Carole
Two strong women
With all my love for you and for the city of Paris

CHAPTER ONE

◆ ◆ ◆

DECEMBER 1933
PARIS

GILLES

The steam train's whistle sounded like a woman's scream. A desperate cry for help that no one heeded as it echoed through the night across the flat frosty fields of northern France. It set nerves on edge as the massive engine panted its way eastward.

Rail tracks tell lies. They seduce us. Their gleaming silver pathways and metal fishplates pretend that life can go in straight lines from Point A to Point B. They make believe that life is orderly and disciplined. All lies. We know that. Yet there is comfort to be found in sitting at a gently shuddering glass window and swallowing the lie.

Gilles Malroux was happy to avail himself of that comfort right now. He stared through the train's window at the blackness thundering along outside and saw only himself thrown back at him. A stern shadowy face of a man in his thirties, skin taut across sharp cheekbones and a moustache straggly enough to hide the scar on his upper lip. Large chestnut-brown eyes, eyes that saw danger. He was tired of those eyes and looked away. He licked his lips and they tasted of soot.

Today was 23rd December. A Saturday. Two days before Christmas.

'I don't like this fog,' the pinstriped stranger seated next to him said to no one in particular in the carriage. 'It gives me the heebie-jeebies.'

'I'm the same,' volunteered the woman opposite. 'But I'm off to visit my son for Christmas and nothing on God's earth is going to prevent it. Not even this damn fog.'

She was middle-aged, fluffy hair with a wisp of burgundy velvet for a hat and an enamel hatpin in the shape of a bird of some sort, a single tight curl of hair in the centre of her forehead. A calm, worthy kind of person. She smiled with sympathy at the stranger next to Gilles. Nice smile, he thought.

A name was thrumming in his head with each turn of the two-metre-wide wheels under him and it wouldn't stop. Dr Antoine Laval was the name in question, churning through the forefront of his brain. Laval, Laval, Laval, the wheels kept it turning. Dr Laval was travelling in the seat at the other end of the carriage, hiding behind today's copy of *Le Figaro*, a man who liked to hide, Gilles sensed. A man who could be startled by his own shadow. He was wearing spectacles, a tan coat with a vicuña collar and a brown homburg and was the possessor of an enormous black furled umbrella that he'd used to lever himself up the high step off the platform on to the train. Gilles had watched him.

The station had been in a state of chaos. Elegantly extended two years earlier, the Gare de l'Est was one of the six large railway station termini in Paris, located in the 19th *arrondissement* and facing the boulevard de Strasbourg. It was the main jumping-off point for all trains heading east and it seemed as if the whole of Paris wanted to scramble out of the city and cram itself on trains in festive mood to visit family and friends for the holiday. The platforms and concourse were heaving with hurrying travellers, harried porters, overstuffed suitcases and wailing infants. Two dogs had launched into a violent fight near the ticket office. Dr Laval had whacked the larger of the animals with his furled umbrella to break its hold on the small terrier's throat, though he seemed to be unknown to either owner. Maybe he just liked terriers. Or underdogs.

Numerous extra trains and carriages had been laid on for the holi-day season, creating frantic fuss and confusion, and over everything at the station hung the delicious aroma of hot freshly roasted chestnuts, drifting on the icy air. Gilles had a weakness for roasted chestnuts, the highpoint of Christmas as far as he was concerned, but he didn't stop for them today. It was too risky.

He took his seat at the window.

Once they left the stop-start suburbs of Paris, the fog reached out with its heavy grey fist and grasped the train more firmly. It dulled the sound of the vibration of the metal wheels and swallowed the blackened steam that was belching from the stack. The train was the evening express scheduled to travel the 500 kilometres from Paris to Strasbourg.

Gilles had done his homework. He believed in being thorough. The train was hauled by locomotive 241.017 with a 4–8–2 wheel arrange-ment. It was a *Mountain* engine and one of the largest locomotives on the French railway system. Powerful. Unstoppable. Like a runaway avalanche. You wouldn't want such a monster thundering into you. The engine driver was *tractionaire* Daubigny and his fireman was someone called Charpentier. Not that Gilles needed these details, but you could never be too thorough, in his opinion.

Attention to detail had saved Gilles's life more than once and as the train cut through the enveloping wall of fog at an unrelenting 150 kph, he experienced a ripple of unease. He glanced along the line of his fellow passengers on both sides of the carriage. There were eight of them alto-gether, bundled up in their winter coats, their cases and colourful gifts stowed above in the luggage nets. Gilles's gaze lingered for no more than a second on the suitcase above Dr Laval's head. It was new-looking, a mahogany-brown one with a hefty black leather strap keeping it nice and snug, but hinting that it contained something that might be worth looking at. The other passengers seemed to be feeling festive, but he wondered about the secretive Dr Laval still lying low behind his *Figaro*.

Do you feel safe, Dr Laval? Or are you terrified out of your mind?

Gilles, who made a habit of studying such things, was well aware that this railway company, *Compagnie de Chemin de Fer de L'Est*, employed an Advanced Warning System that was plagued by safety deficiencies which other railways – such as in Britain where the Hudd system was employed – had overcome. But Gilles believed in doing his job efficiently and cleanly. So here he was two days before Christmas, which he had hoped to spend roasting chestnuts with his sister, seated now behind a metal missile that weighed in excess of 200 tonnes, hurtling itself towards Strasbourg through a blackness that he could neither see nor touch.

In the slick sheen of the reflection of the window he studied the passenger at the other end of the carriage. I can see you, Dr Laval. I can touch you. I can kill you.

Lights flashed, sharp stabs in the darkness, brief pinpoints glimmering through the fog. In the village that had to listen every night to the thundering wheels of the Strasbourg Express as it roared down the track and vibrated the neat rows of graves in the cemetery, old men glanced at their pocket-watches to check that the train was running on time.

Gilles Malroux continued to stare out of the window, focused on the tantalising reflection of the mahogany suitcase above Dr Laval's head. It interested him. Judging by the deep dip it created in the netting of the luggage rack, its contents were weighty. Exactly what Gilles wanted to see. He dragged his gaze away from it and the corners of his mouth gave a brief twitch, his version of a smile.

No one had mentioned the suitcase to him. Not surprising. They didn't trust him, but then he didn't trust them either. Trust was an expensive commodity; it could get you killed. And he always made a point of not getting himself killed. He felt his breathing soften in anticipation. The smart suitcase would be an unexpected bonus when the job was completed and it would make a special festive *cadeau* for his sister on Christmas Day. Yes, a surprise gift, and he almost laughed out loud because he could picture it all tied up with scarlet ribbons that would make Camille's green eyes pop wide open with astonishment. When she saw what it contained, she'd let rip with one of her screeches of delight. That's presuming he was right about Dr Laval, of course.

He could be wrong.

He flicked that thought aside and glanced at the newspaper that his man was holding up as tight as a shield in front of his face. What, he wondered, would it take for Dr Laval to lower his shield? The arrival of the ticket collector? A call of nature? A fracas of some sort in the carriage? Gilles could easily start one of those, a sudden argument with the pinstripe seated next to him or a flare-up of temper with the young woman whose infant had jolted awake, tired and fractious. But no, there was no point.

He was not wrong.

He knew his allotted mark, every detail of him, from his father's name and occupation right down to the three moles on the left side of Laval's face and the careful eyes that had such a clever but distracted look to them. As if the man paid too little heed to life around him and too much to the life inside his head. A dangerous oversight. Gilles believed that was the trouble with thinkers, they thought themselves into dead ends. It had been child's play for Gilles to trace Dr Laval to his apartment in the Vaugirard district, a cosy respectable residential area of Paris in the 15th *arrondissement*, and then to track him today to the Gare de l'Est. Him and his smart new suitcase.

Gilles was wearing gloves, beautiful soft black leather ones that left no fingerprint on anything he touched, and he kept his face turned towards the unrelenting blackness outside. No one would remember him, if questioned. A man in a black hat pulled low, seated beside the window. A dark woollen scarf. Nothing more. A blur. No mention of the scar on his lip or the single white streak in his hair, both hidden from view and hidden from memory.

But one thing was causing Gilles concern. Where did Dr Laval plan to leave the train? At Châlons? Or at Nancy? Or did he intend to continue all the way to Strasbourg? Gilles's instinct told him Strasbourg. The man was leaving Paris in a hurry and Strasbourg sat right on the border, so it would be an easy hop and a step across into Germany or, better still, south to Switzerland.

A finger tapped his knee. 'Don't I know you?'

Gilles stiffened. He turned. The man directly across from him, the one whose knees almost touched his own, was leaning forward, grey eyes keenly interested, his mouth hanging loose as if he'd downed a few too many glasses of something before boarding the train.

Gilles gave him a blank stare. 'No.'

'Come now, Monsieur, I think you'll find we've met before. I have an excellent memory for faces and yours rings a bell.'

'We've never met.'

'I travel all over Europe – I'm in textiles, by the way – so I meet a lot of faces and I am good at remembering them.' He laughed. 'Faces, I mean. As well as textiles.'

'You are mistaken.'

Gilles shut down the conversation by turning back to his window and the milky darkness. He felt another tap on his knee, but he didn't turn this time. The man was getting on his nerves.

'Do you recall a bar in Pigalle called Merci?' the man asked in a low voice.

'No.'

'I wondered if you were still in the market for . . .'

'Monsieur, we have never met before. I have no idea what you are talking about.'

But in reality he knew. Knew exactly. He knew where the sleazy bar was squeezed into a nook behind Paris's Opéra and knew exactly the man's game and merchandise. Gilles had done business with him, briefly, over a wine-soaked table. Textiles, my arse. Inside the ostrich-skin attaché case that the man clutched so tightly on his lap lay row upon row of tiny samples of illegal rum, run at night into Saint-Malo by boat from French Martinique. The man was right. He did have a bloody good memory for faces. It had been more than two years ago and their meeting had been only a matter of minutes. In Gilles's line of work, faces could be the death of you, so he fixed every single one of them into his brain's face-library that he could flick through at will. This man's face, smug and shiny, had until now been obscured under a soft grey fedora pulled down over his eyes while he slept off the booze.

Gilles felt a ripple of annoyance. Of unease. The skin on his palms prickled. He was not a superstitious person, he chose not to believe in crazy signs and portents the way his mother had done, but sometimes the grip of childhood is hard to throw off. It had stuck with him deep down on the inside, so he found it impossible not to see this unexpected crossing of paths as a bad sign. An ill omen. A *foreshadowing*, as *she* used to call it.

Imbécile!

He was being absurd. What the hell was he thinking?

He leaned forward and tapped the man on the kneecap. He felt the urge to tap it with a sledgehammer. In a flat voice he stated, 'I do not know you.'

The man jerked back, startled by the sudden warning in Gilles's chestnut eyes. The bald passenger seated next to him uttered a snort of irritation at the unwanted disturbance, but Gilles didn't shift his gaze from the rum smuggler.

'You do not know me,' he said softly.

The man nodded in instant agreement. 'I don't know—'

Before he could finish, a violent screech of brakes hurtled through the carriage, metal shrieking on metal, eardrum-splitting in its intensity. A noise like thunder rumbled under their feet and sparks danced like Christmas lights outside in the darkness.

There's only one reason a train hits the brakes this hard.

Gilles knew what was coming and was the first to react. He slid off his seat to the floor, pushing aside the rum man's polished feet and curling into a ball, clamping his arms around his own legs to protect them from impact. You can't run if your shins are shattered. His heart was drumming, his ears conscious of the rising cries of panic around him. A parcel fell from above on to his shoulder. A pair of gloves flew off a lap and landed on his head.

Somewhere in the carriage the infant screamed as the sudden shuddering of the carriage tore the child from its mother's arms. Gilles reached out, seized the child from the floor and tucked it inside the protective ball of his body.

Twenty seconds. That was all it took.

Overhead the lights spat and sparked, struggled to regain power and then blacked out completely. The train shook wildly, rattling and rocking as it fought to slow, bucking on the rails. Heavy luggage plunged down from overhead racks. Bodies shot forward in the darkness. Heads cracked against heads. Cries of pain and shock sent bolts of fear leaping from seat to seat.

'What's happening?' a voice panicked.

'The train can't stop!'

'*Mon Dieu*, have mercy.'

'My baby! Where's my baby?'

'Help me!'

Someone flicked a lighter into life, clutched at Gilles's arm. It was the pinstripe next to him. A young man wide-eyed with fear, face whiter than chalk except for a scarlet gash on his forehead.

'We're going to die, aren't we?' The young man's lips were bloodless in the flickering light. 'Pray! Pray with me, I beg you. *Notre Père, qui es aux cieux, Que ton nom soit sanctifié . . .*'

Other voices took up the Lord's prayer, fighting against the thunderous noise of the train, and Gilles was acutely aware that every pulsing second could be his last.

'Get down,' he shouted. 'Cover your head.'

The young man dropped to the floor, arms wrapped over his head, but before the lighter went dead, Gilles cast a glance up at the dim outline of Dr Laval's suitcase. Still there. In the rack. Too heavy to fall out of the net. Its owner was sitting bolt upright, eyes closed, his lips murmuring something inaudible.

So there'd be no festive gift in scarlet ribbons for his sister now. Gilles felt a shiver tight under his ribs, a cruel pause halfway between life and death as grief rolled over him.

'Happy Christmas, Camille,' he whispered.

That was the moment when the Paris–Strasbourg Express slammed into the rear wagons of the stationary Paris–Nancy train at 110 kilometres per hour, at a point between Pomponne and Lagny-sur-Marne, twenty kilometres east of Paris.

It was carnage.

CHAPTER TWO

◆ ◆ ◆

CAMILLE

Twenty kilometres away, Paris gave no thought to hurtling express trains. The city was too preoccupied with Christmas. The greeting of '*Joyeux Noël*' sounded on shoppers' lips as they bustled through the brightly lit boulevards. The scents of cinnamon and sweet chestnut drifted from pavement stalls and in the festive shops on Haussmann the tills rang out as eagerly as the church bells from the ornate tower of the Église de la Sainte-Trinité. There was a sense of urgency and excitement in the city streets, an unaccustomed togetherness, as long as you ignored the beggars huddled on the corner of Saint-Lazare station.

As the daylight drained away, darkness crept across the river. It spread a web of ice that whitened the beards of the stone gargoyles on pont Neuf, while in alleyways it clung to cobblestones to catch out unwary drinkers. Saturday was always a rowdy evening in Paris's bars and restaurants, today more than ever.

Deep in the shadowy streets of Montparnasse district over on the Left Bank of the city, I sat quietly in my rented room up on the fourth floor on rue Didot, doing my best to ignore the city. I shut my ears to the drunken revellers falling over the battered wicker chairs of La Cave à Rosa, the bar that spilled on to the narrow pavement opposite my building with its scrawny Christmas tree and lights that flashed throughout much of the night. I was engaged in polishing my work shoes. I believe implicitly that sloppy shoes betray a sloppy mind. Shoes underpin our daily lives. At their best, at their very best, I am convinced they can even turn us into someone we're not.

I had applied several coats of black Saphir shoe paste on the silk-smooth leather and was polishing round and round in small circles with a strip of muslin wound across my fingers. Every now and again I spat on it, making a sharp *pfft* noise in the small silent room. The water content acted as a lubricant on the polish, so that I could work it with the brush more deeply into the underlying wax to create a mirror-like coating. The painstaking process gave me pleasure. The rhythm. The murmur. The fact that I made no mistakes.

Mistakes.

My hand froze. For a moment I felt my heart twist out of shape. Today I had made mistakes.

With an effort I laid my shoe-brush down on the newspaper that was spread out meticulously on the surface of the small table and picked up a yellow buffing cloth. It was soft and clean. I nodded with approval at the neat black shoe into which my hand was curled, forming a bridge of support under its polished hide. Happy feet are the basis of a happy day, I reminded myself.

I badly needed a happy day.

A light knock sounded on the door, more of a scratch than a knock. I lifted my head and threw down my pencil.

'Not now, Barnaby,' I called. 'I'm busy.'

A grunt came from outside on the landing.

I was still seated at the small table that doubled as my desk, but now the newspaper had gone and in its place a pile of books towered in front of me. Ploughing through them and using a freshly sharpened Conté pencil, I was making detailed notes on a pad. My notes were neat. Elegant even. Not the impatient scrawl of a few years back that shot off in all directions like the tails of feral cats. No, that had been no better than sloppy shoes. That was banished. This hand had been fastidiously cultivated during night after night of laborious practice and – along with my gleaming shoes – it had got me where I wanted to be.

'You have a fine script, Mlle Malroux,' Mme Beaufort, the department supervisor, had said with an approving lift of an eyebrow as she scrutinised my letter of application which lay flat on the desk in front of her. The office was panelled in oak. Smart and dignified, like its occupant. 'Let us see if your typing skills are equally desirable.'

They were.

'And your employment references?' Mme Beaufort pressed.

She was a woman of around fifty with busy eyes and restless hands. Her great mass of hair was held tightly with pins, immaculate, dark but on the turn now, shimmering with silvery threads that she made no effort to disguise by soaking them in black tea the way my mother had done. It was swept up into a stylish chignon that emphasised the narrowness of her face. Her clothes were of quiet good taste and she wore no rings on her fingers despite her Madame title.

'Voilà,' I said as, with a steady stare, I handed over the excellent forgeries.

The scratch on the door came again.

The building was densely occupied because it was dirt cheap. The first three floors had been split up into a number of small apartments scarcely worthy of the name and the upper two floors were let out as numerous individual rooms all crammed on top of each other. The higher you went, the cheaper they became because the roof leaked and the shutters were hanging by a thread. Mine was on the fourth floor along with five others, served by a severely liver-stained bathroom and clanking pipework at the end of the landing.

Barnaby Riverton lived right next to the bathroom. He was young, English, and possessed an Englishman's airs and graces, and he wore very old but very beautiful brogue shoes that I coveted. Despite the quality of his footwear, he was yet another penniless painter over here in Paris. As half of Montparnasse was inhabited by equally penniless artists these days, he fitted right in.

'Please, Barnaby, go away.'

The sound of a body sliding slowly down the wooden panels of the door brought me to my feet at once.

'Barnaby, what are you . . . ?'

I pulled open the door. My friend and neighbour was slumped on the floor, propped against the wall, his handsome face trying its best to grin up at me.

'I'm sorry, old thing,' he whispered and sank his head on his knees. He was covered in blood, as if someone had tipped a pot of Cadmium Red all over him.

I felt a jolt of pain. 'Not again, Barnaby,' I murmured softly and stretched out a hand to raise him to his feet, the way you would a clumsy child.

It was his left wrist again. But not an artery this time. I drew him into my room, kicked the door shut from prying eyes, and gently laid him on my bed, ignoring the mess he made of my bedcover. I fetched a bowl of cold water from the bathroom on the landing, tore a clean pillowcase into strips, kissed his feverish forehead, and set to work.

CHAPTER THREE

♦ ♦ ♦

GILLES

The safest place to be seated on a train that is involved in a front-end or rear-end collision is in the middle coaches. But in a side-impact accident, such as at a level crossing, it's the middle coaches that are most likely to derail. Worth considering. In the end you pay your money and take your choice, but Gilles's choice of carriage was dictated by the choice of Dr Laval, who was a cautious man. True to form, he'd chosen the centre carriage.

That carriage right now was leaping off the rails with its wheels spinning in the air wildly out of control. Gilles was aware of that brief crucial moment of lift, a letting-go of the bonds of earth. His mind fought against it and he cursed his luck.

The darkness exploded into a million jagged fragments. Metal buckled, twisting and shrieking and drilling staves into flesh and bone. Carriages smashed, limbs broke, lungs were crushed. Pieces of flying glass the size of dinner plates slashed through arteries. Screams of panic and pain roared through the trains as the great monster *Mountain* engine ploughed a path through the hapless rear wooden carriages of the stationary Nancy train ahead.

Gilles found he couldn't move. Blackness drenched his mind and he wanted to float down into it. It was the cry of the child that persuaded his eyes to open. Red streaks ripped across his vision. Pain. Where? He forced his brain to function until slowly, slowly, one cog at a time, it started to turn. His left leg. One shoulder. And something wrong with his jaw. Liquid was slithering down his face. Blood? His own? Someone else's? The child's?

He tried to move but couldn't. Darkness robbed him of vision. Fear crept up his throat and he thrust it back down but his heart rate soared. He could feel limbs jammed on top of him; they belonged to bodies that didn't respond when he touched them. He was trapped.

Keep calm. Think straight.

Get your bearings.

Why was he pinned here? It took his mind a moment to work it out. Of course, the carriage had rolled on to its side and he was protected within the footwell between the two rows of seats, but it meant the door to exit the carriage was now up above him. He couldn't see anything in the darkness but he could hear activity. Screams that sounded from hell. Shouts. The groaning of metal. Hands were reaching in from outside, hauling someone out who was sobbing with pain, but Gilles was still blocked inside his cave by the dead weight of a body directly on top of him. The child was wailing. He could hear a woman's voice screaming, 'My baby! Where's my baby? In the name of Christ, I can hear her crying . . .'

Acrid smoke. The crackle of flames.

'The child is with me,' Gilles shouted.

In truth he had no idea whether or not the child was injured, but it was kicking like a harpy against his ribs, so couldn't be too bad. He wished it would stop that infernal noise. He jammed his feet against the footboard, pushed with his uninjured shoulder against the dead weight and felt it shift, not much, but enough to allow him to reach into his pocket for his torch. He flicked it on. Its pinpoint beam picked out a tan-coloured back above him. He felt a thud of recognition. Dr Laval.

He started to shout. 'Help me! I have a child down here.'

Oddly the child instantly stopped yelling in his ear and instead wrapped its small arms around Gilles's neck, so tight he could barely breathe. Its cheek was jammed against his own. Hands and voices reached down to him, pushing Dr Laval's deadweight legs aside, and he passed the child up through the small gap into eager arms. He set about extricating himself, twisting and turning until he squeezed himself from under the body in the tan overcoat.

'Fire!' someone outside screamed as a warning.

His heart slammed into his ribs. His mind's eye could see flames leaping from the engine's red-hot coals, driven by the wind from carriage to carriage. How many carriages back from it were they? Five? Six? He could smell smoke. He quickly flicked the pencil beam of his torch over the limp figure that had been the dead weight on top of him. Yes, it was definitely the tan coat of Dr Laval but . . .

Putain de merde!

Where the doctor's head should have been, there lay a large brown mass. It took Gilles a heartbeat to recognise it. The suitcase, the brown one with the black strap. It must have been dislodged in that final death-spasm of the carriage and been catapulted down on to its owner's head, crushing his skull and hurling him on top of Gilles.

He yanked the case free. Christ, it was weighty. Even in the dark he could make out that Dr Laval's head was twisted at a viciously unnatural angle. Hair matted with blood. Gilles experienced a wave of nausea. Not for the man's death, no, not that, it had saved him the job. But for the way the suitcase had come at the man. As if it knew how to protect itself.

Should he leave it? Walk away. Abandon what it contained. Let it feed on the hapless Dr Laval and be avenged.

Gilles knew this was one of those pin-sharp points that can alter your life, he felt it in his bones, deep in the soft spongy marrow that creates the blood cells of survival. He pictured the wide grin on his sister's face on Christmas Day if he presented her with the brown suitcase, and without hesitation he seized the handle and hauled it and himself up out of the battered carriage.

Gilles breathed in great gulps of air. Once out in the open the night's darkness seeped inside his head and he couldn't seem to see straight. It wasn't just the fog. Figures blurred at the edges. He kept stumbling. He tripped over bodies and fell on metal doors that had burst off their hinges. Broken glass cracked and crunched underfoot and flakes of hot ash spiralled down from the black sky in a kind of acrid snow that made his nostrils sting.

It was like a battlefield. Not that Giles had ever seen a battle, he'd been too young for the war, but there were bodies everywhere, lurching out of the darkness, scrambling and shouting, falling to their knees on the frozen ground with tears and screams or sobbing prayers of thanks. Curses rang out. Blood slithered down faces. Hands grasped at him but he shook them off, only dimly aware they were trying to help him.

He wanted no help.

Up ahead, by the light of the flames that were clawing up into the night sky, he could see the Nancy train crushed into matchsticks and knew that no one, absolutely no one, in those rear carriages stood a cat's chance in hell. Poor bastards. All around the stricken trains stretched flat fields, but right now they didn't look like the usual dull wintry fields of northern France because they had been swallowed by the persistent fog and its milky surface was reflecting the flames. Flaring golden. Like an army of shields advancing on the survivors.

Gilles wove an unsteady path, dragging the suitcase along with him.

'Help me . . . please?'

The voice was so soft Gilles almost missed it in the onslaught of noise. It came from behind him. He turned, almost fell, switched on his torch and saw a man on his back on the ground who looked as if the train had run over him. He was oddly flattened, ribs crushed and his face a mask of blood, yet he had found the breath from somewhere to ask for help. Gilles dropped to his knees.

'Help is coming, Monsieur. It will be here soon. Hold on.'

The man gripped his hand as if Gilles's *Hold on* had been an invitation. So here he knelt in darkness, his knees in wet earth and breath as white as the fog. With a suitcase and a man's hand. Shouts and cries raining down on his head and a ball of anger locked inside his gut.

How had he got in this mess?

Everything has a meaning, his mother used to say. Everything is a lesson. He looked down at the strong blistered hand clutching his and gently squeezed it.

'Hold on,' he said again.

A horrible grunting noise, more animal than human, came from the man and then he fell abruptly silent. His fingers grew slack. Gilles had seen other dead men but felt an unexpected sense of loss for this stranger and kept hold of his hand, unwilling to let him go, though he didn't know why.

The bell of an ambulance erupted into the cold night air, and when Gilles looked up he saw the headlights of a police car carving a luminous path across one of the black fields. Instantly he was on his feet. He was a wanted man and needed to get away quickly. He felt under the man's blood-soaked overcoat to an inner pocket from which he extracted a wallet. He replaced it with his own, then staggered off into the darkness.

Gilles set off across the field but couldn't walk straight because one leg refused to do his bidding. The fog clung to him, fumbled at his cheeks, and the damp slid silently up inside his nostrils. His hat was gone. He could feel the fog gathering in his brain too, the fog and the darkness and something else. He wasn't sure what the something else was but he could feel it moving in there. Something liquid, shifting around within his head so that his balance was off. He stumbled again and again on the uneven ground, mud sucking him in. It took all his concentration to keep both feet going in the same direction.

'Monsieur!'

The voice came at him out of the night, an urgent shout. He gripped the suitcase handle tight with one hand but he didn't slow.

'Monsieur!' Again.

The beam of a heavy-duty torch pinned him in its spotlight, blinding him.

'Monsieur!' A third time. A different voice. Closer.

He stood his ground and faced them. 'What do you want?' His voice sounded odd.

'We heard the crash and raced over from the village to offer what assistance we can.'

The man speaking looked to Gilles like a farmworker, clad in dungarees over his broad butter-fed belly and thick boots caked in cow shit. But the other one. Oh Christ! He wore a heavy black cape over a long flowing black soutane. A priest. A priest who would want to save his godforsaken soul.

'They need you over there,' Gilles said. 'It's bad.' Again there was something wrong with his voice. Gripping the suitcase, he tried to step around them but his balance was all off.

The farmworker seized his wrist in a grip of iron, took the suitcase from him and wrapped an arm around Gilles, holding him on his feet.

'Your name?' the priest asked.

Gilles shook his head. Trapped. Too weak to fight off these determined helpers.

'Address?'

Another headshake from Gilles. 'I can walk home. Go help the wounded, Father.'

The farmworker gave a snort of laughter. 'Wounded? *Mon ami*, you are covered in blood and that great gash on your forehead badly needs stitches.'

Gilles's eyes started to close. They shut the two men out.

'There are others who need you far more than—'

'Don't worry, we'll soon have you home. Here, let's take a look at this now.'

The priest's long, thoughtful face was smiling gently and in his hand lay the wallet that Gilles had stolen from the dead man. He was studying the identity card. How the bloody hell did that happen? Gilles had a feeling he'd missed a moment in time. That worried him.

'Ah, here we are. Christophe Lagarde. You're from the village of Fragonne. *Bon!* Look now, that's not far away. I suggest we drive you home, M. Lagarde, and then we come back to aid other poor souls in need of Our Lord's care. All right with you, Pascale?'

Another slip of time. A missed moment. Gilles blinked and when he opened his eyes he was bouncing along in an ancient farm truck that belched toxic exhaust up through the floor.

'What happened up there?' the worker questioned. 'On the train.'

Gilles thought he'd replied, but the worker asked the question again, so he couldn't be sure. He couldn't be sure of anything right now except the suitcase at his feet, and a powerful desire to sleep.

When he opened his eyes next time, he was standing in front of a door, a good strong one with oak panels and a large brass door-knocker in the shape of a lion's head.

'*Voilà*, Madame,' the priest said in his softly spoken voice. 'He's all yours, your husband, Christophe Lagarde. He will need to be taken to hospital.'

There was more. But Gilles's ears were pounding and he heard nothing, except the voice of the woman in a navy wool dressing gown who stood on the threshold of the door, staring at him. He'd never seen her before in his life. Her dark hair was pinned up in neat sausage curls and she had the look of a lawyer. Someone serious. Someone in control.

'Christophe,' she said in a voice that was pleasantly soothing. 'What is it this time?' Her large grey eyes flicked over him, over the suitcase and back to his wounded head. '*Viens*,' she murmured. With a touch of her hand in his, she drew him inside, accepted the luggage from his rescuers and shut the door on them with a brisk, '*Merci.*'

She moved close to Gilles, so close he could smell the brandy on her breath, took his damaged face in her warm hands and kissed his mouth.

CHAPTER FOUR

◆ ◆ ◆

CAMILLE

It was a brisk energetic morning. The wind had stripped away the fog and was chasing cigarette butts and a child's bonnet up the street as I looked out of the window across the grey zinc roofs of Montparnasse. I sipped my bitter Turkish coffee, wrestled the night's knots out of my long unruly hair and contemplated with a sigh of pleasure the two full days off work that lay ahead of me.

I slipped my favourite emerald dress over my head in readiness for my brother's arrival, and added a thick woollen cardigan for warmth, a bright cherry-red one to look Christmassy. What shocks me is that when I think back now, I wonder that I had no sense of what had happened the previous night. Surely. Something so huge. So destructive. I should have had some faint awareness, some pulling on my heart, some inkling. But I was too preoccupied with keeping Barnaby Riverford in one piece to give my brother any thought that night.

My mother always used to get a tingling at the base of her throat and a coppery taste in her mouth when something big was coming. That's what she claimed. A *sign*, she'd call it. Was it true? I have no idea. But the night that Big Luc kicked the door down and beat the hell out of her, she had crammed Gilles and me inside her wardrobe beforehand and told us not to come out till daybreak. So maybe.

My day – this terrible winter Sunday that would shatter my carefully ordered world – moved forward calmly while I hummed Christmas carols as I checked on Barnaby. He was still fast asleep and snoring in his own room. His golden hair smelled of turpentine as I tucked him up. It was Christmas Eve and I was excited at the prospect of seeing my brother Gilles later.

That was my first mistake.

Expectation is one of the joys of life for me. I love anticipating what will come next, seeking what awaits when I open the curtains at dawn, always certain the day will bring something that will lift my heart if I look hard enough. Is it expectation or is it hope? Hope is needy and spineless. I call it expectation because I have a firm belief in the importance of creating your own future, carving it out of the shapeless rock of life with your own bare hands.

When I told Barnaby this once, he laughed and said, 'Blessed is the man who expects nothing, for he shall never be disappointed.'

'What? You miserable little toad. How can you believe such a thing?'

'Oh, it's not me, *chérie*. It was said by a very eminent English poet.'

Somebody-or-other Pope, apparently. But it was years ago. Barnaby knew a lot of things like that. Sometimes, when he'd fallen out with one of his boyfriends, he'd wander into my room late at night when I was bleary-eyed from studying all evening and he'd read me to sleep. Stories of little Cosette or the Three Musketeers or the dashing Edmund Dantès. When he saw that I didn't own a single work of fiction he almost had a heart attack, poor lamb, so now I had a whole bookcase full of them and I'd read every one.

I climbed on a chair and pinned a bough of holly above my door, getting myself thoroughly prickled in the process, but when I stood back I was pleased at the festive sight of the scarlet berries. I'd chopped it off a tree up in the cemetery. Fleetingly I wondered if stealing from a cemetery brings bad luck, a quick reprimand by the spirits of the dead. I laughed at the thought and turned away. My room possessed the tiniest of fireplaces which I had filled with scraps of holly branch and pine cones for the ritual roasting of chestnuts that Gilles was so ridiculously fond of.

My second mistake was thinking that Mme Beaufort wouldn't notice the folder missing from her office filing cabinet.

A light urgent tap on my door. I opened it and it was Anne-Marie Tamarelle, my friend and neighbour from further down the hall. She breezed into my room, leaving the door half open.

Anne-Marie was twenty-two, dainty as a Christmas fairy and petite in every area except her bosom which was so fulsome it looked as if it was about to topple her over. She possessed a cloud of ash-blond curls and a Clara Bow mouth that the johns took one look at and started imagining the many purposes they could put it to.

'There's someone downstairs to see you,' she announced.

The way she voiced the word *someone* didn't bode well.

'Who?'

'Watch what you say to him.' She murmured the warning under her breath.

'Who is he?'

Before she could reply, the door was pushed open behind her and a tall man in a dark-blue uniform strode in, immediately sucking the air from the room. A policeman. My pulse thumped in my ears and I immediately thought of that folder I'd removed from the office.

'This is Officer Aubert,' Anne-Marie informed me.

I overlooked the fact that he had barged into my room. A polite smile flitted across my face and vanished.

'You are Mlle Camille Malroux?' he checked.

I hate the *flics*. They smell bad. Everything about them. They always take pleasure in harassing the working girls of Montparnasse and demanding kickbacks, either in money or in kind. I knew for a fact that my mother used to pay a hefty fistful of francs each month to keep them at bay.

'I am.'

'*Bonjour*,' he said, but his gaze was on the room instead of on me, as though assessing it for anything of value to pocket.

He frowned. Officer Aubert was young, with an earnest manner and an intelligent expression; he didn't look corrupt. But what does corrupt look like?

'What's the problem?' I asked.

'Do you have a brother called Gilles Malroux?'

I nodded. Nervous.

'When did you last see him?'

'About two weeks ago.'

'Do you have a photograph of him I could take a look at?'

Zut! Did he think I was that simple-minded?

If the police were after my brother, I was not going to hand him to them on a plate, so I shook my head with regret. 'I'm sorry but I lost all my photographs in a house fire a few years back.'

He and Anne-Marie gave me a blank stare. Neither of them believed me.

'Why are you inquiring after Gilles?' I asked. I kept it polite.

'Sit down, please, Mlle Malroux,' Aubert said. He drew a deep breath, as though preparing himself for something unpleasant.

I sat on the bed.

'Mlle Malroux, have you heard about the train collision that occurred outside Paris last night?'

I clamped my teeth tight together to prevent any sound creeping out. I stared at him and nodded.

'I'm sorry to have to inform you that your brother, Gilles Malroux, was travelling on the Strasbourg train.'

Anne-Marie fluttered across the room in a swirl of purple taffeta and stood in silence beside my bed, one small hand gripping my shoulder.

'But the good news is,' the policeman continued, 'that he survived the accident. He is in hospital.'

'How bad?' I demanded.

'I'm sorry,' his voice grew suddenly soft, not a policeman's voice. 'He is severely injured.'

He told me more. About the train crash, the hospital, the injuries. And I could see my hands shaking on my lap, but all I could hear in my ears was Gilles's voice speaking to me on my birthday last month.

'If I should die unexpectedly,' he'd said, 'whatever it looks like, whatever they tell you, it won't be an accident.' He'd poured us both a glass of smoky Armagnac. 'It will be murder.'

'Don't you dare die,' I'd scolded him.

He'd laughed. Hugged me. And promised not to die.

CHAPTER FIVE

◆ ◆ ◆

CAMILLE

Salpêtrière Hospital scared the life out of me. It is the largest hospital in France and it looks like a museum. Huge and important-looking, the kind of place you put a collection of dead things in. The charity hospital was built on a giant powder keg which is how it got its name. Saltpetre, you see, is an ingredient in fireworks and gunpowder, a salty white powder called potassium nitrate, and it was made in this building in vast quantities for Louis XIII and his army, before Louis XIV turned it into a hospital. This was something I was unaware of when I ran, gasping for air, through its massive arched entrance and along its maze of corridors, but it was something I would learn later.

There was much I would learn during the many hours that I would spend staring at its plain blank walls. But right now I was screaming my brother's name.

'Can I help you?'

A nurse in a frilly starched uniform had appeared at my elbow.

'I'm looking for Gilles Malroux.'

'He's not allowed visitors yet, I'm afraid,' she said.

'I'm his sister.'

Her sweet young face melted with sorrow and her voice dropped as though in church. 'Of course relatives are permitted.'

'How is he?'

'Struggling,' she whispered and led me between the rows of regimented white beds.

How bad struggling? I wanted to ask, but I didn't dare.

The ward looked more like I imagined a ballroom would look than a sickroom. It stretched on forever and had a ridiculously high ceiling. All along one wall there was a row of tall arched windows through which light flooded, bleaching the life out of everything in its path despite the greyness of the day. Not a single mote of dust in sight anywhere. I could think of worse places to be sick.

The ward was eerily quiet. Were they already dead under their white shrouds? I didn't look at any of the occupants of the beds, I kept my eyes down, fixed on the shiny black shoes of the nurse as I trailed behind her.

The nurse suddenly stopped at the foot of one of the white metal beds about halfway down. 'Here we are.'

I looked at the patient. No, no. She has made a mistake. This can't be right.

When my brother Gilles and I were small we had a passion for collecting stray sick cats. Dirty mangy creatures with only half an ear or missing a paw, all were filthy and riddled with seething clusters of fleas behind their ears or hiding in their armpits but it never stopped us. The destitute backstreets of Montparnasse provided fertile ground for our passion for these feral strays, even though our *maman* would throw them in the rain butt if she got the chance.

When I look back I can see why two skinny kids would care so strongly about these pathetic animals. I realise now what I didn't realise at the time. That we saw ourselves in them. Ribs like twigs, scabs on limbs, sores on eyes and ulcers on mouths, perpetually ravenous, but most of all possessed by a terror of human beings. It showed in our eyes as much as in theirs.

Roland was our favourite. A big black bruiser of a cat who was always in trouble, in fights with stray dogs over scraps of food. We'd sneak him into our tiny bedroom, mop up the blood on him as best we could and give him somewhere safe under one of our beds to rest up for a few days while he was hurting. The bastard was never grateful, always biting chunks out of us. Some nights when he believed I was asleep he crept up on to my pillow under cover of darkness, pressed his filthy furry cheek against mine and slept. I didn't let him know I was awake. I kept very still. I loved him.

Living a life starved of love, I clung to any scraps I could get, the same way Roland clung to any discarded chicken's foot he could steal. He would defend it to the death.

Now, in the hospital, I felt it again, the burning need to offer safety to someone I loved who was hurting. My brother was swathed in bandages. They wrapped all around his head and face, and my chest ached for him, like it did when I found Roland dead on the roadside outside the cemetery. But this was worse, far worse. I couldn't breathe right. I tasted blood in my mouth.

This is always the price of love.

The Invisible Man. The one with all the bandages.

That image.

That's exactly what my brother looked like, but without the blue eyeglasses that H G Wells gave his hero to wear. I watched every tiny movement of his chest. He didn't move any other part of his body, he didn't twitch, he didn't moan in his unconscious state. His fingers remained limp within thin cotton gloves. I stared mesmerised at the white dressings that lay where his eyes should have been and I asked again and again in my head if he would be blind when they came off. I was desperate to speak to a doctor but no one came, so I sat there in painful ignorance.

'Gilles,' I whispered, 'stay with me.'

No answer. I wasn't expecting one.

Over his nose and mouth curved a triangular rubber facemask with steel valves and long winding tubes that ran from it to a tall metal gas cylinder that stood in a crate beside the bed. All sorts of complicated dials and taps were attached to it and I stared at them with tears spilling down my cheeks, willing them to keep pumping oxygen into his shattered lungs.

I held my brother's hand and didn't let go.

Time passed so slowly, I feared that the day was broken. I watched the light change from a bright ice-cream white to a fuzzy liquid grey as the sun slid at its own pace across the sky. It would not be hurried. New shadows slunk on to the blank wall opposite and then started to crawl from bed to bed like the Angel of Death on the prowl in the ward as the day darkened. Nurses materialised and stuck needles into Gilles's arm or fiddled with the controls on the oxygen tank, always jotting something on the chart at the foot of his bed.

All they'd say was, 'He's holding on.'

An impatient doctor with two tired-looking young men in white coats in tow finally put in an appearance but was condescending to me. He went out of his way to make me feel both stupid and grubby, when in reality I was neither.

'How is he, Doctor?' I asked.

'M. Malroux has suffered severe crush injuries,' he announced, ending the conversation.

'How bad are they?'

'You really want to know details?'

'I wouldn't have asked if I didn't.'

The doctor was tall with a pair of fine gold-rimmed spectacles perched on the end of his nose which he pushed up and down in a gesture of irritation. He peered at me over the top of them. I could see he disliked me. It showed in the way he kept his head averted. Was it because I questioned him? Or was I just another irritant in his busy day? He addressed the exhausted young men in white coats rather than me.

'In addition to M. Malroux's broken bones and superficial tissue damage,' he stated, 'the patient is suffering from crush injury syndrome. The level of muscle injury causes large quantities of potassium, phosphate, myoglobin, creatine kinase and urate to leak into the circulation. Such a sudden release of toxins into the circulatory system can cause renal dysfunction.'

'What does that mean?' I asked.

His heavy eyebrows drew together at the unwelcome interruption. 'Come, Faucher, enlighten the . . .' he paused, such a faint subtle pause, but still a pause, 'young woman.'

'Yes, sir.' One of the white coats explained kindly, 'It means kidney failure.'

'Barbier,' the older doctor continued, 'inform us as to what else this life-threatening condition can entail.'

The second white coat, the eager-to-please one, rattled off, 'Yes, *Docteur*. Cardiovascular instability, arrhythmia and cardiomyopathy. As well as metabolic acidosis, paralysis and paresthesia, plus renal hypoperfusion and—'

'Enough, Barbier,' the doctor snapped and turned curtly to me. 'Any more questions, Mademoiselle?'

'What is the treatment for this . . . syndrome?'

'Rehydration. Intravenous access and fluid resuscitation is the mainstay of treatment for crush injury syndrome.'

'And his broken bones?'

'They will be attended to.'

'What about his bandaged eyes? What is wrong with them? Will they recover?'

For the first time he forgot about me and gazed at his patient. In an undertone he said, 'It is too soon to tell.' He glanced down at my hand still wrapped around my brother's and he exhaled heavily. 'Cleanliness and sterility are essential in cases like this to avoid infection.'

With no further word, he left. It was Christmas Eve and they were all in a hurry to return home to their loved ones and the ritual opening of Christmas gifts. I learned later that each of the white coats was a houseman, which means a qualified doctor but still in training. The self-important doctor wearing the elegant suit and spectacles was a surgeon. He was Dr Arquette. I would not forget Dr Arquette.

CHAPTER SIX

◆ ◆ ◆

CAMILLE

Gilles was going to die tonight. The realisation came to me gradually, little by little, in small signs, a whisper in my ear that was growing louder. Unlike the doctor, the nurses were kind to me.

'*Du thé?*' they offered.

'*Merci.*'

The one with the sweet young face brought me a hot infusion of *thé au citron* when the cold wind outside picked up and they let me sit quietly to one side while they carried out their nursing duties on my brother. I realised the truth when they didn't kick me out as day stumbled into night. They let me stay. They knew he was not going to make it through the night.

A constant bone-aching grief kept me company while all around me sick men were exhaling their night breath and holding on tight to life. I held on tight to Gilles's hand hour after hour, on to Gilles's life, I would not let him leave. It was when the night was at its blackest and my heart at its lowest that the jammed wheels of my mind finally started to turn once more. Slow at first, but gaining speed, and while the shadows shifted and shuffled through the ward, a question slid into my head. Why was Gilles on the train to Strasbourg if he was planning to spend Christmas Day with me?

He would not have abandoned our Christmas Day together without good reason. Our Christmases together were important. To us anyway.

So why the train?

He must have been working and it must have been important or he wouldn't have risked missing our Christmas Day together. But working on what and for whom? I leaned close, my lips almost touching the bandage over his ear, and I started to whisper.

'What happened, Gilles? What is going on?'

I listened hard but there was no change in his breathing and his fingers remained limp in mine.

'I need to know, Gilles. You said that if you died, it wouldn't be an accident even if it looked like one.' I could smell antiseptic ointment on him and I recalled what Dr Arquette said about infection. I pulled back a fraction. 'But this was a terrible train accident. No one could have foreseen it. So what were you working on? Give me a sign.'

I waited.

Someone coughed. It startled me and I swivelled round. The ward was in darkness except for one dim lamp at each end, throwing out more of a shimmering halo than a proper light. At first I saw no one except the formless humps in the beds, but I blinked hard and spotted a dim figure standing in the doorway, half in, half out of the double swing doors under the lamp. I stopped breathing, as if by doing so I could make him vanish. He was in uniform, deep blue. A policeman.

I squeezed Gilles's hand. 'The police are here, keeping watch. Are they after you for something?' I nodded, replying to my own question. 'That's why the bastard came to fetch me. They want me to identify you, in the hope of getting information about you out of me.' I laughed softly but it was an angry sound. 'They don't know us, Gilles.'

I stared openly at the figure in the doorway and after a full minute he withdrew.

'Tell me, Gilles, tell me what I need to know.'

What is going on?

I sat immobile, still holding Gilles with one hand, but I reached with the other to the tiny cabinet beside the bed. It consisted of a small drawer at the top and a narrow cupboard space underneath. The ward was too dark for me to see anything other than rough shapes, but I felt around inside the lower cupboard and found only a pair of shoes, nothing inside them, not even socks. Disappointed, I slid open the small drawer and it grated slightly but not enough to disturb anyone. My fingers explored again. They found a watch, a keyring attached to two keys, a fountain pen, a hair comb and a wallet. Nothing else. I wondered where his clothes were, his coat, the hat he always wore to cover the white streak in his hair, but I assumed they were too damaged to keep.

I extracted the wallet. I knew it well, its ebony Italian leather, because I had given it to him for his birthday five years ago and the memory of how pleased he was to receive it caught at my heart. And now, as soon as I held it on my lap, I started to cry, deep shuddering silent tears that wouldn't stop.

Did he hear me? He gave no sign. I waited for the storm to pass, wiped my face on my sleeve and then fumbled with his wallet in the dark. I could feel money, soft well-used banknotes, quite a fistful of them. I didn't remove any. Something else was with them, a square of stiffish smooth card, slippery on one side, and I realised it was a photograph. I peered at it closely but its image was a blur in the shadows. Tucked in behind it was a scrap of paper. Something important? Impossible to tell. It occurred to me that his identity card was not here.

Why not? Had the police already taken possession of it?

I slipped the piece of paper and the photograph into my pocket, then explored the wallet's loose-change compartment. It contained various coins; I counted ten of them, but I left them there and rummaged further. My fingers caught on something else, something jammed so hard in the bottom corner that I had to scratch at it with my fingernail to ease it out. It sat, light but solid, in the palm of my hand but I couldn't work out what it was. About the size of a ten-centimes coin but without the hole in the middle. An odd shape. I ran my finger over it and I could tell it wasn't made of metal. I felt some kind of indentation in its surface but in this blackness it remained a mystery. I added it to my haul and, after a moment's thought, I pocketed the keys too, then replaced the wallet in the drawer.

I leaned close to my brother again, my palms cradling his hand, aware of the weight of it. 'You won't believe what foolish thing Barnaby did yesterday,' I whispered.

I started to talk and talk, telling him all kinds of crazy stuff inside my head. I talked about Mme Beaufort and the office file I 'borrowed' for him. I talked to keep him listening, to keep him breathing, and didn't stop until dawn shot a shaft of gold on to the polished floor. It was Christmas Day.

CHAPTER SEVEN

◆ ◆ ◆

GILLES

The bedroom door burst open.

'*Joyeux Noël*, Christophe. Merry Christmas to you.'

Gilles woke with his heart racing. He forced a path up through the layers of fog that were crushing his ribs and filling his nostrils with the smell of burning flesh, but the screams and the stench wouldn't stop.

'Relax, Christophe, you're safe now that you're here with me.'

The voice was one he didn't recognise, soft as a breeze. A delicate hand brushed his cheek.

'Open your eyes, Christophe.'

He tried. He couldn't.

'Here, let me help you.'

A warm damp cloth was laid across his eyes. The sensation was pleasurable and dulled the sound of pounding fists trapped under the train's buckled sheets of metal. He felt the warm cloth work its magic and his eyes opened, though no more than narrow swollen slits. Enough to give him sight of a bedcover. It was a pale shade of *eau-de-nil*. Embroidered.

'Merry Christmas,' the voice said again. A woman's voice.

He tried to lift his gaze from the *eau-de-nil* bed linen but it was like trying to lift Dr Laval's dead weight off him in the train carriage. His eyelids gave up the fight and started to close once more.

She laughed, such a musical laugh, so light and gentle it didn't hurt his eardrums. It dawned on him then that every other part of his body was hurting.

'My *pauvre* Christophe, go back to sleep. We'll try again later. They came knocking on the door again, but don't worry. I sent them away.'

Them? Them?

Gilles shivered and sank back into the fog.

CHAPTER EIGHT

◆ ◆ ◆

CAMILLE

My brother is still alive.
I said those words again, out loud this time. 'My brother is still alive.'

The enormity of that statement overwhelmed me and when one of the older nurses brought me a cup of tea as the ward began its daily bustle, I couldn't stop grinning at her. He had proven them all wrong – the nurses and doctors who believed the morgue would be his resting place this morning.

Gilles had survived the night and they said that his 'vital signs' were apparently picking up. They checked his temperature, pulse, respiration rate and blood pressure and pronounced them stable, then blood was taken for further tests and I thanked the nurse. Not for the kind provision of the tea, which I sipped with relief, but for giving me hope. It flickered into life within me.

'You look exhausted,' the nurse commented in a motherly manner. 'Go home and rest now. You can come back this afternoon after the doctor has done his morning rounds.'

'Dr Arquette?'

'Yes, that's right.'

'Is he a good doctor?'

'He's the best there is,' she said with pride.

'So is my brother,' I replied.

'What is that?'

Anne-Marie perched on my bed like a kitten. She was in full war paint with kohl eyes and a slash of carnal red lipstick, and scantily clad in her black lace camiknickers that showed off her tiny waist and milk-white bust. In readiness for her first john. I was fond of Anne-Marie. She was someone who was generous with her friendship, in my opinion sometimes overgenerous to the other girls who took advantage of her good nature.

Most days she gave off the appearance of being a happy young soul to whom laughter and sleep came easily, but I wasn't fooled. There were days when she didn't talk at all. Literally not a word, and I smelled pastis sickly on her breath. On those days I painted her nails for her and spun stories about how we were going to leave this wretched place one day soon and go live on a pretty little houseboat on the Seine with pink geraniums on its deck and a pet white cat called Vénus. But today was not one of those.

My window was open as usual and the room was chill, the way I liked it, but I worried that Anne-Marie must be cold in her flimsy garment and I threw a crocheted shawl over her. She snuggled into it and asked again.

'What is that?' She prodded one lacquered fingernail at the small object on my palm, cautiously as though it might bite. It seemed to be made of coloured stone, a vivid blue.

'It looks like a weird sort of cross to me,' I suggested.

'No, I reckon it's a love token.'

'A love token?'

'Why else would your brother have a piece of junk like that tucked inside his wallet? Look at it. I bet you it's supposed to be two arms joined together in the air.'

'You think?'

'Yes, it's bound to be from some lovestruck girl who tore it off her charm bracelet in a nightclub and gave it to Gilles to remind him of her.' She smiled her dreamiest smile. 'It's romantic really.'

'Gilles is not the romantic type.'

'He cared enough to keep it.'

I stared at the odd loopy sort of cross in my hand and tried to see it as romantic. I failed. It was a peculiar little thing in a shape I'd never come across before. Picture a normal church cross but with its head-piece rising in a tall loop above the central upright. Yes, I suppose it could be a charm of some kind. The longer I stared at it, the more I thought Camille could be right: a love charm.

I pictured Gilles rubbing it like a talisman. My mother had held an unwavering belief in the power of a talisman and had them in all her pockets, constantly fingering them. A fat lot of good they did her in the end. Did this one really mean something special to Gilles? If so, my brother had been hiding a romantic streak, a secret side to him. I knew there had been girlfriends along the way, but nobody really serious, well, none that he'd brought to meet me anyway and I liked to think he would have. Could this tiny charm actually bring him love? But what state will he be in when the bandages are peeled away.

A painful throb started up in my chest and I couldn't make it stop.

'You all right, Camille?'

'Yes.'

Anne-Marie slid her dainty legs off the bed, stood in front of me and wrapped us both in the crocheted shawl in a comforting embrace.

'He'll get better,' she whispered, 'I'm sure he will.'

We both knew she was lying.

I knocked on Barnaby's door in a rhythmic tattoo of four beats. I waited. I repeated it, so that he'd know it was me. I waited an age. It was cold out here on the landing, a raw easterly was ripping through the city and the sky was glazed with a sheet of thin cloud the colour of sour milk. I'd lived in Montparnasse on the Left Bank my whole life and had paced every busy little street. I knew every cobblestone, every shop, I could picture the colour of each door and I'd watched the local *gamins* grow into skinny-legged youths who huddled in groups on street corners, fingers yellow from nicotine and eyes wary as a wolf's. Knives in pockets. They knew me. But they ignored me.

D'accord, I ignored them. But I could smell them. When I had come home yesterday they'd been across the road, hanging around old Barthélemy's *tabac*, loose-limbed under the tattered awning, and I wanted to tell them to go home where they'd be safe.

Barnaby's door flew open. '*Joyeux Noël*, Camille.' His lovely English voice was full of Christmas cheer and his undamaged arm drew me to him. 'I thought you were spending it with your brother.'

I leaned my tired body against his in the sordid little hallway with its cracked tiles and its stink of God knows what.

'Barnaby, I need a drink.'

He laughed, a great gust of good humour that enveloped me. 'At ten o'clock in the morning?'

His blond hair was all tousled and spiky, the white dressing on his wrist already daubed with oil paint, his eyes still soft from sleep. I'd woken him. He showed no sign of the black despair that had driven the blade into his wrist yesterday and he scooped me into his room. I was exhausted and in need of his brainpower. He was the cleverest person I knew, despite being only twenty-four, two years younger than myself.

The room as always smelled of turpentine and oil paint, strong but not unpleasant. He placed me down on his big velvet armchair. It had once been green but was now the colour of dead leaves and it had bald arms that were paint-streaked like a rainbow. Still wonderfully comfortable though; it wrapped around me and I immediately wanted to sleep. The room was a mess of canvases and paints and easels, cloths draped over some pictures which I knew were nudes, plates and glasses abandoned half-full, and its disorder drove me insane. But as always there was an energy in the room that bounced off the paint-spattered floorboards and off the cracked plaster of the walls. An energy that I loved and which came off Barnaby in waves.

'What?' he demanded. 'What has happened?'

'My brother was on the train that crashed near Lagny.'

'*Non!*'

'He's in hospital.'

'How bad?'

I had no words to describe it. I accepted a glass of some heavy *vin rouge* that he placed in my hand and I downed it in one. I shuddered. My empty stomach burned. But I felt my blood start to pick up speed and when Barnaby plonked himself down on his knees in front of me and asked, 'What can I do to help?' I was grateful. That simple caring question made me want to weep with relief. I put my head in my hands and sat there in silence for a long time, while he stroked my knee in a lazy comforting rhythm. I breathed hard. Finally I lifted my head.

'Yesterday must have been a really bad day for you,' I said softly and glanced down at his wrist. I should change the bandage. 'Did your exhibition not go well?'

'Nobody bought a single one of my paintings, not one solitary soul,' he groaned. But he popped a laugh on the end of it to show that today he was rising like a phoenix from the ashes of his dark night. 'One critic called my work "immature daubs". To my face. He had the gall to stand right in front of me and pronounce them "indecipherable".'

'I hope you told him where he can stick his "indecipherable".'

He laughed with genuine amusement and turned his gaze to the bandage on his wrist. He said simply, 'Thank you, Camille.'

We left it at that. For now. When he was ready he would tell me more, he would offer me a glimpse of what demons he was keeping in check this time.

'I have a question for you, Barnaby.'

'Ask anything.'

I reached into my pocket and drew out a clean white handkerchief. I unfolded it. In the centre of the cotton square lay the blue love charm from Gilles's wallet.

'Do you know what this is?' I asked.

'Yes.' He picked up the small object and inspected it with interest.

'What is it?'

'It's an ankh,' he told me.

'A what?'

'An ankh. A-n-k-h.' He spelled it out. 'It's the Ancient Egyptian symbol for life.'

I stared, jaw-dropped. 'Ancient Egyptian? How can you know such a thing?'

He touched the ankh with the tip of his finger, respectfully. 'I read books,' he said gently. 'I go to exhibitions. This is a fantastic city for artists.'

'Is that meant as a rebuke?'

'Of course not, Camille. Don't be touchy, *chérie*.'

'I read newspapers,' I pointed out. '*Paris-Soir*. And *L'Humanité*.'

'I know you do.'

It was Gilles who had introduced me to *L'Humanité*, the Communist paper founded by Jean Jaurès. I even went to a Communist gathering once. Never again.

He placed the blue charm on the palm of my hand and closed my fingers over it. 'It sounds as though your brother is going to need his symbol of life.'

I held it tight, alarmed. I had robbed Gilles of it. I stood quickly. 'I must take it back to him.'

'There's no rush. It's ancient superstition, Camille. Nothing more.'

I rose from the chair and headed for the door. 'Thanks for the drink, Barnaby.' I paused and thought for a minute. 'I wonder where Gilles came across it. Where can I find out more information about ankhs?'

'The Louvre, of course.'

'The museum?'

'Yes, it has loads of Egyptian things.'

I frowned. Intimidated.

'And its painting collection is unbelievable,' he added. 'It's the largest museum in the world and is right on our doorstep. Don't tell me you've never been there.'

'Of course I've been there,' I lied. 'I'm not allowed back into the hospital to see my brother until this afternoon, so I'll hurry down to the Louvre now.'

He chuckled. 'No chance. It's closed.'

'Closed?'

'It's Christmas Day, Camille.'

'Of course.'

I'd forgotten.

'Merry Christmas, Barnaby.'

'Merry Christmas, Camille. What would you like as a gift?'

'My own ankh.'

He sprang over to one of the blank canvases piled against the wall, picked up a long-handled artist's brush from a jar, all bushy and speckled, squeezed out a rich glossy blue on to a palette and with a few skilled brushstrokes he had drawn me an ankh. It glistened. It breathed. It was beautiful.

'There,' he said, placing the canvas in my hands. 'This will keep you safe.'

CHAPTER NINE

♦ ♦ ♦

GILLES

She was in the room. He could smell her. A delicate floral scent. Yet she made no sound, no rustle of a skirt, no sighs or sniffs, so what was she doing?

Sitting in the pretty pink boudoir chair, watching over him?

Or standing at the end of his bed, observing him like a lab rat?

At one point he dimly heard her talking to someone else in the room but the words all crashed into each other.

Who? Who was this someone else? A man?

A policeman?

That thought. It made the pain in his head vibrate against his skull and he was grateful when whoever this woman was placed a cool cloth on his burning forehead.

It was as she slid a cold spoon between his lips and tipped a trickle of bitter medication on to his tongue that an alarm bell started up in his battered head. He struggled. He was sure he struggled, maybe even lashed out, but the alarm bell was deafening him. The fog swept in again and silenced it.

'There,' he heard her say in her fading voice. 'Better now.'

'Who is he?' a man's voice asked.

CHAPTER TEN

◆ ◆ ◆

CAMILLE

'And you are . . . ?'

The question jabbed at me from behind. A light finger tapped my shoulder. I jumped to my feet, startled.

The ward was quiet this evening, just a dull murmur from the other beds and their visitors like the soft buzz of a hive. Plus the relentless rhythmic wheeze of my brother's oxygen mask. I'd been sitting on one of Salpêtrière Hospital's hard wooden chairs beside Gilles's bed for hours, leaning forward to be as close to his bandaged form as possible. I'd again been talking, talking, talking. Telling him anecdotes from our childhood. Not the ones involving a belt and a buckle and screams, no, not those, but the ones where Gilles stole a rowing boat on the Seine and we'd drifted downstream with the current, laughing in the sunshine, or when I used to do his school homework for him and he used to knock the teeth out of any boy who jeered at me in the schoolyard for having holes in my shoes in the rain.

I turned and I found a tall man there. He was standing a step too close to me. His expression was solemn. Dark hair cropped in close waves to his head and a swarthy skin. I could hear him breathing through his nose as if he'd run upstairs too fast. He was wearing a white coat and just for a split second I thought he had a snake draped around his neck but it was a stethoscope.

'And you are . . . ?' he asked again.

'I'm Camille Malroux, Gilles's sister.'

'Pleased to meet you, Mlle Malroux, though not under these circumstances.' He smiled at me and I felt hugely relieved to find a doctor here on Christmas Day evening, one willing to talk to me. In his hand he carried a hospital chart of some kind.

'How is Gilles doing?' I asked at once before he could drift away to another bed.

'He is in a critical condition, but his vital signs are improving. I think you can take encouragement from that.'

'He was always stubborn.'

The doctor gave a small nasal snort and studied his patient for a long moment, as though seeking the location of that crucial streak of stubbornness. He walked round to the other side of the bed, checked the oxygen mask and the flow metre on the gas cylinder and made notes on the chart.

'What about his eyes?' I questioned. I forced my voice to stay calm. 'Will he be able to see again?'

'It is too soon to tell.'

Following Dr Arquette's well-worn line there.

'How bad is the crushing of his ribs?' I persisted. 'How many of them are broken?' It's details I wanted, not platitudes.

But, to my surprise, instead of answering he came back round to my side of the bed and said in a low voice, 'Please sit down, Mlle Malroux.'

Instantly my throat clamped shut. My poor brother. What was this doctor about to tell me?

'Why?'

'Because I have something to discuss with you.'

Again the same low voice. I feared that this was his fatal-news voice, so I sat quickly. My gaze was fixed on his large dark eyes that gave nothing away.

He remained standing. 'How well do you know your brother, Mademoiselle?'

'As well as any sister.'

'Do you know his address?'

'No. He moves around a lot. From place to place. Never stays long in any one apartment. He's restless.'

Did I say it too fast? Did it sound convincing? I looked down at the bandaged face on the clinical white pillow. Oh Gilles, what have you done this time? Have the police sent this doctor into the lion's den to question me? I'm beginning to wonder if I can trust him.

'Mlle Malroux, I'm going to remove the protective glove on your brother's hand for you to see it for yourself.'

He reached for Gilles's limp hand and started to roll down the white cotton glove, and for the first time I noticed the doctor was wearing white sterile hospital gloves himself. As I did now.

'But the nurse told me my brother's hands are burned,' I murmured, 'and need to be guarded against infection.'

'That's true. Third-degree burns destroy the epidermis and the dermis, but I assure you we are taking great care to keep them clear of infection.'

I half-closed my eyes as the damaged skin emerged, afraid of what I would see. It was black. I felt sick at the sight. The burn slashed right across his palm and his fingertips, as if he had tried to haul away a red-hot chunk of metal. The doctor turned Gilles's hand over with professional care. The back of it was barely scorched, just a few blisters that were shiny with purple ointment. I had to look away. I stared down at the doctor's shoes, black brogues, highly polished. At anything other than the damaged hand he was displaying for me.

'Tell me,' the doctor said kindly, 'if you recognise your brother's hand. The shape of his fingernails, the length of his fingers, the size of the knuckles. Is this Gilles Malroux's hand?'

His voice was infinitely gentle, knowing his words might hurt.

I looked up, tears in my eyes. I nodded.

'Are you sure?'

I nodded again.

'Thank you, Mlle Malroux.'

I didn't watch him replace the glove. I leaned forward to the band-aged face in the bed and kissed its cheek.

'I'll return tomorrow,' the doctor informed me. He rested his hand on my shoulder.

Don't touch me, I wanted to say, but I didn't. *You carry death on your fingers. I can smell it.*

I heard the click of his footsteps as he walked away, the swing of the door at the end of the ward. Tears were streaming down my face and I was powerless to stop them, but as I leaned even closer to the figure in the bed, I was smiling.

I whispered, 'Who are you? What have you done with my brother?'

This man is not my brother.

These six words sat in my brain like metal spikes. I could think of nothing else as I continued to occupy the chair beside his white hospital bed.

This man was not Gilles.

How could I be so sure?

Because when he was seventeen a tyre jack collapsed and his thumb was crushed. I know because I was the one who splinted and bandaged it. As a result his thumb sat at a slightly crooked angle and the nail was deformed. This man's thumbnail was smooth as a pebble, despite the impact swelling around it. One glance was enough for me.

This man is not my brother.

'Who are you?' I whispered again.

I wanted to grasp his shoulders and shake him awake, but I let him lie there behind his oxygen mask and bandages, hiding from me.

What happened out there in the crash? In the darkness.

Did you steal my brother's wallet and leave him there at the side of the track to die? Is that it? Did you try to run but a burning section of train carriage fell on top of you, trapping you there?

Is that what happened?

I pictured the scene in my mind. The flames clawing up into the night sky, the sparks racing on the wind, the screams, the bodies of the dead, the locomotives and the carriages buckled and burning. My brother lying there lifeless.

Grief started to form like a hard cold stone just under my ribs, but I refused to give it space. I refused. I would not allow those pictures to exist in my head. I told myself that the images of the train crash that rose in my mind were false. I would not accept that the lifeless form I saw sprawled beside the railway track was my brother.

Gilles is alive.

The ankh had been safe in his wallet.

It was late in the evening now, sleet was needle-sharp in the air, but in Montparnasse even on Christmas Day I had no trouble finding a bar open at this hour. It overflowed with noise and festivity. It wasn't the infamous Le Sphinx club on boulevard Edgar Quinet with its glamour and decadence, always vibrant and self-obsessed, but I slid instead into a smaller, more discreet place across the road, into Rizki's bar.

I nodded to those drinkers I recognised with an attempt at Christmas jollity, but I didn't linger with anyone. I was not in the mood for talk. I needed to think. I slunk into a dark corner, sat at a small zinc-topped round table and huddled over the *vin rouge* that Rizki brought me without even asking. From my pocket I removed the photograph and the slip of paper that I'd taken from Gilles's wallet in the middle of the night at the hospital. I laid them out on the table in front of me but yet again they meant nothing. I drank three glasses of the red wine in quick succession, but still I couldn't shift that hard cold stone.

The photograph was of me. Me windblown and laughing into the camera on the beach at Carnac in Brittany two years ago. I was touched. And surprised that he would carry around a picture of me in his wallet. Surprised not because I doubted that he loved me enough to do so, I knew he did, but because by doing so he could get me into trouble. If he were ever caught on the wrong side of the law, this photograph could drag me down with him. I tucked it out of sight in my pocket once more.

The piece of paper that I'd found alongside it had turned out to be nothing more than an ordinary receipt. I peered at it closely again and read that it was from a *magasin de jouets*, a toyshop called Le Rêve. The Dream. It was across the river. Though why Gilles would be buying a toy I didn't know, because he had no children, no nieces or nephews. But Gilles had always kept his private life very private, so it was perfectly possible that one of his friends might have had a child who required a Christmas gift. A boy clearly. The receipt was for a tinplate model car.

It meant nothing to me and I tucked it away again. What did mean everything to me was whether the man in that hospital bed had stolen Gilles's wallet and replaced it with his own. What was the bandaged man's real name? Who was this imposter?

I struggled to stop my thoughts spinning out of control and forced myself to think calmly. I prided myself on my logical mind, so I laid out the facts one by one.

Fact one. Gilles, it would seem, was on one of the trains that crashed. Unless the man stole my brother's wallet in the street or at the station before boarding the train, but if that were the case Gilles would have turned up at my place on Christmas Eve as planned. Complaining of a lost wallet and berating Paris's guttersnipe pickpockets.

So yes, I did believe my brother was on that train.

Fact two. If Gilles was badly injured or even killed in the crash, he would now be lying either in a morgue or in a Paris hospital. But under what name? How could I track him down in this vast city without a name? Finding out the injured stranger's real name was key to finding Gilles.

Fact three. Gilles could have gone into hiding. He could be in trouble, steering clear of police and keeping his head down. It wouldn't be the first time. But if so, why had he not contacted me? He knew I would keep him safe. The more I thought about it, the more I allowed myself a smile. Maybe tomorrow he would turn up at my door with a big grin and a Christmas *cadeau* all tied up with red ribbons for me. I reached for another glass of wine as relief hit me. Of course Gilles would come.

I was sure he would.

CHAPTER ELEVEN

◆ ◆ ◆

GILLES

G illes was listening to the house.

Its voice was soft and old as it stretched its timbers in the morning, creaking its joints and waking with a sigh and a cough as windows were thrown open to the winter's breath. Its sounds were growing familiar to him. He lay in his sickbed hour after hour in the warm embrace of a soothing feather mattress that rustled when he moved, and slowly he was getting to know this unknown place in which he had washed up. Wherever the hell it was.

Gilles didn't like not knowing. His survival had always depended on knowing. Knowing exactly where he was. Who people were. Where the danger lay.

He now recognised the quiet murmur of the stairs when her feet touched the first tread. The skittering of pigeons on the roof above his head, a clock striking somewhere beneath him, a mellow golden sound. The ticking of water pipes and the clanking of taps turning on and off. They all pecked at his mind while he drifted in and out of sleep on a pillow of dreams from which he could not raise his head.

Dimly he was aware of pain, but it was no more than a muted throb. Of no meaning. Where had it come from?

Somewhere there echoed the throaty crow of a cockerel.

A cockerel? So he was in the countryside. He tried to recall how he had got here but failed. His mind ached with the effort and there was a horrible wheezing sound in the room that irritated him, as though a smelly old dog was curled up in its basket at the end of the bed.

It only stopped when *she* entered the room and the metal spoon touched his lips.

At that moment he felt the kindness of her, warm and alive beside him, and her voice was like a river of molten silver, all light and shiny. His brain failed to grasp her words and they merged with other sounds that came to him as a blur. Carefully, like picking apart a knotted ball of wool, he identified them, one by one. Birds. Wind. Trees. Rain. The tap-tap-tap of hail.

But the process of doing so exhausted him and he let himself sink back on to the pillow of dreams. Sometimes, when the dreams were bad, it felt more like drowning.

The pain woke him. Sharp. Sudden. Excruciating.

'Felt that, did you?'

Gilles's eyes shot wide open. He found himself in a bedroom that felt as if it were underwater; it was all pastel shades of green with one pretty rose-pink chair. The man staring down at him with keen beetle-black eyes was wearing a dark-green suit and had blood on one hand, a scalpel in the other.

'Just tidying up,' the man said and smiled benignly.

Tidying up?

Tidying what up? What the hell did he mean?

'Your leg,' the green suit explained. 'It's a mess, I'm afraid.'

'Who are you?' Gilles asked.

He was shocked. His words had no sound worth a damn, as weightless as good intentions. They emerged as no more than a murmur.

'I'm Dr Grémillon.'

The man paused, pursing his lips. He had sandy hair and pink skin with freckles and looked harmless. Except for those black eyes. They told a different story. He waved a hand at a well-used leather medical bag on the chair, as though it explained everything. The smile slid away. 'More to the point, Monsieur, who are you?'

Who am I?

Secrecy was bone-deep in Gilles. Even in his present state of confusion and mental fog he kept his mouth shut.

'I don't know,' he whispered.

'Poor fellow,' the doctor said. Yet his tone was jovial. He patted Gilles's arm with a show of concern. 'We're taking good care of you and I'm just redressing your leg wound.'

With a scalpel?

'Hurts a bit, I know. I'll give you a shot of something to ease the pain.'

Gilles shook his head. *No shots.*

The doctor stood gazing down at him for a long moment during which he shed a layer of his professional bonhomie. 'You are a lucky man, my friend.'

I am not your friend.

The doctor leaned closer over him, intent and serious. 'You are a lucky man to have Mme Lagarde offer you shelter and kindness at a time like this.' He exhaled heavily and his breath smelled of a woody aromatic tobacco. A pipe smoker. 'To have her protection even.'

'Do. I. Need. Protection?'

Gilles spaced each word, but still they came out blurred.

The doctor laughed softly. 'In this life we all need protection, *mon ami.* Don't you agree?'

Gilles wanted to shake his head. To say no, I can protect myself. But he felt a tiny prick in his arm and the dreams swept him away.

This time. He was ready.

The moment Gilles felt the cool metal of the spoon touch his lips, he twisted his head away. Sticky liquid crawled down his chin.

'*Zut!*' she exclaimed. 'Don't, Christophe.'

Christophe. Who is this *Christophe?*

Prayers.

Unmistakable. That intonation. That self-satisfied church drone of words spilling over him. Scraping his soul. He recalled that cadence from his childhood and recoiled.

A priest. She'd brought a priest into his room. Was he dying?

Through the narrowest of slits under his eyelids Gilles could make out a strip of black soutane. It was stained and draped over a fleshless figure. One hand, made of nothing more than bone and gristle, clutched a large black Bible, its ancient edges softened by a lifetime of prayers and tears, and the other hand was curled around an ornate brass cross that dangled from a chain around his neck. With great effort Gilles lifted his own hand from the bedcover and tried to clutch at the man's wrist but he was clumsy. His fingers found the cross instead.

He heard the priest murmur softly, 'May the Holy Ghost lead us in truth.' A pause, then in a louder voice, '*Sois béni dans le Seigneur, mon fils*. Our Lord's blessings upon you, my son.'

'I have to get out of here, Father.'

'What? Out? What do you mean?'

'I need to leave this place.'

'You are wrong, my son. You are in the safest of hands here. You are in God's hands.'

There it was, the unanswerable. You couldn't argue with that kind of logic. Gilles's head was pounding and bolts of pain snaked relentlessly up from his leg, but he gripped the sheet and struggled to raise himself off the pillow. Instead of aiding Gilles, the priest placed two strong hands on his shoulders and gently but firmly flattened him against the pillow once more.

'Sleep, *mon fils*.'

CHAPTER TWELVE

◆ ◆ ◆

CAMILLE

Paris is a city that doesn't just steal your heart, it dazzles you. I see it in people's eyes as they walk the streets, gazing. It is called the City of Light for good reason. It was the first city in the world to introduce streetlamps and it has always flourished as Europe's beating heart of culture and Enlightenment.

Its grace and grandeur know no equal, thanks to the genius of Georges Haussmann. Fine boulevards and tree-lined avenues boast an abundance of the most magnificent buildings to be found anywhere in the world, so that style and beauty meet the eye at every turn. Chic and sumptuous, handsome and artistic, as well as downright bawdy if you know where to look. But above all, the city is elegant. As supremely elegant, I do believe, as a pair of Charles Jourdan silk shoes. American tourists call Paris *swell* and the British term it *agreeable*. But, of course, they don't know its hidden rancid corners.

I worked each day in an office beside the Seine alongside twenty-seven other neatly dressed women and twenty-seven industrious Royal typewriters, French *machines à écrire*. These were big brutish machines with extra-long carriages for government documents and hefty keys that clattered and yacked and rattled all day long. Their voices filled every corner of the huge high-ceilinged room till the air tasted metallic and saturated with sound. It was breathable but it wasn't pleasant.

My job was as a typist in the government department of the Ministre de la Marine marchande. The Ministry of the Merchant Navy in

Chautemps' socialist government was overseen by Minister Eugène Flot and it handled the comings and goings of all the ships and their cargoes into the great port of Paris. It always amazed me that many people had no idea that Paris was a busy port, but then many things about people amaze me.

'Watch out,' Louisa whispered out of the side of her mouth, as she scurried past my desk with a sheaf of blue files in her arms. 'Mme Beaufort has got a face on her like thunder and she's heading this way.'

'What's the problem?' I asked without allowing my fingers to pause.

'There's a policeman with her.'

A collective intake of breath disrupted the relentless rhythm of the keys.

'I hope he has polished his boots and oiled his hair this morning or he'll receive a Beaufort reprimand,' someone joked and laughter rippled through the room. But not mine.

Police. What did they want here? In the sudden chill in the air I felt my fingers speed up to outpace my nerves. By the time Mme Beaufort entered, we were all seated demurely at our desks, eyes down, fingers flying over the typewriter keys at the required eighty words a minute. I didn't look up until I saw her stylish suede shoes come to a halt in front of my desk and even then I didn't pause, willing them to walk on to the next one. She was dressed in chic black today and I had a sense of a crow landing to pick my bones.

'Mlle Malroux.'

I stood immediately, as we'd been trained to do.

'Officer Garot wishes to have a word with you. But first let me say this, young woman.' The way she said the word 'woman' was the way you might spit out 'scorpion'. 'Never in all my years here at the Ministry have I had to suffer such indignity. The police in our midst. You have brought shame on our department.'

'I have done nothing wrong, Madame. I don't know why—'

'Mlle Malroux,' the officer interrupted. He was young and keen and placed a hand flat on my desk next to my ruler to establish his control. 'I am here today to request that you accompany me to the gendarmerie for questioning.'

No polite *s'il vous plaît*. No shrug to indicate the interrogation was just a formality, nothing serious. I was tempted to pick up my ruler and rap his knuckles.

Mme Beaufort released a long, frayed breath and strode away towards the door, past the four rows of identical government desks, seven typists in each row. The gendarme in his dark navy cape followed her. I picked up my bag and followed at his heels like a dog. Twenty-seven pairs of eyes watched us.

'Who is the man in the bed in the Salpêtrière Hospital? The one whose hand you hold hour after hour.'

'My brother,' I answered. 'You know that. It was one of your own officers who came to my room on Christmas Eve and informed me he was there.'

'Ah yes, of course. Injured in the terrible train crash. I'm sorry.'

He was clever, this one. Older and smarter. He spoke quietly and shook his head in sympathy and asked simple questions that we both knew the answers to.

'Your name?'

'Your address?'

'Your brother's name?'

'When did you last see him before Christmas Eve?'

'Is he recovering?'

'Has he spoken to you?'

'Is he conscious?'

'What is his address?'

'His job?'

Those last two were trickier.

'I don't know his address, Captain Durand. He moves around . . .'
I let a sob escape, 'I mean he *moved* around so much because of his
work that he was never in one place for long.'

'His job?'

'He was something in sales. Buying and selling goods.'

'What kind of goods?'

'I'm not sure exactly. He travelled the country to shops of various
kinds. But now he is so injured he may never again be able to . . .'

My words seemed to die in the small stuffy interrogation room, with
its dark oak floorboards scuffed and in sore need of a polish. My head
was splitting and my mouth felt dry but I was sticking to the script that
Gilles and I agreed on long ago. I scooped a clean handkerchief from
my pocket and held it to my eyes.

'What is it you suspect my brother of doing?' I murmured.

'Murder,' he said.

The handkerchief slid from my fingers, my eyes shot wide open
with shock, my hands covered my mouth to stifle my cry. I shook my
head, over and over. 'No, no, you're wrong.'

His quiet face was stern. 'Am I, Mademoiselle?'

'Yes. Who is he supposed to have murdered?'

'An undercover policeman!'

Murder.

The police captain's voice spiked in my mind as I stepped out on to
the pavement. The air was bright and brittle as an icicle but it rid my
lungs of the stench of the police station. The city had paused. It was
lunchtime and for Parisians that meant the moment had come for a
glass of *vin rouge* to take priority.

Murder.

No, Gilles, no.

The street was quiet, the bustle muted. I set off in the direction
of the nearest Métro, Madeleine station, with the intention of

returning immediately to the office and to Mme Beaufort's watchful eye before she—

'So where is he, Mademoiselle?' The man's voice caught me by surprise. 'How much did you tell the *flics*?'

Against the wall of the building just ahead of me a man with his jacket collar turned up was leaning and smoking, staring at me.

'I don't know you,' I said and walked on past him.

He fell into step beside me. A big man though not tall, in a half-decent suit, a cap pulled low over his forehead, tobacco-stained fingertips. Unpolished boots, I noticed. I could hear a low sound coming from him, like the snarl from one of the street dogs before it attacks. You learn to recognise the point at which you are in danger.

I swerved, stepped off the pavement and dodged between traffic to cross the road. When I looked back from the other side, he was still standing there staring at me, and as I watched he launched himself into the road, looking neither right nor left, but aiming in a direct line for me. He didn't hurry. He ignored the blast of car horns and kept his gaze on me.

I could run. I was good at running. I'd done plenty of it in the past, but I needed to know who this man was and how he knew Gilles, so I chose my spot and stood my ground. By the time he reached me I was standing in the shop doorway of a smart men's tailoring establishment with colourful Christmas waistcoats on display, where I was in full view of the proprietor behind the till.

Attack was my first line of defence.

'Who are you?' I demanded.

The question bounced off him unheeded. 'So where is he, Mademoiselle?' he asked again. 'How much did you tell the *flics*?'

'Where is who?'

He gave me a look. 'Do not act the simpleton.' He exhaled smoke in my face. 'Where is your brother?'

'I have no brother.'

'Lies will get you nowhere. Is that what you told the *flics*?' He tossed his head towards the police station.

'What I told the police is my business. Not yours.' I stepped forward, crowding him in the small space of the doorway. 'Who are you?' I repeated. 'If you want me to talk to you, I need your name.'

'Robespierre,' he said with a laugh loud enough to bring the shop proprietor out from behind his counter to stand by the side window through which he could observe us both more closely. He folded his arms with annoyance over one of his own portly waistcoats. I was happy with that, in case my companion decided to bring his clenched fists to our discussion.

'Mlle Malroux, I am seeking your brother.'

He knew my name. My name. He knew I had a brother. He knew I'd been inside the gendarmerie. What else did he know?

'And,' he continued, 'it's up to you whether we have this conversation right here, over and done with quickly, or whether we continue it in Montparnasse.'

He knew where I lived.

My mouth went dry. Gilles, what have you done? Where are you?

'A drink,' I said, 'I need a drink.' I pushed past him and marched into the bar next door.

He sat opposite me, the man who called himself Robespierre. Elbows on the table, bulky shoulders hunched like a boxer, his fingers constantly on the move, tapping and twitching, as impatient as his slate-hard eyes. He let me drink my wine in peace, but he watched me the way a cat watches a rat before it strikes.

The bar wasn't busy, just a few old men in fingerless gloves playing dominoes and in the corner a pretty woman with absinthe eyes dealing out tarot cards for anyone who tossed a few centimes on her table. My companion lit another cigarette.

'Where is he?' he demanded for the third time. 'He is not the man in the hospital bed.'

'Where is who?'

The hand holding the cigarette shot out and stabbed its burning tip down on the surface of the table, grinding it into the wood. So close to my own hand that I felt the heat of it. Tiny sparks prickled against my flesh. When he removed the cigarette, the wood beneath was blackened. A warning. Under the table a tremor shook my legs and I was glad I was sitting down.

I lifted my empty wine glass, smacked its lip down on the table next to his hand that was still clutching the dead cigarette, and I watched an ice-shower of glass splinters dive on to his skin. One nicked a vein. A tiny bead of blood sat there, dark and shiny.

'Now we're even,' I said.

His lips drew back from his teeth but it wasn't a smile. 'You are your brother's sister,' he said with a hint of respect and nodded.

I sat back and slid my hands on to my lap in case any more tremors sneaked up. This man scared the hell out of me.

I sighed, as if capitulating. 'Now let's talk. You are seeking my brother and so am I. Maybe we can help each other.'

'Where is he?'

'Let's be certain that we are talking about the same man. Tell me his name.' I sounded ridiculously reasonable.

Again that low growling sound deep in his chest before he answered, 'Gilles Malroux. Your brother. And don't say he's in Salpêtrière Hospital. I know better. Where is he?'

'I wish I knew. But I don't. He seems to have disappeared.'

'So what were you doing at the gendarmerie?'

'The police think Gilles is in hospital and want me to identify him.'

He gave me that slate-grey stare again. I couldn't tell whether or not he believed me.

'What is your connection with my brother?' I asked, using the same brisk tone Mme Beaufort used in the office when any of us fell below her exacting standards.

Again the baring of the teeth, each one Gauloises-tinted. 'We do business,' was all he said.

'What kind of business?'

He licked the bead of blood from the back of his hand. 'Ask your brother.'

'I would if I could.'

'He has something that belongs to me. I want it back.'

Instantly I was transported to my old schoolyard in the rain. A boy's freckled face thrust into mine, my pigtail wound into a vicious knot around his fist. '*Gilles has something that belongs to me*,' the boy had hissed at me. '*A place in the queue of johns outside your mother's front door*.' He and his *imbécile* friend had cracked up with laughter. I'd spat in his eye and yelled, '*I know how and when you're going to die, Éric Farnet. Because I'm the one who's going to kill you*.' But as soon as Gilles learned to punch and to punch dirty, no one teased me any more about my mother's backstreet occupation.

'What is this *something* that Gilles has of yours?' I asked. 'I may be able to help trace it.'

Under my bed in Montparnasse lay a scruffy old khaki rucksack. 'Keep it for me,' Gilles had instructed. That was three weeks ago. Set me to guard something and he knows I will do it.

'It's part of an Egyptian statue,' my companion said reluctantly.

'A statue?' I wasn't expecting that. 'What kind of statue? A gold one? A silver one? Which part of it is missing? Its head?'

'Its hand.'

He rose to his feet, as stiff-limbed as a fighting dog, and he tightened the scarf around his neck.

'Camille Malroux, your brother stole it. I am giving you two weeks to find it. Then I will come to you and I will take what I am owed.

A hand for a hand.' His gaze shifted to my woollen glove that lay discarded on the tabletop. He gave it a meaningful stare before turning abruptly away. He left the bar.

I continued to sit there. Stunned.

A hand for a hand.

I badly wanted to order another *vin ordinaire* but resisted the urge. Instead I walked out and around the corner of the block to a side street where I pressed my back flat against the wall. To prop me up while the tremor took hold. I didn't trust myself. Breathe in, breathe out. Like Gilles taught me.

When it had passed, I straightened my beret and stepped rapidly back into the flow of humanity that keeps Paris turning. I headed straight for the Louvre.

CHAPTER THIRTEEN

◆ ◆ ◆

CAMILLE

I had never seen a god before. Until now.

Of course I'd had my fill of images of Jesus Christ in the many churches of Paris. Who hasn't in France? But they had always struck me as either overflowing with gentleness or torn by suffering. Sweetness or agony were carved into the core of the marble, depicting the emotions of a human being. Not a deity. More often than not, a damaged and sad-eyed figure, bloodied and slumped on a cross.

Here in the Louvre's great hall of Egyptian Antiquity I came face to face with my first real god. I felt an overwhelming urge to bow down in adoration, to buckle my knees, so vast and so monstrously intimidating was he. An Egyptian colossus. A massive statue hewn out of darkness. All-powerful. I knew nothing about him except what was printed on a ludicrously small plaque at his feet. It told me that this was the magnificent Rameses II, the great and glorious pharaoh who ruled over Egypt for sixty-six years from 1279 BC until 1213 BC and at the height of his power declared himself to be a living god.

I believed him. If you saw him, you would too.

'Can I help you? You wish to speak with me, I'm told.'

I spun around. I had to drag my mind out of the hot Saharan sands and back to the present.

I nodded. 'Dr Delamarche?'

'That's right.'

When I was told at the Louvre's front desk that a Dr Delamarche from their Egyptian Antiquities department could spare me a few minutes, I had pictured a dusty old man with thinning hair scraped over a shiny scalp and a soft faraway look in his eyes. I didn't expect a young woman who could have stepped out of *Vogue* magazine. Not that she was flashily dressed, far from it. Her two-piece costume was a demure navy-blue and her cream blouse was buttoned high to the throat, but the jacket was exquisitely styled to her slender figure and the blouse melted in a spill of silk and pearl buttons.

'You are?'

'Camille Malroux.'

In a beat of silence I watched her bright blue eyes assess me. She possessed an intelligent angular face, one that looked as if it enjoyed the process of digging deep under surfaces. An attractive smile that made me think life came easy to her.

'I can give you five minutes,' she said pleasantly. 'Come.' She moved away at a brisk pace.

I trailed behind her, observing the way she walked. Each two-tone shoe was placed on the floor as if she owned the spot it landed on.

I'd lived in Paris all my life, yet never once had I stepped inside the Louvre Museum before. I admit it now, to my shame.

The largest museum on earth, Barnaby had told me. Sixty thousand square metres of it and containing over 30,000 objects from the past. But why would I go there? What was the attraction? A load of old Roman gods hacked out of Italian marble, I'd thought. A pile of Greek bits and pieces of dusty pottery. The broken Venus de Milo. Was she Greek or Roman? I had no idea. And the *Mona Lisa* with her secret sinful smile. Probably some ancient jewellery and room after room of dull paintings showing off the might and pomp of Louis XIV and Napoleon Bonaparte at the head of his victorious army. That's what I thought.

I thought wrong.

I turned into one of the Paris tourists I used to laugh at, gazing about me, eyes wide with wonder. The museum itself was exactly what I imagined a palace to be. All marble and pillars and painted ceilings and gold everything. I was surrounded by objects whose existence both baffled and bewitched me. Strange beautiful stone jars which had the brightly coloured head of a monkey or a falcon growing out the top, statues with bizarre crinkled hair styles or with great rectangular beards jutting from their chin.

As I followed Dr Delamarche I passed what looked like a tiny ivory baboon and an ancient chair with lion's feet that I wouldn't have given houseroom to, it was so decrepit. I caught glimpses of bits of things, broken things, small boats and buttons, hair combs and cracked bowls. Yet here they were displayed in glass cases to be admired. It was a mystery. Here they had power. I could feel it.

But it was the gigantic sphinx that stopped me in my tracks. I stood in awe. A vast oppressive monument that seemed to crush me. I became nothing.

'I know. Magnificent, isn't it?' Dr Delamarche's voice was suddenly beside me. 'It has that effect the first time you see it. The head of a human, the body of a lion. It's the Great Sphinx of Tanis. It was discovered in the ruins of the temple of Amun-Ra. Tanis used to be Egypt's capital during the 21st Dynasty.'

'Why is it here and not in Egypt?'

She gave a rueful smile. 'A sore point. We can thank Jean-François Champollion for that. He persuaded King Charles X to buy an Egyptian collection and this part of the museum opened in 1827.' She gazed around her and murmured softly, 'It is a privilege to work here.'

She drew me away and I was struck by the way this woman unconsciously trailed a finger across some of the glass cases as she passed them or smiled up at one of the huge statues, as if at a friend. Such intimacy. With gods. With pharaohs. On equal terms. I felt something tighten in my chest and it took several deep breaths for me to recognise it for what it was. Jealousy.

Dr Liliane Delamarche.

That was the nameplate on the door. I was nervous as I stepped inside. Behind the door lay an office brimful of what Dr Delamarche, with a casual wave of her hand, termed *artefacts*. The word was new to me but it was obvious that she meant old stuff, things that had been dug up out of the ground. I studied her fingernails. No sign of dirt.

'Please be seated, Mlle Malroux.'

I didn't want to be seated. I wanted to go over and peer at the shelves where she kept her treasures to look for ankhs. But I did as she asked, I took my place in the chair opposite hers at a sweeping oak desk whose surface could barely see the light of day between the abundant piles of papers and buff files that had colonised it. All tidily stacked. I liked the neatness.

'How can I help you, Mlle Malroux?'

'I have a small artefact,' I borrowed her word, 'that I need to know more about. I would be grateful if you could . . .'

'Show me.' She held out her hand.

I liked the directness.

I drew from my coat pocket the small blue ankh that I had found in Gilles's wallet and let it lie on my palm for her to see.

'It looks as if it's carved out of some kind of unusual stone,' I pointed out.

Instantly she grew alert like a hound on the scent. She leaned forward, flicking her dusky-blond hair behind her ear. She wore it smooth on top and brushed out into a swirl of curls at jaw level like the film star Carole Lombard in *Fast and Loose*. Dr Liliane Delamarche looked very . . . very what? I studied her closely and considered my choice of word. Very modern.

'May I?' she asked, and lifted the object from my hand.

'I believe it's an ankh,' I said, so she wouldn't think I was totally ignorant.

She nodded. 'Yes, you're right, it's an ankh. What can I tell you? It's a fascinating symbol deeply rooted in ancient Egyptian culture. It's known as the key of life, but it can symbolise both life and life after death.'

'Eternity?'

'Ancient Egyptians were as eager to provide for their afterlife as they were for this life. That's why their tombs were crammed full of utilitarian everyday objects like food and drink, farming tools or hunting spears and even chariots or combs and mirrors. But entry into the afterlife was not guaranteed. The *ka* of the dead had to negotiate a dangerous underworld journey and face the final judgement before they were granted access which . . .' She checked herself and smiled. 'Don't get me started. I never know when to stop.'

I laughed. 'I'm interested. Please go on.'

'Well, the ankh was commonly depicted in the hands of ancient Egyptian deities, you see it a lot in the tomb paintings. It represents their power to sustain life, but also to revive human souls in the afterlife. There are depictions of the gods actually handing the ankh to the pharaoh.'

'Like Rameses II?'

'Oh yes, old Rameses possessed a powerful life force. But let's get back to your particular ankh.' She ran a finger over its blue surface speculatively. 'Where did it come from?'

'I found it inside the wallet of my brother who is now missing. I'm trying to find him and wondered if this ankh might be significant.'

'Has he travelled to Egypt?'

'No.'

I said it too fast. She glanced up from the ankh and fixed her gaze on my face. 'Missing, you say?'

'Yes.'

'What makes you think this ankh is significant?'

'He is not a man who holds on to useless things. If it's in his wallet, it's there for a reason. Could it be a love token?'

'It's possible. An expression of eternal love.'

'Is this one old?'

'It looks fairly new. Egyptians churn out hundreds of them these days for the tourists who travel out there.'

'If it were old, would it be valuable?'

'All items from ancient Egypt are of value to our understanding of their civilisation.'

We both stared at the small looped cross in her hand. She knew that's not what I meant. I waited.

She sighed, disappointed in me. 'As for its monetary value, let's take a look. At first glance, it's nothing special. Though they are not usually made of faïence these days.'

She reached into the top drawer of her desk and brought out a jeweller's eyeglass through which she proceeded to examine the ankh. After a moment's inspection she nodded to herself and removed the eyeglass.

'It's made from faïence coloured with cobalt,' she announced.

She replaced the ankh in the palm of my hand and in that brief flicker of time I heard my name. As clear as I am standing here, I heard Gilles speak my name.

The wind had picked up and swung to the north. So when Dr Delamarche and I walked past the Élysée Palace, the official residence of the President of France on rue du Faubourg Saint-Honoré, the *tricolore* was snapping and cracking its red, white and blue stripes at us with an energy that matched our own.

'Come,' Liliane had said to me in her office. She'd snatched her camel coat with its silky sable collar from the coatstand behind the door. 'Walk with me. I have an appointment.'

So we continued our conversation on the move. The street was busy, with large black ministerial Citroëns and a sleek blue Delage purring past us, but we ignored them. I was discovering that my companion was very single-minded. She was exactly what I wanted. Someone who knew things I didn't.

'What you have to understand,' Dr Delamarche was saying as we crossed avenue de Marigny, 'is that an ankh was a form of protection. Did your missing brother need protection?'

'Yes, he did.'

I glanced at her curious face. She wore a new-style slouch hat with a rolled brim that dipped over one eye and made her look mischievous. My old-fashioned cloche suddenly seemed inadequate. Or was it what was under it that was inadequate?

'But he knew,' I added, 'how to protect himself.'

'Maybe this time the forces of evil were too great for a little Egyptian charm in his wallet.'

I couldn't tell whether she was teasing me because just at that moment she halted in her tracks and announced, 'Here we are.'

Here was a pair of grand double doors with fluted pillars on either side. The words La Maison were picked out in discreet brass lettering above them, and a liveried doorman was already swinging the private club's door open for her.

'Good afternoon, Dr Delamarche,' he said with a welcoming smile. 'Your father has not yet arrived.'

'Typical,' she laughed. 'He's always late for everything.' She turned her head and informed me over her shoulder, 'Papa is something or other in President Lebrun's government,' as if that explained everything. 'Come on in and we'll finish our conversation before he arrives.'

The doorman gave me a look as I traipsed into the club's hallowed interior in her wake. He was certain I was here to steal the silver.

The carpet felt like an animal under my feet, its dark ruby pile was so deep. Inside, La Maison was sumptuous, all polished mahogany, glittering chandeliers, gilt-framed oil paintings and an imposing staircase that swept in a great curve to whatever secrets lay on the upper floors. This was a club for the rich and famous and I was like a nettle in a bed of lilies. Conspicuously misplaced.

But I liked it here. I liked it a lot.

'A *soixante-quinze* for me, please, Louis,' Dr Delamarche said to the barman, 'and one for my friend.'

My friend. It spilled so easily from her lips.

'You happy with that?' she asked me with a smile.

I nodded. I'd never drunk a *soixante-quinze* but I knew about it all right. A French 75 was a cocktail created in Paris, by Scotsman Harry MacElhone in his infamous Harry's Bar in rue Daunou where all the shiny American celebrities like Ernest Hemingway, Mary Pickford and Jack Dempsey gathered like starlings. So yes, I could manage to down a cocktail if offered. At three o'clock in the afternoon.

The bar wasn't busy at this hour, a few elderly men murmuring in low voices or ensconced in leather armchairs with their newspapers. Behind us against the far wall, dominated by row after row of solemn oil portraits of French politicians through the years, stood a bank of wine-coloured velvet booths for privacy. But my new *friend* sat herself down on a high stool at the bar and patted the pristine gloss of the polished surface in front of her.

'Let's take another look at it,' she said.

I removed the little package from my pocket and unrolled the layers of cottonwool in which Dr Delamarche had cocooned it. Before us lay the bright-blue ankh. We both leaned closer. Why had it been in Gilles's wallet?

'What are those markings on it?' I asked. There were odd notches on its sides.

'They are curious, I admit.'

On our walk from the Louvre to La Maison she had enlightened me on the making of Egyptian faïence. It was a form of ceramic created without the use of clay. It consisted of crushed quartz or sand, with calcite lime and alkalis added to produce a superb range of figures and pots and exquisite objects. But after a while I'd stopped listening to her words. I listened instead to her voice. It was so passionate about its subject that at one point she would have stepped out in front of a tram if I hadn't seized her.

And at that moment I'd wanted to be her. With all that enthusiasm and all that knowledge and all those pearl buttons. To be Dr Liliane Delamarche. I didn't want to be me.

'Do you know that an ankh was always laid on a dead pharaoh's lips? To help them open the door to the afterlife.'

I thought of Gilles and a shudder shot through me. What had happened to him? Please, Great Rameses, don't let him have need of an ankh. Or a door.

'You all right?' she murmured. 'All this talk of death can be too much for some. The ancient Egyptians were obsessed with death and the afterlife, so I am used to it. I forget sometimes that others can find it . . .' she threw back her head and laughed, shattering the muted mood in the bar, 'weird.'

Our drinks arrived and I took no more than a restrained sip. I nodded my approval of the champagne and gin mix, instead of knocking it straight back and calling for a second.

'Dr Delamarche, do you know anything about a missing hand from an Egyptian statue?' I asked.

'What?' She frowned at me over the rim of her coupe glass. 'Which statue are you talking about? Many of the statues are damaged, as you saw in our display hall.'

'I don't know which statue. Someone mentioned it to me. It seemed important.'

The silence came out of nowhere. One moment we were talking, the next moment we were not. Instead our eyes were locked and her blue gaze had lost its laughter. Neither of us touched our drinks.

She lowered her voice but each word was crystal-clear to me.

'What is going on?' she asked. 'Who are you? What is it you want?'

Before I had time to think up a lie, a man's voice boomed out behind me, 'Now who do we have here?'

As Dr Delamarche twisted on her stool, her face broke into a grin and I slipped the ankh off the bar into my pocket.

'Papa!' she scolded. 'You are wickedly late.'

A tall elegantly suited man leaned forward and kissed her forehead. I felt the blade of jealousy once more. To have a father. One who kisses you so sweetly.

'My apologies, *ma chérie*. Blasted Chautemps just wouldn't shut up and kept us all pinned in our seats while he droned on and on about the unemployment rate and getting the destitute off the freezing streets at night. He even regaled us with the charming story of seeing a man on the Champs-Élysées pick up and eat a bonbon that had been dropped on the road and trodden flat. Such was my day, Liliane.' He directed his smile at me. 'Enough of that. Now please introduce your friend.'

I held out my hand. 'I'm Camille Malroux. I came to see your daughter about some information on . . .'

'Ancient Egypt,' he finished and his laughter rattled the glasses that gleamed behind the bar. This was a man used to big spaces and big audiences. He stood ramrod-straight. Ex-military. Equipped with the moustache to prove it. I was instinctively wary. He represented the immutable backbone of authority and the harsh eye of the establishment, both of which I was raised to mistrust. 'It's always about some dig in Egypt,' he said, 'or a query about which vengeful god slew his brother or a request to translate the hieroglyph text of a new-found stela or to give a talk to a bunch of grubby postgraduates at the Sorbonne.' He rested his hand on his daughter's slender shoulder. 'Liliane is much in demand, Mlle Malroux.'

I could hear his pride.

'I am not surprised by that, M. Delamarche.'

'What is it you do?' he asked as if he had a right to know. 'Burrowing around in the museum too, I assume.'

'No, I am a *fonctionnaire*. I work for the civil service at the Hôtel de la Marine. As a typist at the moment, but I am studying for my exams to advance further within the system.'

I'd said too much. But I didn't want him to think I was a nobody.

'Don't tell me,' he responded, 'that you're one of those delusional women who expect to end up running a civil service office.'

'Yes. That is exactly my aim.'

He snorted his disgust. 'We're having that same problem in government. Women trying to access positions of responsibility. In the civil service it's absurd to even consider it. Women are too emotional and disorganised to work as effective civil servants. We all know that they let their feelings take precedence over professional considerations. This leads to difficulties within the management of the service and staff.'

He was lucky he didn't get the remains of my cocktail in his face.

'M. Delamarche,' I said angrily, 'women possess exactly the same feelings and abilities that men have. Who do you think kept this country running during the war when the men were off shooting each other?'

He treated me to a slow condescending smile. 'You prove my point exactly. Far too emotional. It's why we don't allow women the vote in this country. And there is the question of authority that is problematic. How could a woman command men? And how could men obey a woman?'

'Ask Lady Astor?' I snapped.

'Ah yes, the first female Member of Parliament in England.' He chuckled and brushed a finger along his luxuriant moustache. 'Such trouble. How the House is regretting that move. *Mon Dieu*, thanks to good French common sense we have to suffer no women in our National Assembly.'

'Papa,' his daughter scowled at him, 'you are a disgrace.'

'Your daughter is living proof right under your nose,' I pointed out with more heat than I intended, 'of women's ability to achieve high positions. And look at Marie Curie. She won the Nobel Prize in Physics in 1903 for her research into radiation. And she was the first woman in France to teach at the Sorbonne, telling male as well as female students what the hell to do. In 1911 she won a second Nobel Prize in chemistry. The only person in history to win a Nobel Prize in two different disciplines. A woman.'

Mentally I thanked my dear English friend Barnaby for feeding me such educational books. In the bar I squared up to this arrogant bastard, not caring whether or not I lowered my voice. 'Of course women are as clever and capable as men. *Merde*, this is 1933, you need to come out of the Dark Ages, Monsieur.'

I turned to his daughter. 'Thank you for your time and for your help. I will leave you in peace now.' I downed the last of my cocktail, slid off my stool, ignored the father and walked out of the bar.

His voice followed me, unaware of its own volume as he commented to his daughter, 'She seems a bright enough young woman. Ambitious, obviously. Her head full of nonsense though. But she won't get anywhere unless she cleans up her mouth and stops wearing that awful cheap perfume. Utterly nauseating.'

I didn't hear Dr Delamarche's murmured reply.

CHAPTER FOURTEEN

◆ ◆ ◆

GILLES

'Christophe.'

A woman was calling to someone. Gilles recognised the voice. It was her. He moved his head on the pillow to see if he could see this Christophe anywhere, but no one else was in the room. Just her.

'Christophe,' the voice was gentle, 'wake up.'

A hand nudged his arm.

He took a deep breath and dragged himself to the surface. It was like fighting his way through wet sand. His eyes opened fully and there she was, leaning over him, smiling. Silvery-grey eyes bright with concern.

'Hello,' he mumbled.

Relief softened the edges of her face. She was around mid-thirties, he guessed, with a high shiny forehead, the kind that is packed with knowledge. Her hair was dark and rolled into sausage curls that made her look older than she was.

She stood up straight and took his hand between hers. '*Eh bien*, Christophe, there you are at last.'

'I'm not Christophe.'

She smiled indulgently. 'What does a name matter?'

Slowly, bit by bit, images of a doctor and a priest trickled into his mind and with it came again the trickle of fear. 'What am I doing here?'

'You were injured in a train crash and you are recovering.'

'Why here?'

A jolt shot through him as the mist and the sand gradually cleared from his mind and he realised that there were no drugs in his system today to keep it shut down. She'd forced no spoon to his lips. She wanted him awake. Awake meant in pain.

'Why here?' he asked again and watched her watching him closely.

'Dear Christophe.' She stroked the back of his hand but it was more disturbing than comforting. 'I am here to help you. I believe it was a sign from God that you were brought to my door. Let me help you.'

'But why would you want to do that?'

She smiled at him and though she would pass unnoticed in a crowd, her smile was beautiful. It lit up the dreary little room. 'Blessed are the merciful, for they shall obtain mercy. Blessed are the pure in heart, for they shall see God.' She gently tucked his hand under the bedcover. 'You were brought to me, Christophe. By God. For a reason.'

'What reason?'

'Ah, that is for us to discover.'

Gilles had seen what happened to the merciful and to the meek on the backstreets of Montparnasse when he was a child. They got beaten into the ground. It seemed to him that people who are unable to make a success of what life has to offer here on earth console themselves with the hope of heavenly rewards afterwards. It helps them deal with the pain of life. That was fine. He had no objections to that. Everyone needs a little consolation along the way, but he did object to them ramming it down his throat. This woman seemed to be seeking salvation by saving him, body and soul. But why him?

'What is your name?' he asked.

'Mme Rosa Lagarde.'

'Is there a M. Lagarde?'

'No. He passed away.'

'I'm sorry.'

'I'm not.'

'And where are we?'

'In God's embrace.'

'And where exactly is God embracing us? In which town or village?'

'That is not important right now.'

'It is important to me.'

She firmly straightened his bedcover that didn't need straightening. '*You* are important to me, Christophe. Remember that.'

Things changed after that.

The spoon still materialised each day but its contents were reduced. Gilles no longer spent the day in a drugged coma. On the other hand, it meant the pain in his leg swept in like lava, burning up all else, and he found himself longing for her footstep on the stair and the chink of glass on metal. The taste of the liquid was as bitter as death itself. He was no fool. He guessed it was laudanum but found it impossible to deny himself the relief it brought, at least for now.

'Open the window, please?' he asked her.

'So you can jump out?' she laughed and he liked her laugh.

'So I can breathe fresh air instead of stale sickroom leavings.'

'We're on the first floor up here.'

'Are we in a house or an apartment?'

'This is a separate house, away from other buildings.' She gave him a long serious look. 'So no chance that others will hear you, if you shout.'

'Why should I shout? I am being well cared for.'

That made her smile.

'The window?' he prompted.

She obliged and opened the sash window. The day was overcast, the sky like a dirty sheet of ice, but the scent and taste of the air was nothing like the thick fumes of Paris. This air smelled of animals instead of people, of loamy earth instead of the familiar filth of the city streets. Gilles didn't like it.

But she was right not to trust him. He had seriously considered jumping.

CHAPTER FIFTEEN

◆ ◆ ◆

CAMILLE

They gave me no warning. I walked into the ward unaware, my head still pulsing with rage.

I'd entered the hospital and hurried through its maze of corridors knowing that the only way I was going to find my brother was by discovering the identity of the man lying in the hospital bed. The one masquerading as someone he wasn't. The one with the name Gilles Malroux typed on his medical chart. My hopes that the ankh would lead me to the whereabouts of the real Gilles had hit a brick wall, and a sick churning in the pit of my stomach dulled my senses. When I entered the ward, I was only half there.

I'd stopped in one of the hospital washrooms and scrubbed with their harsh institutional soap at my wrists and under my ears to scour away the perfume that my sweet Anne-Marie had given me for Christmas. I saw my cheeks burning with shame when I glanced in the washroom mirror.

The ward was busier than usual. The late afternoon light had split into shafts that streaked on to the white bedcovers like spears, pinning them down. I paid them little attention as I headed further along past the metal beds, my thoughts on the strange object in my pocket and on the man who'd said to me, *You prove my point. Far too emotional.*

What if he was right?

Could I change myself? Could I become as calm and as collected as his elegant daughter? Was that what I needed? To progress? Was it lack of control that my supervisor, Mme Beaufort, saw peeking out from under my neatly polished shoes and—

I halted. I snatched a quick breath. The oxygen mask was off. The bandages were gone.

I saw his face.

His hand rested in mine on the bedcover as I sat quietly in the chair, while a nurse fussed with a thermometer.

'You must be pleased,' she said sweetly, 'to see your brother improving.'

'Yes.'

'As he's awake, I'll bring a small bowl of broth for you to feed him. I'm sure you can manage that, can't you?'

'Yes.'

'He'll be sore, so take care, won't you?'

'Yes.'

I was the very model of calm and collected.

The spoonful of broth slipped between his blistered lips and he swallowed, his swollen and sore-looking eyelids at half-mast. Bloodshot eyes watching me. It must have been a good-looking face. Before.

Before the train leaped off the rails. Before the fire ripped through the carnage. Before the screams in the darkness and the raw fear. It set my heart hammering and a cold sweat lay clammy on my skin. Had Gilles been there alongside this man? In those flames?

This face had strong cheekbones and a long jaw that was patched with gauze dressings held in place by strips of white tape. On his forehead too. The areas of skin that I could see were an angry red and shiny with ointment, his eyes a deep honey shade. His unswerving gaze made me uneasy. I was feeding a complete stranger and he must be wondering why.

'I'm glad you seem to be a little better,' I said softly. 'And that you are awake.'

He said nothing. He hadn't yet spoken. I eased the spoon to his lips again. It is an extraordinarily intimate act, to be feeding someone like a child.

'I'm sorry you are here,' I murmured. 'Sorry you are in pain. Did the nurse tell you that you were in a train crash and that the doctors are doing their best for you?'

Very slowly his eyes closed. Leaving me behind. Was he remembering? I wanted to stroke his brittle crisped hair and tell him he was safe now, not to be frightened, but I didn't. Instead I fed him three more spoonfuls and gently dabbed at his lips with a muslin cloth. I kept my breathing calm, but I could see his was ragged, his chest jumpy.

'What is your name?' I asked.

'I don't know.' His voice was low and scratchy. His eyes didn't open.

'You don't know?'

'I can't remember.'

'You don't remember your own name?'

The faintest of nods.

'Do you remember anything? The crash? Your home? Your work? Your family? Your life . . . ?' I made myself stop.

A slight shake of his head on the pillows.

'*Mon Dieu*, that must be frightening. I'm so sorry.'

His eyes opened, wider this time, tired and troubled, but the corners of his lips twitched into the faintest smile. 'Of course you are, Camille.'

'Well now, M. Malroux, this is excellent news. You are awake and that is encouraging progress. We are pleased with you.'

It was Dr Arquette, the surgeon. His voice of authority issued from behind the curtain that the nurse had whisked around the injured man's bed. Dr Arquette was conducting his ward rounds and had dismissed me from his patient's bedside with a curt gesture of his long skilled fingers. I waited outside the curtains, tucked against the wall where I could observe who came into the ward and who left.

'Your injuries are responding well to treatment,' Dr Arquette's voice continued. 'But we still have concerns, so I think we will request that your visitor leave you in peace today. You need total rest.'

I heard no response from the man in the bed. Was he staring at the surgeon the way he'd stared at me? A questioning and wary gaze, assessing what he saw. Examining each word. The surgeon strode away with barely a glance in my direction, followed by a flurry of white coats and stethoscopes eager to keep up with him. A nurse drew back the curtain and smiled at me apologetically.

'The doctor has prescribed total rest for our patient, so I'm afraid I'm going to have to ask you to leave, Mlle Malroux.'

'Nurse Laurent,' I said, 'if you woke up in pain, not knowing who the hell you were, don't you think you'd want your sister to sit and hold your hand? Isn't that the kindest thing to allow.'

She flushed slightly. 'The doctor has ordered it, Mademoiselle. I'm sorry but you must leave.' Her fingers gave the curtain a final embarrassed twitch.

'No.' It came from the man in the bed. 'No.' His voice was weak. 'I want her here.'

Quickly I moved closer to the bed and rested a hand lightly on his shoulder. It was surprisingly muscular. The hospital pyjamas felt rough. 'I'll stay, Gilles, I promise,' I said, and dropped a kiss on this stranger's thick chestnut hair. I tasted blood.

He looked up at me, his honey-coloured eyes fixed on mine. 'Stay,' he murmured.

The nurse regarded us uncertainly.

'I'll be good.' I smiled.

She glanced up and down the ward to ensure no doctor was in sight. 'Very well,' she said with reluctance. 'Half an hour.'

'Thank you.'

She bustled off to another bed whose occupant was fussing about having no water in his jug and I sank down on to the hard chair. I took my so-called brother's bandaged hand in mine. It felt like that was where it belonged.

'Now,' I whispered softly, 'let's see what you can remember.'

CHAPTER SIXTEEN

◆ ◆ ◆

CAMILLE

'I am in darkness. I remember nothing. My past is gone.'

The voice of the man in the hospital bed, the one with my brother's name on the chart at his feet and the look of restraint in his striking amber eyes, sounded bleak and raw. Yet there was no self-pity in the way he said it. He was quietly stating a fact, one so terrible that it wrenched something deep inside me. Our past is who we are. It is our identity. Without knowing who we were before, how can we know who we are now? Or who we want to be in the future.

'Don't look so shocked,' he murmured. Talking was clearly an effort. 'Dr Arquette says retrograde amnesia is not uncommon. After a traumatic event and a blow to the head. He says I could recover my memory. Given time.'

I don't have time.

'Do you remember anything at all?'

'I remember you. Your voice in my ear hour after hour when I had nothing else to hold on to.'

I smiled. 'That's a start. Anything more? From before the train crash.'

'Bits and pieces. Floating around in my head.' His breath grew short. Distressed. 'Everything is disconnected. No order or time. Sometimes I get a picture. Or part of a picture.'

'What kind of picture?'

'Of a garden. Of my foot on a spade. Burying a black cat.' His eyes flickered. Physical pain or mental pain? I couldn't tell.

'I'm sorry,' I offered, but it felt so little. 'Let me help you.'

His face changed. His strong features settled into a new calmness beneath the blotchy gauze patches and his eyes shed some of their pain. 'Why would you do that, Camille?'

I leaned closer and dropped my voice to little more than a whisper. 'If you were able to hear me when I first came here, you'll know I thought that under the bandages you were my brother. You had his wallet and the police informed me that you were Gilles. I talked to you, I . . .' I hesitated, 'I said things because I believed you to be my brother. Do you recall?'

'I recall. And I recall you saying, "Who are you? What have you done with my brother?" So I know you are not my sister.'

'Have you told the police that?'

'No, not yet. I wanted to talk with you first.'

'Thank you.'

There was a long silence except for a rattle like loose nails inside his lungs.

'My brother has disappeared and I have to find him urgently, but he is already on the wrong side of the law, so I don't want to set the police looking for him.' I wanted to say so many things to this man who studied me with such intensity but it was too early to explain everything, he was too sick. I kept it simple. 'I need to know how you came to be in possession of my brother's wallet. Where did your paths cross?'

I heard a faint sigh and the nails shifting behind his ribs. He shook his head. 'Camille, I'd tell you if I knew.'

Could I believe him? I wanted to.

I looked at my hand wrapped around his on the white sheet. His was a broad capable hand, a hand that could do things, bearing no wedding band, and I wondered whether a nurse had removed it when placing the gauze dressing across his palm, or if there had been no ring to remove. For a full five minutes we remained like that, isolated from the murmuring of voices in the ward. I had never considered before how essential memories are. How do you face each day if you no longer know who you love? Or what kind of person you are. Or what you do for a living. He could be a murderer or he could be a doctor or a taxman or a jazz player. How can he tell?

Merde, he must be in a cold sweat.

'Don't panic,' I said with a reassuring laugh. 'Together we'll reconstruct the person you are. Piece by piece. You need rest now, like the doctor said. You look exhausted.'

Exhausted was too small a word. His face looked drained of all hope, haunted and gaunt. Who was this man?

'But I will come back this evening,' I promised, 'and we'll start your reconstruction.'

By the time I returned to the Salpêtrière the sky was filthy with unshed rain. Paris was looking miserable. The wind had not abated and through the tall windows of the ward I could see trees thrashing their bare branches. The sound of their violence was eerie within this place of quiet. Voices were kept low. There was an unspoken acceptance that the healing process required silence to do its work, and the air hung heavy with whispers and with the scent of unknown medications. I sat wrapped around by the silence and waited for the mystery man in the hospital bed to wake. He was moaning softly in his sleep. There was so much I needed to ask him but I forced myself to patience.

When he finally surfaced from whatever nightmares he was fighting his way through, I welcomed him with a smile and gently rubbed his undamaged wrist to bring him back to the reality of where he was.

'First,' I said, 'let's give you a name.'

'What do you suggest?'

'Something memorable. We don't want you to forget it again, do we?'

'Like what?' His eyes could barely stay open. They were muddy with fatigue. Or was it pain?

'Any preferences?'

'No. You choose one.'

'Let's name you Beauregard.'

I wanted him to laugh at the irony. He looked anything but handsome at the moment. He managed a small indulgent smile.

'I'll call you Beau for short,' I added.

'Beau it is then.'

'Now, Beau, let's find out what kind of man you are.'

From a bulky canvas holdall that I had placed on the floor, I extracted a bundle of *La Vie Parisienne* magazines that I'd scrounged from Anne-Marie, my friend in Montparnasse, and which I placed on my lap, but first I laid out Barnaby's colour wheel on the bed. A colour wheel, Barnaby had explained to me, was useful to artists because it showed colours arranged in a circle according to their relationship with each other. Who knew colours had relationships?

'Your favourite colour?' I asked.

His finger travelled unerringly to one of the triangles of colour and rested there.

'Royal purple.' I smiled. 'Interesting. Power and mystery.'

He lifted a sceptical eyebrow but winced, as even that simple movement of skin caused him pain.

'Get ready for more,' I warned.

I held each magazine up for him to see and I slowly turned the pages. He studied the pictures closely. They depicted life in France, a wide variety of houses and fashion and advertisements, and all the time we talked about the images, so that bit by bit we learned more about him.

Cottage in the country or town apartment? Cottage.

Dog or cat? Cat.

Book or film? Book.

Smart shoes or walking boots? Boots.

Bible or Baudelaire? Baudelaire.

Blond- or dark-haired women? Both. We laughed.

Wine or cognac? Both.

Game of cards or game of football? Tennis.

Trilby or cap? Neither. Grey felt fedora.

French *chansons* or American jazz? Édith Piaf.

Favourite city? Venice.

Favourite fruit? Cherries.

Hot weather or cold? Cold.

Travelling by train or car? He started to shake.

I held a cup to his lips and slowly he sipped the water.

'Thank you, Camille.'

'Feeling better?'

He said nothing.

It struck me that he was a thinker. I had a boss in my office at the Hôtel de la Marine, Captain Moreau, who was the same. He thought things through in detail before voicing any words. Not like me. I speak too soon.

'So,' he said quietly, 'what do you make of me now that you have found some pieces?'

'You lead a good life, Beau. You are educated. You have travelled. You most likely ski in winter and play tennis in summer. You read poetry and you live in a village where there is good clean air to breathe and birdsong in the trees. Probably a cockerel wakes you up in the—'

'A cockerel.' He blinked. Again and again, as though squeezing out a memory.

Something had clicked.

I stayed silent. Slowly, I watched him drag something up to the surface from the murk in his brain.

His eyes fixed on mine and for the first time I saw a flicker of fire in them as a real memory emerged. 'A big boastful cockerel,' he said and a smile began behind the gauze patches. 'Maximilien. Jade and coppery-gold feathers and bright scarlet wattles.'

'You remember a cockerel? Called Maximilien. But not your house. Not a wife?'

'Maximilien lived nearby.'

'On a farm?'

'No. In a . . .' His hand with the dressing across its palm reached up and tapped the side of his head to chase away trails of mist. 'In a garden. A woman used to feed him. Old.' His eyes narrowed with effort. 'Someone . . . someone else . . . hated him.'

'Which someone, Beau? Your wife?'

Again the long pause. I could feel the pain vibrating through him. The battle he was fighting. I brushed my hand over his, just a brief touch to soothe.

'Forget the cockerel for now,' I murmured. 'I have something else for you to see.'

I opened my other hand and on my palm lay the ankh. 'I found it in my brother's wallet.'

He said nothing, gave me no admission of recognition, but he didn't need to. He started to shake again and I felt guilty. Was I pushing too fast? I closed my fingers over the strange cross to hide it from view but he held out a hand, palm up. I laid the artefact on the gauze dressing and he continued to stare at it with the kind of attention to detail that I give to shoes.

'What is your connection to my brother?' I whispered. 'Was this yours, not his? Did he take it from you after the crash?'

Beau's breathing had become laboured. There was a new and terrible sadness in his face that was painful for me to observe because I knew I had put it there.

'It's an Egyptian ankh,' he said. Almost inaudible.

'You've seen it before?'

He nodded.

'But how?' I asked.

'I don't know, Camille. I have no idea. But just the sight of that ankh makes my skin go cold. And when I see it in your hand,' he lifted his sombre gaze from my hand to my face, 'my skin goes cold for you too.'

'You believe it's dangerous in some way?'

'Yes.'

'Maybe for Gilles too?'

'Yes.'

I hadn't told him about the man who had stopped me in the street outside the police station. The one with the unpolished boots who called himself Robespierre. Nor had I mentioned that he had threatened me and promised to return in two weeks. I shuddered. So why did Beau believe the ankh was steeped in danger? What did he know? Locked deep inside his head.

'I've been to the Louvre Museum,' I informed him, 'to the Egyptian Antiquities hall, but it got me no further forward. I have only one more slender thread to chase unless you can remember something, Beau. Like why you were on the train. Or whether you were riding it alongside my brother. Did you agree to swap identities for some purpose?'

'I remember lying in the dark and a man gripping my hand like you are. It was his grip that kept me from sliding into . . .' He stopped.

'Into what?'

'Into all kinds of hell. There were screams. The howling of devils.' His eyes closed and I waited for him to come back to me. When he finally opened them he added, 'He might have swapped wallets then, I don't know.'

'If it was Gilles, it means he survived the crash. But where is he now?'

At that moment a nurse in her stiff white headdress drifted softly through the ward, murmuring, 'It is time to leave. Visiting time is over.' There came the sound of chairs shifting and *au revoirs* being said.

I didn't want to leave. I liked the stillness here. The sense of safety. I wanted to sit here longer, holding the bandaged hand and helping to reconstruct Beau from scratch. I realised I was starting to like this man.

'Camille, an ankh is supposed to be the key of life.'

His eyes filled with sudden compassion and he dragged in a thin breath. I leaned closer.

'This one,' he whispered, 'is the key of death.'

How far could I trust him?

I am not a gullible person. As the child of a *putain* on the streets of Paris, I'd seen too much of life in the raw and had all gullibility knocked out of me. The question that kept plaguing me was this: had Beau really forgotten his past, had it all fallen into a black abyss? Unreachable. Or was he holding out on me? Hiding the truth for reasons I couldn't begin to guess at.

What exactly was going on here?

That night I sat on the bed of my painter friend, Barnaby, alongside the lovely Anne-Marie whose madame had given her tonight off work because a bastard client gave her a split lip and a black eye yesterday. We were drinking a bottle of something that tasted as if it had been drained from the waters of the Seine and watched Barnaby wielding his brushes. He was painting a nude. The model was sprawled in his lovely old green velvet chair and kept bursting into song, so that Barnaby had to shout '*Tais-toi!*' but to no avail. The model was male. As blond and beautiful as the picture of the son of Zeus pinned on the ceiling above the bed, so Barnaby couldn't bring himself to get annoyed with him.

As I lolled against Anne-Marie, the expression I'd seen in Beau's eyes wouldn't leave me. It hovered at the corner of my line of sight so that every time I moved my head, I saw it. I emptied my glass and Anne-Marie refilled it. Beau's eyes had held such compassion. Its warmth reached inside me.

'He's not lying,' I said out loud to no one in particular.

Barnaby dabbed a smear of Scarlet Lake on the canvas, setting the young man's thigh on fire. 'You mean your mystery amnesiac? It sounds to me as though he's in serious trouble if all the poor chap can remember is burying a black cat.'

He picked up another brush and dragged it through the pool of Prussian Blue on his palette. I knew the weird names of these colours now and was in awe of the magic that Barnaby could make them perform.

'And the ankh,' Anne-Marie pointed out, twisting her blond curls around her pretty fingers. 'It seems he remembers the ankh from somewhere.'

'Yes, but where?' I slumped flat on my back on the bed. Even its cover smelled of turpentine. 'Does it mean that he and Gilles must know each other? Unless Gilles just came across the ankh by chance in Beau's pocket and stole it. I wouldn't put it past him.' I sighed heavily. 'I'm starting to get angry with him.'

'Angry at the stranger?' Barnaby queried.

'No, at my brother. I don't want to be angry with him, but if he really did escape from the crash, why hasn't he been in touch with me? He knows I would be worried sick.'

'Face it, Camille,' Anne-Marie said, 'Gilles has a history of getting on the wrong side of the law. He has probably just gone into hiding. Stop worrying. One day he'll come bounding up our stairs again, bearing gifts.' She laughed. Anne-Marie had always had a soft spot for Gilles. 'You know what he's like.'

I hadn't told them about the man. The one who had demanded a hand from me. Two weeks. I lifted my own hand up in front of my face and stared at it. It was spotlessly clean and its nails had been manicured by Anne-Marie. 'I fear for his life,' I whispered.

In his rucksack under my bed I had found an elaborate leather volume called *The Book of the Dead*. Gilles's name, in handwriting I didn't recognise, was scrawled in large letters on the inside cover.

CHAPTER SEVENTEEN

◆ ◆ ◆

CAMILLE

The next morning I did something I'd never done before. I called in sick. I hurried through the rain past the old green metal pissoir to the telephone at the back of Simone's Bar at the end of the street, dialled my office number at the Hôtel de la Marine and told them I had a raging fever. Simone, wearing a shin-length khaki apron, watched me lie through my teeth with a grin on her face and a breakfast glass of wine in her hand. I hung up, feeling genuinely sick. Sick to my stomach. I had done all in my power to appear to be the perfect employee, the perfect choice for further advancement up the civil service ladder. And now this.

Gilles. Where the hell are you?

I had to work fast. Make every minute of my stolen day count. First I hopped on the Métro, line twelve, across the river to Madeleine, a station in the 8th *arrondissement*. The Madeleine itself dominates the area, big and showy, a huge Catholic church that looks for all the world like a Roman temple with its mass of Corinthian columns. I'd never been through its great brass doors. I expected gladiators to be slitting each other's throats inside but there was more than enough throat-slitting going on out here on the street.

I stood on the pavement and observed for a while, acting like a typical tourist. Gazing up in awe at the fifty-two massive pillars that surround the church, but at the same time keeping a sharp eye on the point where the place de la Madeleine ran into rue Tronchet. Right on the corner lay a large shop with a wide glass frontage and over its doorway was blazoned the name Le Rêve in shiny gold letters. It was a toyshop. In my pocket lay the receipt I had found in Gilles's wallet.

The rain had ceased, but its efforts had darkened the pale Lutetian limestone that is the mark of this city's buildings. *Paris stone* is what we call it, a creamy greyish stone that gives the city a unique attraction, but right now I failed to see the city's beauty. I feared I was wasting my time here.

I crossed the road and entered the shop, watchful. The bell over the door tinkled. Paris was the first city in the world to install electric streetlights and was proud of its bright arc lamps, but whoever owned this shop had taken it all a step further. Everything glimmered and glistened under a barrage of lights. I was drowning in glass cabinets of gleaming lead soldiers, shelves of boxed model cars, dolls with dead porcelain faces and hair like sheets of gold, metal toy trains and shiny fire engines. Skipping ropes, puppets, wind-up monkeys, farm animals and an ugly pull-along wooden duck. I stood transfixed. I'd never been in a toyshop before in my life.

When I'd slunk as a child through the backstreets of Montparnasse, I'd have given my right eye to own one of those cap guns on display in front of me under a glass counter. The one with the gunmetal-grey barrel that looked like it meant business and bone-cream handle. A bucking bronco etched on it. I shoved my hand in my pocket to stop it reaching over to snatch it. I stared instead at a fancy red pedal car that years ago Gilles would have taken a whipping to ride in, given the chance, and got my bearings.

The shop was large, extending far back beneath an archway, with numerous counters and display units. Neat piles of board games and balsawood model sets made me recall our childish attempts at playing draughts in the dirt of the cemetery and Gilles's newspaper aeroplanes flying free on the wind. Even at this early hour the shop was busy, one fur-coated woman drooling over a pink doll's house that made me want to throw up.

A man in a sleek pinstriped suit glided up to me, as oily as his slicked-back hair. He wore thin wire spectacles and what looked like a sleeping ferret under his nose.

'Can I help you, Madame?'

'Yes, I hope you can.' I removed the receipt from my pocket. Not for a moment did I think it would lead anywhere but I was all out of other options. 'My brother bought a toy here recently. It says toy car on it. I'd like to purchase another one the same if you have it still in stock.'

He smiled a big well-practised smile. 'I do indeed. Please come this way.'

He led me to a shelf with an array of brightly coloured tinplate cars on it and picked one up. Larger than I expected.

'*Voilà.*'

He presented it to me on his palm with a flourish. It was a blue-and-cream saloon car with great big headlamps and an opening boot which he demonstrated. About the size of a shoe.

'Do you recall selling one to my brother?' I asked.

'I will check my records,' he said obligingly.

'*Merci.* I'd appreciate it.'

He placed the car on a counter for me to inspect and vanished into a back room. There was a low hum of chatter in the shop as other customers browsed the toys on offer, but no one looked my way. I edged towards the cap gun collection. That was when I caught sight of a display of little highly coloured blue and gold tin boxes stacked in the shape of a pyramid. I hurried over to them and picked one up. They were trinket boxes no bigger than my palm, made from a light metal and designed in the shape of King Tutankhamen's coffin, twinkling royal gold and lapis-blue under the lights. Egypt had followed me here.

I opened one, lifting the top off. Of course there was nothing inside it, of course not. What was I thinking? I carried it over to the counter and placed it beside the tinplate car and I didn't like the way my hand shook. The manager returned from his back room; in his hand lay a sheet of paper.

'It seems that the purchase was made three weeks ago,' he informed me.

'Can I speak to the person who served him?'

'It was M. Sarrazin. He is busy in the stockroom at the moment. Ah, Madame, I see you have selected one of our Tutankhamen boxes. A delight, are they not? The public cannot get enough of anything from Ancient Egypt ever since Howard Carter's discovery of the tomb. Everyone is keen to buy something connected to the young pharaoh and his beautiful funerary objects that were—'

'Monsieur, I am short of time.'

His oily smile slipped a fraction.

'I'll take the cap gun with the bone handle as well, plus a box of caps.'

He rang up my purchases on his till and I paid, but as I did so, I murmured, 'And M. Sarrazin?'

'I will fetch him to wrap them,' he said more brusquely.

He vanished again and returned with a wide-shouldered man in tow who proceeded to cocoon my toy car, trinket tin and toy pistol in snowy tissue paper while the manager looked on with approval. M. Sarrazin was courteous and answered my questions quietly. No, he didn't know why my brother picked that car and no, he bought nothing else. No, he'd never seen him in the shop before or since. Paid in cash and didn't seem at all agitated.

But I was agitated. So agitated I could barely catch his replies. There was a frantic buzzing in my ears. This man, this *M. Sarrazin*, wrapping my parcel so neatly and tying it up with string, was the same man who in the bar opposite the police station had threatened to cut off my hand in two weeks' time. It was M. Robespierre.

I tore at the string. Snagged it so hard it cut into my finger and drew blood. I ripped open the brown paper the way an animal claws at its prey, pieces flying away in the wind like feathers. I'd hunkered down behind one of the Madeleine's vast columns because I could wait no longer. I had found myself in the shadowy world where nothing is as it seems, where you grasp at something and suddenly it isn't there anymore.

Like Beau and his memories. Wisps of nothingness.

The tissue paper fluttered as the wind snatched at its white folds and I heard its rustling as a warning, a clear warning, but I told myself to ignore such foolishness. I was not my mother. I didn't believe in super-stition. I raked my fingers through it to reach the little tin coffin of Tutankhamen and as I lifted it free of its wrappings, I heard something inside it rattle. My heart stopped.

An elderly couple on their way to morning coffee hurried past me, hunched against the chill wind, but they were no more than a blur to me. A bristle-furred dog came and sniffed at my shoe but something about me made him back away and retrace his steps the way he had come. Was I becoming toxic now? Is that what the dog sensed in me?

I opened the tin coffin.

Inside lay a miniature figure made of some kind of stone, exquisitely carved and painted in gold and black. Its body was wearing an elabo-rate ankle-length tunic with what looked like tiny jewels embedded in it, so that even in the heavy shadows of the church it threw darts of light at me. The figure's long hair was painted jet-black with a fringe like Cleopatra's. It looked like an Egyptian woman, similar to ones I'd seen in the Louvre. Her arms were folded across her body but there was nothing at all defensive about it.

My mouth went dry. Her head lay loose and unattached. Severed from the body. Robespierre had placed them there. He was sending me an unmistakable message.

CHAPTER EIGHTEEN

◆ ◆ ◆

GILLES

She was shaving him.

It was a disturbingly intimate action, her fingers touching the skin of his face as she manoeuvred the blade, but innocent enough. Yet he would have preferred to continue unshaven.

'Christophe, I cannot stand your stubble for one more minute,' she had announced as she cleared away his breakfast tray. 'It is time for a shave.'

He had assumed she intended him to shave himself, but no.

'Your hand is still far too shaky,' she insisted. 'I will do it. I used to shave my father after his stroke.' Her eyes shone with anticipation. 'Don't worry.'

He had been shaven by a barber on occasion and thought nothing of it, but this woman? She could slit his throat. She soaked a towel in hot water and wrapped it over the lower half of his face. It was scalding hot.

'Christophe, what were you doing on that train?' she asked, patting the towel against his skin.

When she removed it, he answered, 'I would tell you if I could, but I have no memory of why I was on that train.'

'Where were you going? To Strasbourg?'

'Maybe. I wish I knew.'

Did she swallow the lie?

She soaked the badger shaving brush in hot water, then using a small amount of shaving soap from a pot, she mixed it with the brush into a lather in a shaving bowl. Her movements were easy and rhythmic, something she'd done many times before, but he could sense that her mind was still on the train.

'Was this your father's shaving equipment?' he inquired to shift her thoughts elsewhere.

'No. My husband's.'

He regarded the crisply stropped blade of the cut-throat razor and wondered if she had shaved him too and what he had died of.

She gave him a smile. 'Ready?'

He nodded.

With a swirling motion she began to lather the lower half of his face, avoiding his moustache, and tipped his head back to spread the soapy cream under his chin and jaw.

So far so good.

'Do you remember the crash?' she asked abruptly.

'No.'

She lifted the brush from his face and her silvery eyes darkened to the colour of the birch-tree bark outside. 'Really? You don't recall the train accident?'

He stared at her, blank-faced. 'No. It's gone.'

But he did. He remembered it. Every single raging second. The wild panic. The chaos. The fear that burned like wildfire. The sudden impact that shook your bones loose and the child's cries, the crushing weight of Dr Laval in his metal spectacles. His neck snapped. The carnage outside and the dying man's *Help me . . . please*. How could anyone forget? It was branded forever on his mind, along with the screams and howls that would echo through his dreams.

She held the blade at the correct thirty-degree angle and it ran as smooth as silk along his face in the direction of his stubble's growth. A light pressure, nothing more.

'Do you remember arriving here?' The question was half under her breath as if not to upset the rhythm of the shave.

'Yes.'

Her fingers lifted his chin, tilting his head back, so that she could draw the skin taut as the blade glided down towards his throat.

'Who brought you here?'

'A priest and a farm worker.'

She nodded. The blade rested on his throat. 'Who are you running from?'

'No one.'

'What is your job?'

'I buy and sell things.'

'What kind of things?'

'Anything that people will pay good money for.'

'What is your name?'

'Christophe.'

She relaxed her hold on him and smiled. 'Would you buy and sell things for me?'

'If the price is right.' He smiled back at her.

'How did you get the white streak in your hair and the scar on your lip?'

'A knife fight in Marseille.'

She laughed. 'You are a terrible liar.'

She rinsed off his face with cold water, then splashed aftershave on his skin so liberally that he winced.

'Sting?' she asked.

'Like a scorpion,' he answered.

CHAPTER NINETEEN

◆ ◆ ◆

CAMILLE

'What is so important about the hand?'

I considered Beau's question. I had hurried over to the 13th *arrondissement* again, to the hospital, and made my way to his bedside faster this time. I was getting used to the vastness of the place, the immense scale of Salpêtrière. I'd learned from one of the older nurses that as many as five thousand unfortunates used to have beds here sixty years ago when it was a charitable hospital for infirm and insane women. In those days sewers and rats overflowed down on the lower levels. It gave me the shudders. No sign of that now in this quiet sterile ward.

'Robespierre claims that Gilles has stolen it from him,' I said. 'Part of a statue. But I have no idea how large or small it is meant to be or what its value is. He wasn't exactly informative.'

I had told Beau about M. Sarrazin. Or Robespierre, as he called himself. I'd hoped my description of him might trigger a memory, something I could work with, but no. Another dead end.

Beau reached out with one of his injured hands and gently wrapped it around my wrist. 'I think you have done enough, I am concerned about the consequences. Go to the gendarmerie and report your M. Sarrazin to the police. Stay away from that shop.'

'Where I come from, you don't go to the gendarmerie unless you're dragged there by force.' I gave him a wry smile and reached into the canvas bag at my feet. 'I've brought you some news papers.'

He made an effort to raise his head a little.

'How are you feeling today?' I'd asked when I'd arrived. 'Your colour is better.' I smiled to encourage him to believe the lie.

He'd nodded. 'My thoughts are clearer. Today I intend to dig for buried treasure in this useless head of mine.' Hope glistened so brightly in his eyes that my heart went out to him and I was determined not to let his words be pipe dreams.

I dumped a bunch of the newspapers on to the bed cover.

'Take a look. The train crash is all over them. Maybe the reports and photographs will trigger something.'

I sensed something that felt like an electric shock pass through him when he touched the printed pages. I tried not to show it but I had high hopes. Surely the graphic details would open a door in his mind. He started to shuffle through the various papers but his movements gradually slowed, his fingers grew sluggish, and I knew that somewhere deep inside, in the damaged part of his brain on which the crash was forever imprinted, it was all too much.

'Read them out to me,' he whispered. 'Please.'

'Are you sure?'

'Yes.' He said the word fiercely.

'Very well. Let's start with a look at the facts.' I discarded some of the more lurid accounts and began to read aloud in a low unemotional voice.

'The 23rd December 1933 was a nasty winter day in Paris, with blistering cold and heavy fog. Many say it was an accident waiting to happen because of underfunding in the rail service.

'A local train, service number 55, had been added to the schedule from Paris to Nancy in order to deal with the extremely high passenger volume ahead of Christmas. The East Company was forced to include older, wood-bodied carriages in the train as the increased traffic saw them running out of passenger carriages. Behind it ran the express train from Paris to Strasbourg, service number 25, the most powerful steam train in Europe with a top speed of 120 kph.

'*The local train was running late. It left Paris behind the scheduled 5.49 p.m. departure and when it reached Vaires-sur-Marne where the line slims down from four to two tracks, a rail bus was sitting in the outside track. The local train, service 55, was forced to stop at a red signal to let it go first.*

'*Following behind service 55 was the Paris–Strasbourg express. The driver failed to see the trackside signals that ordered it to stop at Vaires-sur-Marne due to the stationary local train up ahead and sped through the station at full speed. Disaster was by then unavoidable. The heavy express slammed into the back of the local train after passing through the station at 8.12 p.m. The wooden bodies of the regional train's rear five carriages were obliterated. Two hundred and four people were killed. One hundred and twenty injured.*'

Silence. It drowned us. We both sat there in the peace and quiet of the ward, seeing the tragedy unfold in front of our eyes.

'Don't stop now, Camille,' he murmured. 'I need to hear it. All of it.'

'No, Beau, you know the facts now, that's enough. You don't need—'

He snatched up *L'Écho de Paris*, holding it awkwardly with painful hands, and started to read aloud in quick jerky sentences. '*We saw outstretched hands, a face covered in blood with wide open eyes, and the stiffened legs of a naked woman.*' Beau uttered a deep moan. '*Another woman lay buried under twenty other dead bodies, with her ribs smashed, both legs crushed and her skull partly split open. Severed heads, torsos, and limbs lay strewn on the ground. From all around came the unforgettable howling of the injured and—*'

'Don't,' I said and eased the newspaper from his grip.

He seized another and read aloud, '*Twenty-four children under twelve years of age perished in the disaster; the youngest casualty was eight-month-old Gérard Deguingue.*'

'Enough, Beau.'

'How can I not remember such tragedy? How is that possible?' His hands were shaking so hard that the newspaper crackled and fluttered.

I gently removed it. Instead I read out snippets from the big five Parisian dailies – *Le Journal, Le Matin, Paris-Soir, Le Petit Journal, and Le Petit Parisien*. All were right-wing publications, so I rarely trusted a word they said, but they all picked up on the fact that lack of resources and poor organisation had hampered rescue efforts. They reported that stations at Vaires and Lagny were equipped with only two stretchers. Rescuers had to load the injured on to benches torn from the wreckage.

I paused and our eyes locked. Imagining the crippling chaos in the darkness.

'Who rescued me, I wonder?' Beau whispered.

'We'll never know. But you're here. You're recovering. Let's be thankful for that.'

'Camille.'

'What is it?'

I watched his face and the bright anger in his eyes. The way his sore lips moved.

'Camille, the more I think about it, the more I am convinced it was your brother who held my hand that night. Gilles Malroux. Maybe he robbed me of my wallet then, I don't know and I don't care, but I do know that the hand that was holding mine stopped me sliding down into a terrible blackness. I wouldn't be here without that hand. I would be stone-cold on a marble slab somewhere, waiting for my turn in the queue for Père-Lachaise cemetery.'

A sadness rose and fell inside me. Gilles, was it you? If so, where are you now? Give me a clue, my brother.

I continued to read. Several papers reported that two ambulances sent from Paris hospitals couldn't find the site of the accident and turned around. They claimed that between 8 p.m. and 10.30 p.m., all casualties admitted to hospitals arrived there in private cars or taxis. The rescue effort was condemned as haphazard and uncoordinated.

'This is a disgrace,' I muttered.

'All disasters are immediately politicised by the newspapers,' Beau pointed out. 'This appalling tragedy will be meat to their grinder.'

He was right. In *L'Humanité* the Communist Party's voice was strongest in condemning the railway companies. It attacked their cost-cutting and redundancies for putting the lives of railway workers and passengers at risk for the sake of profit. The axes were out.

'There are even reports of over five hundred passengers being injured,' I told him.

Was Gilles one of them?

'It's too early to trust the figures,' Beau said. 'They snatch them out of the air at this stage.'

'How do you know that?'

For a moment he closed his eyes. He held his breath, as if staring at something that surprised him inside his head.

'There was a suitcase,' he whispered.

'Your suitcase? Where is it?'

There had been reports in the newspapers of belongings thrown everywhere. Scattered throughout the wreckage were cameras, gloves, keys, handbags, suitcases, walking sticks, Christmas packages, all dipped in blood.

'Not *my* suitcase.' He frowned deeply, dragging the image from under the weight of mental fog. 'A brown one. One I recognised. The man who held my hand was gripping it. But it belonged to . . .'

We waited. We willed the memory to resurface. Willed a name to run off his tongue. But when his eyes opened they were full of loss and I grieved for this man who had been robbed of his core self.

'It's like the burning of a library of precious books,' he said abruptly. But instead of weeping or thrashing his pillow in anger, he gave me a smile of sorts, a twitch of the corner of his mouth and a flick of his chin. 'I shall have to write new ones, won't I?'

I leaned forward, so close I breathed in the medication on his damaged skin, and I pressed my lips to the side of his head where his dark hair was singed. 'Are you able to do that?' I murmured.

'We both need to find Gilles,' he told me. 'So yes. I shall rewrite the pages of my life. Now tell me more about what kind of man your brother is.'

CHAPTER TWENTY

◆ ◆ ◆

GILLES

The nights were hard. The pain in Gilles's leg reached up like the devil clawing for his soul, but Rosa had left a glass of laudanum at his bedside if it became too much. By the early hours of the morning it became too much. But he didn't touch the glass. He needed his brain to be sharp if he was going to think his way out of this.

'God bless your dreams,' she'd whispered to him as she settled him for the night. She'd touched her lips to his forehead and now in the darkness he fingered that spot, wondering if he bore the mark of Cain.

What was it she wanted from him?

What part did she intend him to play?

Was it a walk-on role in her mission to spread the Lord's gospel and love, or something much darker? More sinister?

Gilles's mind shifted to his sister. She was good at seeing through women's smoke and mirrors, and would laugh at him. 'Isn't it obvious?' She'd say when a woman he'd bought a drink for in a bar turned out to be a good-time girl on the lookout for bigger fish. His sister would know what to make of Rosa Lagarde.

'Camille,' he murmured aloud. 'What are you doing now? I'm sorry we didn't spend our Christmas together and I bet you're mad as hell at me. Or are you studying so hard for your exams that you barely notice I'm not around? Think of me, Camille, when you lift your head from your books.'

Gilles was his mother's son. However much he tried to deny it. She had been a believer in second sight and in the thinness of the veil between this world and that of the spirits. So he closed his eyes and conjured up an image of his sister walking at his side, her arm bumping against his, matching him stride for stride on boulevard Raspail in Montparnasse as they dodged between stalls in the market on a Friday morning. Snatching an orange. Hiding a potato up his sleeve. Once Camille made off with a whole pannier of melons. They had gorged till the juice turned their chins and their school shirts orange.

Come to me now, Camille. He summoned her the way his mother used to summon her spirits. *Come to me. I need you.*

But another memory came at him like a train out of the darkness. His blood thumped in his ears as a pain, sharper than the one in his left leg, started to chip a piece out of his heart.

'I'm sorry, Camille. I'm sorry I couldn't stop the bastard.'

One of his mother's johns used to take his belt to Camille down in the cellar when she was only six. Night after night. It was when the john's friend tried to do more than just beat her that Gilles had put a stop to it with a screwdriver. Through his throat. Gilles and his two good *copains* had dumped the body at night in Montparnasse cemetery. That was his first killing. He was eleven. The first was the hardest. After that it got easier.

That was when his sister's tremors had started. She'd learned to control them now. Almost. He shifted position in bed to ease the pressure on his leg but didn't reach for the glass. With a grin he remembered suddenly that his Christmas present to Camille was going to be the suitcase all tied up with red . . .

He felt the breath sucked out of him.

The suitcase.

Gilles swung both legs over the side of the bed and placed his good right foot on the polished wooden floor. He stood up. He reckoned he had an hour. Maybe more if she met up with a friend.

Rosa Lagarde had gone to market. She was confident enough of him now to risk leaving him in the house alone, but only after she had dosed him with a generous shot of laudanum to send him to sleep. He could have refused it but it would have been a simple matter for her to pick up the phone and turn him over to the police. They both knew that was the ace in her hand.

So he drank it. And the moment she was out of the room he stuck two fingers down his throat and made himself vomit up trails of the reddish-brown liquid into his bedpan. Now she was gone and he had to make every minute count.

He tested his damaged leg on the floor but the pain was so intense it forced him to sit again while he gasped for breath. It would bear no weight. He tried once more on one leg and this time used an ungainly hopping movement to reach the door but each time that he landed on his right foot, a jolt of pain ripped through his suspended left leg. But he made it and turned the doorknob. Locked.

He had expected that. Whenever she went out for any length of time, she turned the big old key in the door but left it in the lock. Not for one moment did she believe him capable of even getting himself across the room. It was impossible. But that just showed she didn't know Gilles well enough yet. He smiled grimly. The impossible was his speciality.

After a diversion to the room's dressing table, he had acquired a pocketful of tweezers, nail file, nail scissors and, crucially, hairpins, plus a page torn out of a magazine. This was far from his first encounter of wrestling with a lock, so it was the work of a moment to retrieve the key, open the door and ease himself out. On the landing he took his bearings. There were four other closed doors on this level. It seemed that the house was long and narrow and spotlessly clean.

He leaned his weight against the wall, breathing hard, and slid himself to the first door on his right which he quietly swung open. An unoccupied guest room. Neat, tidy, unlived-in. White bedcover, flowered curtains, silky rug. Gilles dragged himself into it and inspected the inside of the wardrobe but it contained nothing but a man's suits and shirts. Why had she kept her dead husband's clothes? Perched on his one decent leg, he bent over and peered under the bed. Nothing. Not even dust. On top of the wardrobe? No suitcases. He looked out of the window and saw a barren back yard with the nearest house well out of shouting range. Beyond that stretched winter fields, the earth dark and bleak and empty. That's where he was heading.

The bathroom next. Smart, modern, with a woman's toiletries. When Gilles caught sight of himself in the mirror he experienced a faint ripple of shock. He looked appalling. There was a long fresh scab on his forehead and bruises on his jaw. His eyes looked half-dead and oddly out of focus, while his features seemed chiselled out of granite. Like one of the headstones at a graveside.

A fear that the facial muscles had forgotten how to smile swept through him. Into his mind strode the funeral director who had come to collect his mother's body from the whorehouse when Gilles was twelve years old. The man had been clad in black, wore a tall top hat and had a nose like a crow's beak. His face was grey and stone-still. It had terrified young Gilles. And yet here it was again. In the mirror. He looked away and dragged himself to the final door where he allowed himself a few seconds to slump against the doorframe as the landing blurred around him. His leg was on fire.

He opened the door with a jerk and found himself in her bedroom. It smelled of her scent. Stylish in black and white. A lavish art-deco dressing table of ebony wood and gleaming chrome dominated the room. Mirrors and glass shelves and a pair of tall amber lamps. This was the bedroom of a woman who liked to spend money. And had money to spend.

No trace of a husband, not even a photograph. Again Gilles checked under the bed and in the wardrobe.

No suitcase.

Out on the landing again, he collapsed at the top of the stairs and sat there with his head in his hands for a full minute, bringing himself back under control. Then with a grunt he slid himself down the carpeted stairs, skiing at speed down the slope on his bottom with his bad leg raised in the air until he smashed into the flagstones at the bottom. He let out a screech of agony but crawled his way to the front door where he halted, taking in his surroundings.

The ground floor was a different world. No modernity down here. He was in a large hallway that was furnished with exquisite Louis XV pieces, a beautiful inlaid oak armoire, all curves and cabriole legs, and a grandfather clock with gilded mounts and three cherubs cavorting on top. Gilles knew furniture. He had made it his business to recognise quality. This was quality.

He tried the front door. Locked. No key. This one was a strong heavyweight version that would require far more expert tools than a hairpin. His only way out was through a window but, *merde*, he was reluctant to give up on that suitcase of Egyptian treasures. He had time.

The dining room was pretty and raised his hopes. The table was draped with a tablecloth that reached down as far as the floor, a perfect place of concealment. But no, a stray pair of fluffy slippers underneath. The living room offered no hiding places for suitcases. He was tempted to collapse on an ornate chaise longue covered in green velvet, but even more tempting was a delicate rosewood writing desk in the corner.

He tried its drawers. They were locked. He could easily pop one open with a knife from the kitchen but at this point the suitcase was his priority.

The kitchen and scullery also drew a blank. But in the dark cupboard under the stairs among the brooms and mop bucket he thought for a minute he had struck gold. Three suitcases. Hallelujah! He ducked his head and rummaged quickly to remove the pile of old bedsheets lying on top of them and felt his hopes plummet. One black suitcase and two grey ones. No mahogany-brown ones. None had a strap. He flicked open their locks nevertheless, in case she had transferred the contents of the brown case to them, but all were empty.

He cursed and clambered back out into the hall.

There was one more door. It had a key in the lock. Gilles struggled over to it, turned the key and pulled open the door. In front of him lay a flight of rough wooden stairs that descended into chilly darkness. A basement of some sort. He felt for an electric switch but found none. Time was running out fast, but he took a quick hop down one of the steps, stumbling and cursing his clumsiness. Clearly he needed a candle. He remembered the ones on the dining-room table.

He backed up the step and was just hauling himself towards the dining room when he heard the sound of an engine outside. A car.

She was back early.

Gilles hurled himself at the stairs and scooted up them the same way he had come down but in reverse. On his bottom, pushing himself up one step at a time with his good right leg. He reached the top, drenched in sweat, his pyjamas sticking to his skin, his leg vibrating with pain, just as Rosa Lagarde walked through the front door. He had dropped to the landing floor but if she looked up she would see him.

She didn't look up. She was too preoccupied with what was in her arms. Not a woven basket of fresh farm produce, leeks and cabbages, as he'd expected, but instead she carried a large object wrapped in brown paper. It looked heavy. She placed it on the hall table and peeled away the paper, her fingers eager and impatient. Gilles lay where he'd fallen, watching her through the slats of the bannisters.

Rosa let the paper drift unheeded to the floor, a dull flush creeping up her cheeks. In front of her stood a terracotta statue, around a metre tall. It was an exquisite carving of an Egyptian pharaoh with beautifully figured features and the long royal false beard that only pharaohs were permitted to wear, to signify their status as a living god.

As Gilles gazed down he felt a twist in his gut at what he saw.

The statue was missing one of its hands.

And each stair to the hallway bore a smear of blood, as though a dead body had been dragged from top to bottom.

CHAPTER TWENTY-ONE

◆ ◆ ◆

CAMILLE

I had brought a drink for him. For Beau. A proper drink. Not that cat's piss the nurses kept pouring into him. Nor our rotgut that tasted like sludge from the Seine either. This was the good stuff, from a proper vineyard in the Loire Valley. Simone let me have a bottle of it on the house when I promised to persuade Barnaby to paint a picture of her beloved bar. Though I knew perfectly well that Barnaby would slit his wrist again before he stooped to painting a city bar.

'Have they issued a list of the names of the dead?' Beau asked.

'No. It's still chaotic. If you go to the police with a name, they'll tell you if they've found anybody's identity papers that match it. That's the best they can do at the moment. A gendarme told me that the trouble is that children don't carry identity papers with them, so they're having horrible trouble finding out the dead children's identities.' I knocked back a shot-glass of deep burgundy wine and felt it stop any tears in their tracks.

Beau sipped his. I admired his restraint. In his position I'd have emptied the whole damn bottle. His face seemed to grow more gaunt by the hour. Battered, bruised and in pain, he should be hiding under his sheets, but he wasn't. He was grinding through it, seeking out answers, and his eyes told me exactly how much he wanted them.

Did he see the same in me? The same ferocity? I don't know but there was something between us, hooking our nails into each other. I could feel it.

'There is a connection between you, Gilles and the toyshop man who called himself Robespierre,' I pointed out.

'What's that?'

'Ancient Egypt.'

He stared at me. He didn't look away even when a nurse came to take his temperature and administer some painkillers to him. When she'd left, he said, 'You're right. Gilles had the ankh in his wallet. Your Robespierre had the Tutankhamen coffin tin box. And I seem to know precisely what an ankh is and have seen your brother's before. But I don't know where.' His hand took hold of my wrist. 'Start there,' he urged.

'I did. I went to the Louvre and got nowhere.'

'You didn't ask the right questions.'

'What questions?'

'Go back to your Dr Delamarche and ask if anyone from her Ancient Egypt department was connected in any way at all, however remotely, to the Ligny–Pomponne train crash.'

I looked at this man, so sick and exhausted, locked inside his own personal hell, and yet whose mind could make these connections. I squeezed his hand in mine and was gone.

The Louvre Museum is designed to intimidate. That's how it seems to me. To put us peasants in our place. Its glorious marble palace is bursting with gilding and glitz, and the vast works of art are the royalty that visitors come to bow down before. But I wasn't here to seek out the *Mona Lisa*. Nor the *Coronation of Napoléon*. I was here to seek out answers and I wasn't going to be intimidated this time.

I marched up the wide marble staircase to the Egyptian hall and headed straight to Dr Liliane Delamarche's office. This time I made each footstep own the marble floor under it.

'Come on in, Camille. Sit down. What a pleasant surprise. What can I do for you?'

She didn't mention the fact that her desk was piled high with books and papers, that she had a red pencil stuck behind one ear and a fountain pen poised in her hand. Obviously very busy. She just offered a warm smile of welcome and gestured to the chair opposite hers at the desk. I noted that this time she was wearing a pale wool dress, the colour of pastis when you mix it with water, and a short navy jacket hung on the back of her chair. Only a few wayward locks of hair that had strayed from her neat chignon betrayed any stress she might be experiencing. I sat down.

I didn't waste her time. I got straight to the point. 'Is there anyone among your staff here who has a connection to the Lagny–Pomponne train crash?'

An unexpectedly deep line formed between her brows as she frowned and put down her pen, replacing its lid. 'Are you basing that question on the existence of the ankh? Is that your evidence?'

Her scientist's mind was all about gathering evidence. Not like my hunches. Clear hard evidence was required.

'Yes.'

'Well, it so happens that you are right. One of our staff was actually travelling on the express train and died in the crash. We are all very shaken by the tragedy.'

'Who was he?'

'He was one of our best curators who had worked here at the museum for years. Dr Laval. A hard-working and dedicated man. We shall feel his loss.'

She brushed a hand across her eyes, but I didn't think it was tears she was brushing away. More like tiredness. Or maybe concern about filling his shoes.

'I'm sorry,' I said.

But was I sorry? Really? Or was the shiver that ran through me the same as what a hunting dog feels when he picks up a scent?

'Thank you, I'm sorry too,' she said. 'For his poor wife as well.'

'Of course.'

'So you think there was a connection between Dr Laval and your missing brother?' she asked.

I shrugged. 'I have no idea, and I guess I'll never know now. Another dead end.'

She leaned forward, pointed elbows on her desk. 'Don't give up hope, Camille,' she whispered. 'Your brother could still be somewhere out there. Waiting for you to find him.'

I was touched by my new friend's concern. I rose to my feet. 'I won't keep you from your work any longer. Thanks for your help.'

She came out from behind her desk, and when she came close to hug me I could smell the elegant scent of her perfume. Nothing nauseating about it, that's for sure.

It took me an hour of scouring the Paris newspapers in the old Bibliothèque Mazarine set on the quai de Conti on the Left Bank, the oldest and the grandest public library in France. But I found it. The funeral announcement.

The notice had been set out discreetly in a quiet bottom corner of the paper and I almost missed it, but my heart jumped when I read the name M. Antoine Laval.

Curator at the Louvre Museum.

It was him.

It was today.

I hate funerals. Dark. Bleak. Rain-spattered. Tear-soaked. Raw black earth ripped open. They take me back to my mother's funeral, Gilles and I side by side on the edge of a gash in the ground on a blustery autumn day with dead leaves chasing around our feet.

My mother's burial took place in the huge Montparnasse cemetery with the tombs of Baudelaire and Gaston Maspero, the leading French Egyptologist of his generation, as company for Maman. She might decide to walk the cemetery's alleyways at night seeking out spectres the way she used to prowl the streets of Paris seeking out business. We were eight and twelve years old. I was shaking with fear and Gilles held my hand so tight it had a purple bruise on it that night. It took us four years of scrimping and stealing to pay off the debt for the burial plot.

Dr Laval's funeral was altogether a grander affair. In the 20th *arron-dissement*. A horse-drawn carriage for the fancy mahogany coffin and sleek black cars that purred close behind it like cats on heat and emp-tied the mourners in their unsuitable footwear on to the pathways of the Cimetière du Père-Lachaise. It was the largest cemetery in Paris at over a hundred acres. Bare tree limbs clawed at the grey sky above the marble tombs which were so numerous that the place felt like a silent city of the dead. Molière hid out here somewhere. And Chopin too. But I left them to their peaceful solitude and edged closer to the large group of mourners gathered around the graveside of Dr Laval.

She wasn't hard to spot, the widow. Behind a black veil, supported by a young woman I took to be her daughter, given space around her by others as if her grief needed air to breathe. I circled them while the priest droned on, listening to muted conversations, observing the men in dark suits looking bored and women clutching their handkerchiefs. But the moment the ceremony was over and the prayers were drifting their way up to heaven, I approached two men I had singled out. Both youngish and both looking awkward as if they didn't quite belong here.

'Pardon me,' I said in the low tone that I deemed appropriate for the occasion, 'are you from the Louvre Museum?'

Give a man a smile and you pique his interest. Buy a man a drink and you raise his hopes. Ask about the details of his work and he is yours. It is a fact.

This was something my mother told me when I was a child and I have never found reason to doubt it. Jean-Paul and Georges Lament were brothers. Both worked at the Louvre and both liked a fine cognac. I was buying. A handful of the mourners had drifted to a smart nearby bar, myself included, and the Lament brothers were happy to share a table with me when the bottle of vintage Godet and three glasses materialised.

Jean-Paul was involved in laboratory work on the ancient artefacts and brother Georges termed himself an exhibition preparator. Both were happy to speak to someone they believed to be doing research for a university paper on the skills required to be a curator at the Louvre. Once on to their second glass of cognac, they did not even think to query the suitability of conducting that research straight after the funeral of their esteemed colleague.

Jean-Paul was the quickest. The sharper mind. I had to watch him. His brother Georges, older by two years, darker hair but the same square jaw packed with overlarge teeth, was more interested in explaining the various requirements of display cabinet lighting in the exhibitions he mounted. I eased the conversation around to the direction I needed.

'Was Dr Laval a good curator?' I asked innocently.

'The best,' Georges assured me.

'How long had he worked at the Louvre?'

'Around twenty years.' Jean-Paul narrowed his eyes thoughtfully. 'I thought you knew him.'

'I did, but not well. He gave a talk to my class at the Sorbonne once. From then on he let me contact him when I had any questions. He was very kind.' After that whopper, I knocked back a mouthful of silky-smooth cognac to scorch the lie off my tongue and tried not to think of the cost. 'Did you find him kind too or did he have enemies at work? I imagine curators are sometimes jealous of each other.'

The brothers laughed. I liked them. Committed to each other and to their work, and to their dead colleague, it seemed.

'He had no enemies,' Georges asserted. 'He was quiet and mild-mannered, always helpful to his staff. A brilliant mind. He will be greatly missed within the museum.'

Jean-Paul gave his brother a look, so fleeting that most would have missed it, but I'd had my senses honed on the backstreets of Montparnasse. I saw the look. It was a warning.

'What do you think, Jean-Paul?' I asked, topping up his glass with the amber liquid that had been aged in the very best oak barrels

'About what?'

'About how much Dr Laval will be missed?'

'He was good. At putting exhibitions together.'

'But?'

Jean-Paul shrugged. Not yet ready to spill whatever was buzzing in his head.

'Was there a problem?' I asked.

The cognac had loosened Georges's tongue. He leaned forward, glanced about us to make sure none of the family was in earshot and murmured, 'He had gone a bit weird recently.'

'Weird? In what way?'

'He became very . . .' he paused, seeking the *mot juste*, 'very secretive.'

His brother lost patience. 'Paranoid is what you mean.'

'Why paranoid?' I asked.

'The old fool thought we were spying on him.'

'And were you?'

Jean-Paul laughed, a loose drinking laugh. 'You're quick, you are, Mlle Malroux. Laval was acting strangely. Out of character. Keeping to himself. Bolting his office door so no one could walk in on him, locking his desk drawers, which is something none of us did, and claiming all sorts of absurd things.'

'Like what?'

Georges stepped in. 'Like that he was being followed every day.'

'Paranoid,' Jean-Paul repeated and threw back the last of his drink in one. His dark eyes glistened. He was enjoying himself. I would be too if I were emptying slugs of cognac at that speed.

You didn't ask the right questions. Those were Beau's words to me earlier. I sat back in my chair and considered what the right questions were this time.

'Who did he think was following him?' Keeping it easy, as though asking out of idle curiosity.

They both piled in.

'Some man who he claimed spied on his house every morning.'

'Followed him on the Métro to work each day, so he said. Sometimes Laval used to jump off at an earlier stop, at Concorde, but this shadow of his came too apparently.'

'He was hallucinating.'

They both chuckled, which didn't feel quite right. In the present circumstances.

'Was Dr Laval upset about this?' I inquired.

'Yes, very.'

'We told him to go to the police.'

'Did he?'

'No. But he used to scuttle like a rabbit when he left the museum. Do you remember, Georges?'

His brother nodded and stared pointedly at his empty glass. 'On rare occasions he left early.'

'Did you ever see this shadow-man yourself?' I wondered aloud as I picked up the bottle and let it hover over their glasses for a moment, tempting them.

'No, of course not,' Jean-Paul snorted. 'He didn't exist.'

I smiled, as if in agreement. 'Did Dr Laval ever describe him?'

'Oh yes. Apparently he was tall and lean, long black coat. Black hat. Early thirties.'

I smiled. 'That describes half the young men in Paris.'

'Laval said this one felt sinister.'

'He was just paranoid,' Jean-Paul repeated.

'Don't forget his white blaze,' Georges reminded his brother.

A dart of excitement streaked through my palms and I wrapped them around the bottle. 'White blaze?'

'*Mon Dieu*, yes.' Jean-Paul burst out laughing. 'That was going a step too far with his imaginings. Laval claimed that one day the man's hat was sent flying by the wind. The man chased it into the road and when he bent to pick it up, Laval spotted a stripe of white hair on top of his head like a badger. It was ridiculous. Laval was just acting weird.'

I poured myself the smallest of shots, concentrating on not letting my hand shake. 'I knew a man with a white streak in his hair,' I said softly. 'He got it defending his sister when they were both kids, from an attack by a drunken layabout armed with a brass poker. The layabout drowned the next day. But where the boy's head was cracked open, the hair grew back white.'

Why did I tell them that?

I pushed the cognac away but they were both staring at me with interest.

'He's dead now,' I said quickly.

But my mind was racing. So Gilles was tracking Laval. Gilles had taken that fatal express train to follow the curator. But where was Laval going and why? What was Gilles's involvement with him?

'Was anything new going on at the museum that might make Laval act oddly?'

'There were rumours,' Georges muttered and reached for the bottle.

I let him take it and refill his glass. 'What rumours?'

'That he had his fingers in the artefact till.'

This time I had asked the right questions.

Dr Antoine Laval's wife was not so forthcoming and had no interest in cognac. An austere woman. She liked to tilt her head back and look down her nose at you. No fun to live with, I'd imagine, though when you've just been to your husband's funeral I accept that you have good reason not to put fun at the top of your priorities.

The funeral reception was held just near the cemetery at the Grand Hotel Agathe, so we tumbled out of our bar and into the hotel's smart function room. It was in one of those beautiful five-storey blocks in Haussmann style, graced with elegant wrought-iron balconies and stone facades that are the essence of Paris, but inside it was all fancy ornamentation. Light and airy paintings of nature and sweeping curves everywhere. Even the chandeliers were ridiculously exuberant. Barnaby would know what to call this style, but I just thought it clashed with Mme Laval's heavy widow's weeds. It was altogether too cheerful.

Mme Laval worked her way around the room, accepting a few sympathetic words from everyone. She was good at it, with her cool smile and her determination not to collide with her grief, so that when her gloved hand shook mine, I murmured, 'I'm sorry for your loss,' and meant it.

'How did you know Antoine?' she asked.

'He helped me with my research into Ancient Egyptian artefacts.'

This new word *artefacts* seemed to go a long way in convincing people I knew what the hell I was talking about.

'He was very kind and generous with his knowledge,' I added to make her feel a scrap better.

'Sometimes overgenerous,' she commented.

'I expect he had to travel a lot for his work.'

'Not in recent years, no. He got others to do the legwork.'

'So may I ask where he was going on the train?'

She drew herself up straighter, 'No, you may not.'

In a jerky movement her hand rose to her veiled forehead and I feared that at the mention of the train she was going to cry, but she didn't. She gripped her broad forehead between thumb and forefinger as though taking a firm hold of herself, and I felt bad, triggering her grief with my questions. But I had more to ask.

'Was your husband travelling with his passport? Was he leaving the country?'

She clearly thought the question strange, but her mind was elsewhere now, so she answered anyway, 'It would seem so. Why do you want to know?'

'Was he fleeing from someone?'

Her eyes widened in shock. 'Why would he do that?'

'If he was involved in criminal activity. Mme Laval, was your husband involved in theft from the museum?'

Behind the spider's web of her black veil I saw tears brim in her eyes and slowly slither down her shadowy cheeks.

'No,' she hissed at me. 'You are mistaken. No. No, of course not.'

But her head forgot to lie. Instead of shaking, it nodded the truth. Yes.

'Goodbye, Mme Laval.'

I hurried from the room and out of the hotel. On the steps outside in the cold, Georges was slumped in a semi-stupor with his head in his hands. I could smell the fumes rising from him.

'He paid me, you know, old Laval,' he slurred, 'to keep my mouth shut. He did. When I caught him falsifying the catalogue numbers. It was after that he started locking his door.' He gave me a wonky smile of sorts. 'But be a good girl, don't tell Jean-Paul, will you?'

'I won't tell your brother if you tell me what he stole.'

Ask the right questions and you get the right answers.

CHAPTER TWENTY-TWO

◆ ◆ ◆

CAMILLE

From Père-Lachaise I took the Métro, line two, just as far as place de la Nation and then I set off, hunkered down inside my coat, to find a bus across the river to Salpêtrière. It was a bitterly cold day. A raw wind had set awnings flapping and shutters rattling, and the streets were half empty because no one wanted to be out in this.

But my mind was not on the dismal weather, it was too busy running through all I'd learned today. I was looking forward to hearing Beau's response to this new information. We both badly needed it to trigger fresh memories for him. The pleasure I felt at the thought of talking it over with Beau took me by surprise and I realised how much I was looking forward to seeing him. It caught me off-guard.

I pulled my woollen hat further down over my ears as I hurried across the huge circular place de la Nation with its vast melodramatic bronze statue of Marianne in her Liberty cap, the bare-breasted embodiment of the spirit of France. It's ironic that during the Revolution, more people were guillotined in this square than anywhere else in Paris. And here I was now, striding its bloodied pathways with death in mind.

I was picturing Gilles on that express train hurtling through the darkness two days before Christmas and Dr Laval riding in a separate carriage. Or maybe even in the same one. It was possible. The thought struck me then for the first time that they could have been escaping together, working together, stealing together. In danger together. '*If I should die unexpectedly, whatever it looks like, whatever they tell you, it won't be an accident. It will be murder.*' Gilles's words echoed in my head like stones in a can.

Did that apply to Dr Laval too?

So deep was I in my thoughts that I failed to notice a man approaching from the boulevard Voltaire direction. Failed to register his green coat with a hood that covered half his face. Failed to prepare for the speed of his strike.

A cobra could not be faster.

His hand seized the strap of my bag on my shoulder as he came alongside me and tore it from my arm in one smooth snatch, the violence of it knocking me off balance. I reached for my vanishing bag and for the ankh within it, but all I caught was air. The thief was already running off behind me in the direction of cours de Vincennes, a broad thoroughfare, but it was too straight and exposed for him to be able to shake me off, so the green hood ducked down a side road.

I am a decent runner. I've run all my life. To things and from things. Mainly from things. This man looked easy game. I set off after him with a long rapid stride. But when I realised he was heading for the nearby Picpus cemetery where the many tombs and statuary offered plenty of cover for him to hide, I cut across a side street and was at the entrance first. Startled, he veered back down avenue Saint-Mandé and dived into the back alleys.

I stuck close. But not close enough. I was mistaken about his speed. His long legs covered ground fast and he must have been younger than I'd thought because his stamina held up. By the time we reached boulevard Diderot I was breathing hard but I wasn't giving up.

'*Au voleur!*' I shouted with my last scrap of breath. 'Stop, thief!'

A passing pedestrian made a grab for him. He dodged. Crashed into a pavement table. Lost ground. I was almost on him when we raced past a barber's shop and he slipped down a dark narrow passage at its side. I was right on his heels.

It was a dead end. He could run no further.

He spun on his heel instantly and came at me. Because I am a woman, don't think that I can't fight. Gilles taught me well. My first punch landed full on his throat, stopping his breath, my second in the soft underbelly of his solar plexus, paralysing his diaphragm. He went down with a horrible choking sound. He was crouched on the filthy ground, bent over and fighting for air, hands scrabbling at his throat. I snatched my bag from the dirt and at the same time pulled off his hood, grabbed a handful of his thick wavy hair and yanked his head back hard, so I could see his face.

Merde, it was the doctor.

Was I angry?

Of course I was.

Did I listen to his story?

Of course I did.

Did I believe him?

I left that one wide open for now.

I'd recognised the thief and helped him to his feet but I was wary, hackles raised. He was the doctor from the hospital. Not the unpleasant Dr Arquette with his cohort of white coats, but the other one, the one whose manner was gentle, his voice soft, his skin swarthy. The one who removed the protective bandage from the injured hand so that I could see if it matched my brother's and for that I was grateful.

But why attack me? Why steal my bag? It was only an old canvas thing with very little money in my purse. Nothing of value. Unless you count the strange blue ankh as of value, but what could he possibly know about the ankh?

We were seated side by side on a bus rattling down boulevard Diderot, heading towards the Jardin des Plantes on the Left Bank. The seats were mostly empty and the windows were grubby. Thankfully the shudder of the old engine kept our voices well masked.

'Why did you steal my bag?' I demanded.

'To find out who you really are and how much you know.'

'How much I know of what?'

'Of what happened on the train during and after the Lagny–Pomponne crash.'

I turned my face to study his strong elegant profile and tried to make sense of this. 'Why are you interested in the Lagny–Pomponne crash? You're a doctor. Did you tend many of the wounded?'

'Ah, Mlle Malroux, in a hospital anyone can be a doctor if they are wearing a white coat. A stethoscope around their neck and a clipboard in their hand.' He shrugged. 'People believe what is in front of their eyes. As a doctor it is simple to gain access to a patient who is allowed no visitors other than family.'

His dark eyes, almost black, observed me with warm amusement. 'Don't look so shocked. I did the patient no harm.'

'You are not a doctor?'

'No.'

'But you unwrapped his hand.'

'I was careful to wear sterile gloves. You understand, it was my only way to find out whether it was Gilles Malroux under all those bandages.'

'And did you? Find out?'

He smiled quietly at me. 'Yes. You told me.'

'I did no such thing.'

'You love your brother, Mlle Malroux. You could not hide your relief that the injured hand did not belong to Gilles.'

His voice was soft and convincing. It had a slight foreign accent but I couldn't place it. Maybe Turkish. He was tall and lean, and I could feel a need in him to connect with me, though I had no idea why. I was seated next to the window and as the boulevard's shops and cafés bobbed past, I was aware of streetlights starting to flicker on; winter days were painfully short now. Daylight was escaping. I was running out of time.

I laid a hand on his arm, pinning him to me. No escaping. 'Why were you so eager to find Gilles?'

The bus slowed, approaching a stop, halted, and another passenger climbed on. My companion regarded him keenly, an older man bundled up in furs, but when the newcomer ambled to the back of the bus without so much as a glance in our direction, the man at my side relaxed and, to my surprise, leaned close. His breath was warm on my cold cheek.

'Gilles was my friend.'

My heart tripped. At last, someone who wanted to help my brother, not kill him.

'We worked together,' he added.

'What kind of work?'

'Mlle Malroux, listen to what I have to tell you.' Suddenly his tone was urgent, though his voice was barely a whisper. 'I am from Cairo.'

'Egyptian?'

'Yes. I am employed by Pierre Lacau, the director-general of the Department of Antiquities of Egypt. We are working to track down the networks of criminals who are illegally removing valuable finds out of Egypt. Gilles was assisting me.'

'How do I know whether to believe you?'

He nodded. 'That's a fair question.' He thought for a moment, his solemn face softening with whatever memories he was sifting through. 'If I told you that when Gilles and I were sailing on the Nile in a dhow – the traditional Egyptian triangular-sailed boat – he told me about an occasion when you both stole a rowing boat and went rowing on the Seine, only just avoiding being mown down by the haulage barges. You remember?'

'I remember.'

'And do you also remember him hurrying over on Christmas Day to eat his favourite treat?'

'Hot chestnuts.' I smiled.

'I hope that I have convinced you now that we were good friends. So listen to me.' His smile faded and I listened. 'Pierre Lacau was appointed director-general of antiquities. He followed in the shoes of the greatest Egyptologist of his time, Gaston Maspero, who excelled in Sanskrit and hieroglyphics. Pierre Lacau is now attempting to stop the rampant illegal export of Egyptian antiquities by collectors and by agents for the world's museums. Even by overenthusiastic tourists. All without licences. Everyone who can carry a suitcase is plundering our heritage in Egypt.' Colour had risen in his cheeks. 'It must be stopped.'

I glanced out of the window of the bus to give him a moment to gather himself. A filthy December sky was spitting drizzle on the streets, turning them into glistening black sheets of jet, the gemstone of death. Of grief. I looked away.

'Where did you meet Gilles?'

'Our paths first crossed in Marseille. That's where I discovered his exceptional skills which, as I'm sure you know, are many.'

'You hired him?'

'Yes. To infiltrate one of the networks shipping antiquities from Egypt to France and beyond. To New York and London. Dangerous work for him to get involved in, I admit.' The Egyptian gave me an odd look. 'But Gilles, as you must know, is drawn to the smell of danger. I'm wondering if his sister is too.'

I shook my head hard. Maybe too hard. 'I like my life to be quiet and orderly. That's why I work for the civil service.'

His large dark eyes gazed at me and he laughed softly. 'I would never have put you down as a *fonctionnaire*.'

'You don't know me.'

He left it at that. He sat back in his seat and winced as the bus driver wrestled with the gears when he took a corner. 'I am concerned for Gilles,' he said in a tight low voice. 'The question is, where is he now?'

I shifted round on my seat to look him straight in the face. I felt a stab of annoyance. 'The question is, who is in this network and where do they operate out of and do they have Gilles as their prisoner? Those are the questions I would like you to answer.'

We were crossing the river. It never failed to surprise me that even at its greyest and most hostile, the Seine was always beautiful. A seething, shifting mystery that flowed through the heart of the city. Our conversation paused while we crossed it. Its swirling depths, speckled by the ancient lamps on the bridge, held secrets I did not care to contemplate, so I gazed instead at its *quai* walkways, deserted in the rain, and at its riverside profile of imposing buildings.

That brief distraction was why I missed what happened next. I would give anything to take it back, that moment. In a heartbeat.

Because my face was turned to the window, I was only dimly aware of a figure hurrying from the back seat as the bus slowed and lurched to a halt at the next stop. Only dimly aware of sudden movement at my side. I missed that moment. And I will never know whether I could have changed it. Made that moment turn out differently if I'd been paying attention.

I didn't see the dagger plunge into the side of my companion's neck. All I saw was his body in its green coat slumped across my lap and my second-best skirt turning scarlet.

Another police station. Another police officer. Another stream of questions.

I sat there on the hard wooden chair in a brown pitiless room, stunned. The weight of my grief for the gentle Egyptian, whom I scarcely knew, was crushing me. My leg was trembling uncontrollably but I was powerless to stop it. All I could do was stare down at his blood. It had darkened the weave of my wool skirt. Coloured my cuffs. My coat was thick with it. I pictured his heart pumping it out until life was abruptly suspended and it had slipped into stillness.

'Mademoiselle?'

The police officer. He was talking. I looked up. His lips were moving, thick and mobile. I imagined his blood flowing within them, it would be bright as a rose if I pricked them with a pin. I scarcely heard what they said because my ears were deafened by the drumming of my own blood in my head.

'Mlle Malroux, do you have any idea why he was on the bus? Where he was going?'

'He was going to his death,' I whispered.

It was waiting for him.

Was it waiting for me too, so close I could smell its fetid breath?

A glass of water materialised in front of me but I needed something much stronger than tap water. There followed question after question.

'Where did you meet him?'

'How long have you known him?'

'Why were you travelling together?'

'Did he seem distressed? Frightened?'

'How much do you know about him?'

'Where was he going?'

'What did you talk about, heads so close together?'

'Did you see his killer?'

I don't know what my answers were. Words tumbled off my tongue but they were disconnected and meaningless. The only thing that had space in my head was the sight of a decent man slumped across my lap, the ornate handle of a dagger sticking out of an artery in his neck. Blood, blood and more blood. It flowed. It spurted. It spilled over my hands and down on to my shoes as I held him and rocked him and keened over him. I thought the blood would never end.

Finally the police let me go.

'I don't know his name?' I cried out at the door.

'Omar Youssef Ahmed,' I was told.

Omar Youssef Ahmed, may your soul find peace.

CHAPTER TWENTY-THREE

♦ ♦ ♦

CAMILLE

I walked into the Salpêtrière Hospital ward. Breathing under control. Calm footsteps, no tremors, clean clothes, skin scrubbed to within an inch of its life, hair washed and shining. Yet still he knew. Beau knew. One look at my face and his expression was brimming with concern.

He reached out to me. 'What's happened?'

I sank down on the chair beside his bed and he took my hand. I told him everything. Everything. It spilled out like the blood. And then he asked me to tell it all again. I didn't weep, but only because I was holding on tight to his hand and I wanted to show Omar Youssef Ahmed the respect he deserved. Not a snivelling sodden decimated mess.

'What will they do with his body?' I asked.

'The police will keep it in the city morgue until they have fully investigated the crime.'

'But they have nothing to go on. How can they solve . . .' I made myself say it, made my tongue grapple with the word, 'solve the murder?'

'No, Camille,' a gentle caress of my name, 'they have a lot to go on. They have the dagger, a very distinctive one according to what you say. They have eyewitnesses on the bus. They have the victim's name, so can trace where Omar was living and which people he came in contact with. Someone wanted him dead. The police will question his friends and associates.'

'Friends and associates,' I echoed. 'That includes Gilles.'

'Exactly. But the police are already searching for him without success. However painful it is,' Beau said, 'you must go over and over in your mind everything that happened on the bus today, again and again. Replay every second of it in your head. Look closely at the smallest detail. That way more will come to you of what you saw. Concentrate hard. See what else you can come up with.'

'Beau, if Gilles and Omar were working together as Omar said they were, that means the people running the illegal import network might want Gilles dead too.' My right knee started to shake. We both knew he could already be dead.

'No, Camille.' He gave me a reassuring touch on my hand. 'You have told me your brother is clever and resourceful, so let's believe he can outwit them. We will help him stay safe. But first we have to find him.'

I loved him for saying we instead of you.

That evening I did what Beau had urged. I concentrated. I lay on my bed, eyes wide open, stared up at the cracked ceiling, listening to a jazz trumpet sounding off in a nearby bar, and I replayed in my head today's extraordinary meeting with Omar Youssef Ahmed. From the very first moment.

A cobra. In a green coat with a hood covering half his face. Stealing my bag. I focused harder. Smart leather shoes. Dark trousers. Clean-shaven. No gloves. Hands empty, no umbrella or package of any sort. Strong hands. The seizing of my bag was fierce, a fully committed snatch that was unstoppable. Fast on his feet, quick in the alleyways. Until cornered. Then Omar had turned to face me.

Would he have attacked me to escape from the passageway? At the time I thought yes, I believed I was in danger, which was why I attacked first. But now? I'm not so sure. The Omar Ahmed I had spoken to on the bus did not strike me as a man who would attack a woman, but how could I ever know the truth of that? Once he had regained his breath, he'd shown no resentment that I had thrown two punches at him. Instead he'd leaned back against the wall, inspected me and nodded to himself.

'I should have known better,' he'd said and smiled. 'You are your brother's sister.'

He was not the only one to voice that opinion.

'What are you doing here?' I demanded.

'I need to talk with you.'

'I'm heading for the Salpêtrière Hospital.'

'Then so am I.'

'I'm in a hurry.'

So together we'd caught the bus.

This was where I had to work harder. Much harder. I made myself climb on to that bus time after time after time, seeking something new among the images lodged in my head. I focused on the other passengers, the ones already seated on board. There were three right at the back, a couple more on one side and four singles dotted mainly towards the rear. It took me an hour to come up with that much. I struggled with the faces. The couple were elderly and bundled up in hats and scarves. The singles? A girl, youngish and dark-haired. She had been staring excitedly out of the window as if she was going somewhere special. The others were vaguer. Three men, I think, varying ages, nondescript, one with long legs that stuck out into the aisle. Dark coats, one in a pale trench coat. Nobody I recognised.

The three at the back?

One sat apart, smoking a pipe. I recalled the aroma of it, strong and fragrant in the cold air. The final two were seated together but I couldn't summon up their faces, however hard I tried, until I stopped trying, closed my eyes and let my battered mind float free. Newspapers, they were both reading newspapers. That's why their faces were hidden from me. Accidental or intentional?

That left the man who got on when the bus pulled up at a stop, wrapped up in fur coat and fur hat. I couldn't see past them. Beaver, I think, a rich dense brown that must have been costly when new, but now looked old and as if it had been nibbled by foxes. His face? There was only a blank in my head where his features should be, so I kept revisiting that moment. But nothing came. Just a pair of wire spectacles.

All this effort had got me precisely nowhere. So I grabbed my coat. No, not the blood-soaked one which was now floating in a bath of cold water down the corridor. Anne-Marie had lent me her green one, as a client had recently decked her out in a posh new one with a velvet collar. I shot downstairs and along the street to Simone's bar. She greeted me with a kiss and a glass of something that had a kick like a mule, and let me use her telephone.

In my hand I held Dr Liliane Delamarche's calling card.

CHAPTER TWENTY-FOUR

◆ ◆ ◆

CAMILLE

'*Bienvenue*, Camille. Come on in.'

'Thank you, Dr Delamarche, for seeing me so late.'

'You're welcome. This is an unexpected pleasure. Please call me Liliane.'

But I hesitated to enter. She was wearing a full-length emerald silk gown that shimmered like fish-scales as she moved, plus a broad bold necklace and wide gold wrist-cuffs. Who wears wrist-cuffs? Her earrings and her heavy eye make-up were a vivid green and black but most striking was the cobra's head that rose from a golden band that crossed her forehead. Her dusky blond hair was slicked down straight.

'You look spectacular,' I said.

She laughed. 'Come on in.'

She led the way into a spacious hallway, decorated in what it dawned on me was Egyptian style. Geometric tiles on the floor. Large sculptures of pharaohs' faces were placed under spotlights that emphasised their strange headgear, and a row of oversized scarab beetles in bright enamel blues and golds appeared to be scuttling across a marble shelf. Until that moment I didn't realise that Ancient Egyptian artefacts could be used to decorate a home. Not just kept in museums.

Liliane said cheerily, 'Don't worry, they're just plaster reproductions, you know. Not real. Copies of ones in the Cairo Museum. That one with the elaborate nemes, the striped headcloth worn by pharaohs, is Amenhotep III and that bizarre one over there with the pointy head is the splendid Akhenaton.' She threw open the door to the living room.

Immediately I knew I'd made a mistake. I shouldn't have come. The room was crowded and every person there was in fancy dress. Egyptian fancy dress. My heart sank. I was wearing my dark-brown office suit and I felt like a cockroach at Cleopatra's ball. Gowns were diaphanous, fluttering like butterfly wings around the room, and the men wore long white linen tunics with wide gold or black belts, from which a strange strap of material hung down at the front. All the men wore what looked like striped tea towels on their heads and heavy pieces of gold metal across their chests and on their arms and ankles.

I had walked into another world and I did not belong here.

'You have company,' I said. 'I'll come back another time.'

'Nonsense.' She slipped her hand under my brown serge elbow, steered me through the chattering crowd to a table of drinks and placed a cocktail glass brimming with some kind of green concoction in my hand. She took one for herself and sipped it with relish. 'There.' she smiled warmly at me. 'Better. Now what is so urgent you had to come out on this filthy night?'

In Paris there are apartments fit for people and then there are apartments fit for gods. This one was the latter. It was hiding discreetly just off the Champs-Élysées and, though old, it was sumptuous. I was in a huge, high-ceilinged room that dripped money. Obviously her father's money. Politicians had their palms greased as regularly as ducks took to water and the members of this Chautemps government were up to their necks in it.

I had telephoned Liliane and said, 'I have something I need to show you.'

'Is it urgent?'

'Yes, it is.'

'Then come straight over.' Always direct.

She'd given me her address but no mention of a party.

'Have you got it with you?' she asked now.

I nodded and watched two women with brass snakes spiralling up their arms applaud a bare-chested man who was performing some strange kind of dance. Or was it a ritual? The room vibrated with laughter. Music was playing from a record player and its sounds and rhythms were unfamiliar, bringing with them the whisper of the wind over the desert sands of Egypt. I studied these people who even smelled expensive, the confident set of their mouths, the way they stood, their air of entitlement, their certainty that the ancient gods of Egypt would smile down on them with favour.

Was this something you could learn? The way you could learn to read or to type or to use the right knife and fork. Or was it God-given?

'Come on then, Camille. Let's find somewhere quieter.'

Liliane led me from the room, but not before I'd snatched another glass from the table. I could feel the green concoction humming inside me. If this is what Ancient Egyptians used to drink, it's no wonder they created the pyramids. We settled into a much smaller room off the hall. A much more serious room, yet one in which I felt just as uncomfortable. It was full to overflowing with books. A green-shaded lamp, a desk and books. That was it. I would die to have a room like this and to have read all these books. I thought of my tiny table, my little hillock of shabby volumes and my second-hand fountain pen back home. It churned up that burning feeling of jealousy in my gut again, the same as last time. I knocked back the green concoction to douse its flames and turned to Liliane with a smile.

'Take a look.'

From my bag – not the canvas one that poor Omar had briefly stolen, that one was cursed by his blood – I removed an object that was swaddled in a sheet of tissue and handed it to her. It was about the size of a *petit pain*.

She unwrapped the paper and gave a light chuckle when she saw what it contained. It was the little Tutankhamen trinket box, the one from the toyshop. Made of tin and shaped to represent the boy pharaoh's spectacular coffin, it was coloured a vivid gold and turquoise and a rich royal blue that even in the dim lighting gleamed enticingly.

'The whole world has gone Tutankhamen-mad since Carter discovered the tomb,' Liliane laughed with intense pleasure. 'Even kids. It's good to get them interested in Ancient Egypt at a young age. There are so many fascinating stories about the gods like the wise Osiris and his fight with his evil brother Seth, and about rituals like the weighing of the heart against a feather after death.'

'A feather? What happened then? A heart must be heavier.'

'If the heart was found to be heavier than the feather, it was fed to Ammut, the Devourer, and the soul was cast into darkness. Wonderfully dramatic and graphic, isn't it?'

She shivered with delicious glee and her emerald gown shivered and shimmered with her. I liked this woman who had such a passion for her work. I couldn't see my hefty Royal typewriter ever in its lifetime giving me the shivers, except of boredom. Her clear blue eyes flicked up to me, suddenly serious, questioning.

'Is this why you came? To show me a child's trinket box?'

'No.'

'Why then?'

'Open it.'

She opened it. Her perfectly arched eyebrows shot up. She reached in and removed the headless little figure that lay inside.

'A *shabti*,' she exclaimed.

'What's a *shabti*?'

A frown creased her brow as the tiny severed head rattled loose in the tin container. 'Where did this come from? And why is it broken?'

'I bought the little Tutankhamen piece in a shop and found the broken figure hidden inside when I unwrapped it.'

I watched her discard the tin coffin. She cradled the figure and its separate head on her palm with respect, as though it were something precious.

'It looks old,' I added.

'About three thousand years old.' She couldn't take her eyes off it.

'What's a *shabti*?' I repeated.

'It's a funerary figure.' She balanced the head on the body and held it up for me to see. 'They are small figures that in Ancient Egypt were placed in tombs among the grave goods.'

'Why did they do that? Instead of flowers?'

Liliane laughed. 'No, much more useful. All the grave goods and *shabtis* were for the person to use in the afterlife. *Shabtis* were intended as servants who carried out the tasks required of the deceased in the underworld. That's why many of them carry hoes and baskets. The richer you were, the more *shabtis* you had. In Tutankhamen's tomb four hundred and eighteen were found, while Seti I, who perished in 1278 BC, had in excess of seven hundred *shabtis* buried with him.'

'That's a lot of servants.'

'This one is a beauty. Some are just made of rough stone or wood, but this one is formed out of exquisite faïence and, as you can see, gilded in parts. You see it's in the shape of a mummy with an inscription on its torso.'

I peered more closely. 'That's writing? I thought it was decoration.'

'No, it's miniature hieratic writing. A shortened version of hieroglyphics.'

'Do you know what it says?'

'Yes, I've read it many times before. Most *shabtis* are inscribed with it. It's the name of the deceased person plus the sixth chapter of *The Book of the Dead*.'

My skin seemed to tighten as if it were suddenly a size too small for me. *The Book of the Dead*. Even more of a warning than I'd realised. Did Omar receive a *shabti* too, I wondered, before he climbed on the bus?

'Read it for me.'

'Happy to. The deceased's name was Nimlot. It says, "Oh *shabti*, allotted to me, if Osiris Nimlot be decreed to do any work which is to be done in Khert-Neter" – that's the Underworld – "let everything which standeth in the way be removed from him, whether it be to plough the fields, or to fill the channels with water, or to carry sand from the East to the West". The *shabti* replies: *"I will do it, verily I am here when thou callest".'*

'So the dead person gets a free pass.'

She smiled. 'Yes. *Shabtis* certainly come in useful.'

I held out my hand. 'I'd better have it back then. Just in case.'

Reluctantly she released it. 'It pains me to see it broken.'

'What is *The Book of the Dead*?'

'It's a set of instructions as to how to navigate the long and challenging journey through to the afterlife, the Duat.'

'You'd only need them if you were about to die, right?'

'Well, yes, I suppose that's . . .' Her words halted. A look of shock froze her features. 'Camille, what are you saying? That someone is threatening you?'

'First the ankh, a symbol of life. Now the *shabti*, a tool for after death.'

'No,' she whispered. 'You are imagining things, my friend. The ankh you came across by accident and this *shabti* must have been put in the miniature coffin as a sick joke. People react very strangely to all the extraordinary tales and beliefs of Ancient Egypt and someone is just being foolish.' She chafed my arm in its dull brown sleeve as though to bring me back to life. 'Take no notice. Don't let it—'

At that moment the door burst open. Into the study strode a tall imposing pharaoh, king of all the Egyptians in the drawing room with his proud bearing, his royal headdress and the large cobra head with its flared hood rising menacingly from the gold band on his forehead. Like his daughter's. For it was Liliane's father again. He stared at me, taken by surprise.

'Good evening, M. Delamarche. What a splendid costume,' I commented.

Over his flowing white ankle-length tunic he wore an elaborate burgundy robe that rippled around him with an inner energy, and on display was an array of chunks of gold that would feed me for five years.

He recovered quickly. 'Which is more than I can say for yours, Mlle Malroux.' The insult spilled into a laugh, to hide the barb within it.

'Monsieur le Ministre, I am not here to attend the party.'

'So why are you here?'

He held a large balloon glass of brandy in his hand and raised it to me before taking a good swig. By the ruby tracery of veins on his cheeks, I'd guess it wasn't his first.

'Papa, behave! I invited Camille over.' She turned to me. 'It's Papa's birthday party. Come and see what he asked for as his gift. You'll love it.' She swept me out of the room through a small side door that led into a tiny sitting room that was empty except for a large metal cage that took up most of the floor space.

A ferocious hissing and spitting greeted us and a beautiful creature launched itself in our direction, but its attack was blocked by metal bars. I blinked to make sure I was seeing right. It was a leopard. I'd only ever seen pictures of them and was not prepared for how intensely wild it seemed in this domesticated setting. Or for the smell of it. Its huge golden eyes were mesmerising as they fixed on us and its pelt was marked with black rosettes that I longed to stroke. But no, Liliane was wrong. I didn't love it. Because it shouldn't be here. It didn't fit in any more than I did. It should be roaming wild in a jungle.

Augustin Delamarche stood in the doorway with a look of impatience on his face. 'I was told it would be tame, but look at the animal. It would tear your arm off if you got too close, but yes, my sweet,' he smiled at his daughter, 'it is a magnificent beast.'

We all retreated to the study, leaving the poor leopard in peace, and as we did so, Augustin Delamarche noticed the small broken figure still in my hand.

'Here for more free information from my daughter, I presume.'

He released the air as a laugh but there was nothing humorous about it, his ice-blue eyes shrewd and suspicious. Was it the thought of the free advice his daughter was giving me or the sight of the *shabti* that had sharpened his mood? We stood there, the three of us, listening to the sounds of revelry in the next room. There was a tension in the study now that had swept in alongside M. Delamarche and I knew it was time to leave.

I picked up the colourful little Tutankhamen coffin from the desk but again I heard a great gust of air come from Delamarche.

'Where did you get that?' he asked.

'In a toyshop. Le Rêve. Do you know it?'

Liliane uttered a whoop of surprise. 'Know it? Papa owns it.'

I felt an odd sense of falling. A sudden lurch under the soles of my feet, though I hadn't actually moved. As if I'd stepped off a cliff.

CHAPTER TWENTY-FIVE

◆ ◆ ◆

CAMILLE

M y room was icy. Outside the temperature had dropped and the night sky over the city was heavy, storing up snow for tomorrow, but right now it was the kind of cold that cracks your bones. I didn't put the light on.

I hung up my jacket, pulled on my thickest jumper and wrapped myself in my dressing gown. Gilles had given me the dressing gown for Christmas two years ago. It was beautiful merino wool, a soft dove-grey with a cosy hood and deep pockets, and I loved it. Gilles reckoned that I'd live in it all day if only they'd let me wear it to the office.

I locked my door. But I didn't bolt it. Not tonight.

I had long ago installed a sturdy bolt at the top and bottom for increased safety in this ramshackle building, but tonight I didn't shoot them across. In the dark I removed a blanket from the bed and enfolded myself in it like a mummy.

I lay down and waited. A carving knife in my hand.

The click was so soft I barely heard it. My breathing stopped. I listened so hard I could pick up the skittering of a cockroach under the floorboards, but no human footsteps. The darkness felt alive pressing on my skin.

Whoever he was, he was good.

The wait was endless. Nothing after that initial click of the lock. No movement. No shift of the night shadows or murmur of the boards under his feet. The intruder kept himself to himself and his patience seemed inexhaustible because he made no further attempt to enter my room. He must be standing by the door, as silent as the grave that he no doubt intended to send me to. His patience against my patience. I matched him, silent breath for silent breath.

Thirty minutes? An hour? More? I don't know, I lost all sense of time and place until it was just the darkness and me and the click of my door lock on a never-ending loop. Nothing else existed. My fingers ached, their grip too tight on the handle of the knife.

Protect yourself, Beau had urged. *Be prepared*.

I am prepared.

The attack, when it came, was swift. In total silence.

I heard no footsteps, but suddenly I could smell stale cigarette smoke very close. My heart was thundering fit to break my ribs but I wasn't tremoring. I was ready for him.

He hurled himself at the bed. Something slammed down on it with such ferocity that its ancient iron frame vibrated and squealed, rattling my teeth. At that same moment he flicked on a torch. In the half-light of its beam, from my hiding place curled on my side under the bed, I could make out the lower part of a man's legs in silhouette. Without hesitation I plunged my knife deep into his calf muscle and felt the blade drive through one side of it and out the other.

He screamed. It was a noise that belonged to a feral animal rather than a human. I scrambled out from under the bed, abandoning the blanket, but by the time I reached the door he was already tumbling down the stairs at speed, clinging on to the rusty bannister rail for support. I raced after him and was shocked to realise the knife was still in my hand. There must have been blood on the stairs but in the darkness I saw only the yellow beam of the torch hurtling down into the stairwell.

'*Arrêtez!*' The man's voice rose in pain. Or panic. 'Stop where you are!'

I stopped. Breath tearing in and out of my lungs. I stopped on the very last stair. Not because I was unwilling to plunge my knife into his other leg, far from it, but because the torchlight was trained on a spill of blond hair and a face as bone-white as the snow falling outside.

It was Anne-Marie. She had just returned home from her evening of servicing the johns of Montparnasse and as she opened the big front door, eager for her own bed, she must have been seized by my attacker in the hallway. He was holding an axe to her throat.

An axe?

A small hand-axe admittedly, but still an axe. What was he planning on doing with it? Chopping me up into small pieces in my own bed?

'Let her go,' I said immediately.

My friend's blue eyes were huge, glazed with terror and fixed on me.

'Let her go,' I shouted at him.

He grunted. In pain. Scarlet ribbons trailed all over the floor. He was well hidden inside an oversized grey coat and a black balaclava, so that only his deep-set eyes were visible. I had thought my attacker would be Robespierre – M. Sarrazin – but this figure was too tall and moved like a much younger man.

'You bitch!' he screamed at me. 'Get back up to your room and when I hear your door close, I will release this *putain*.'

'You swear?'

He laughed crookedly and edged the axe blade tighter, producing a thread of crimson from her throat. I had no choice.

'Don't cry, Anne-Marie. It's me he wants, not you. But he's too injured to handle me now and can't afford the police descending, so—'

'Go!' he yelled.

I went. I had just reached the dim landing on the third floor when I heard the front door open and slam shut. I flew back down the stairs again to find Anne-Marie slumped on the floor weeping, dry chest-wrenching sobs, but unhurt. Outside there was the sound of a car engine starting up and being driven away at speed. I dashed into the road but saw nothing but tail-lights skidding around the corner.

Anne-Marie and I were alive. That was the best I could say.

CHAPTER TWENTY-SIX

◆ ◆ ◆

CAMILLE

I hit the wrong key. *Merde.*

Bills of lading. I hate them. They go on forever. I had been typing them all morning and kept making uncharacteristic errors because my mind was stuck. I couldn't drag it away from pounding down the stairwell after the fleeing figure. Still seeing the milky-white throat. The thread of crimson. The axe.

When early on I'd told Beau where I worked, his poor damaged face had lit up.

'You work where?' he'd exclaimed.

'In the Hôtel de la Marine.'

'You work inside one of the most beautiful buildings in Paris?'

'Yes.'

'How very *glamour.*'

My office wasn't glamorous. It was strictly functional. Unlike the facade of the building with its twelve glorious Corinthian columns that stare down on the place de la Concorde and up the Champs-Élysées, with the angular Eiffel Tower visible in the distance. Inside it was even more *glamour.* The state rooms lavishly gilded, plus chandeliers, mirrors and sculptures to dazzle the eye. What goes on behind it all is hidden from sight, the same way the blood in my room is hidden from sight.

Bills of lading. Concentrate.

I knew when I started work for the Ministre de la Marine marchande, the Merchant Navy, that it might not be wildly exciting, but it had exceeded even my well-honed tolerance for tedium. Typing out lists of the entire cargo contents of merchant ships as they traded across the globe was like drilling holes in your head. All original thoughts or ideas leaked out under my desk. These bills of lading were crucial documents used in international trade for import and export of goods, so yes, I was contributing to boost the economy of France, but no, I was not contributing to boost my own mind. To expand my knowledge. I thought of Dr Liliane Delamarche and all the millions of pieces of knowledge crammed inside her head.

'Malroux. In my office.'

I'd missed Mme Beaufort's arrival at my desk. I was slipping. I rose quickly and followed her brisk pace to her office in silence. Others watched, some raised a sympathetic eyebrow. Mme Beaufort shut the door.

'Sit,' she said.

I sat. Knees together, hands in lap, head up, shoulders back. I gave her my best how-can-I-help-you? expression. Calm and controlled. What had she heard about me? Had the police returned? Surely not. I hadn't reported last night's attack, but if she'd learned that I was riding a bus to Salpêtrière yesterday when I was meant to be too ill to work . . .

'Well, Malroux, it looks as though we are going to lose you.'

No.

Why?

'I'd be sorry to leave, Madame,' I said. I kept it quiet. By brute force.

'But first I wish to discuss the fact that files have been going missing from this office.'

My mouth turned dry.

'Files?'

'Yes, Malroux. Files. Three to be exact. Disappearing and then reappearing.'

Thirty-five to be exact, but let's not quibble.

'I know nothing about missing files, Mme Beaufort.'

She was wearing a pale-grey dress and slate-grey jacket, no jewellery. Smart without advertising the fact. Her hands were always on the move and she touched her abundant dark hair, patting it in place, in a rare gesture of uncertainty.

I took advantage of the moment. 'In what way can I help?'

'I will talk straight with you, Malroux. I believe that Mlle Hélène Durand has been removing the files. Taking them for reasons unknown and then returning them in the hope I hadn't noticed their absence. I regard you as a sharp-eyed young woman, observant and quick-witted, who is likely to notice if one of our employees is committing such acts of felony.'

Her shrewd eyes studied me intently.

I didn't look away, I kept my breathing smooth, and I didn't swallow but there was a burning in my throat. I liked Hélène Durand.

'Mlle Durand is a loyal and committed member of staff, Madame, I don't for one moment believe she would do such a thing.'

A faint sigh whispered across the desk. 'You disappoint me, Malroux. I didn't think you would let your friendship with her blind you to the obvious.'

'What makes you suspect her?'

'I found her in my empty office when she had no good reason to be here.'

I remember. Hélène had gone there to report that she'd sent an important document upstairs in error. She would have suffered consequences. I'd quickly retrieved it, silenced the mouth of the secretary upstairs with a bottle of Burgundy, and we didn't speak of it again. She wasn't in Mme Beaufort's office to steal files. That was my job.

I had been taking the files that listed imports and exports through the port of Marseille for the past year, copying them at home and passing the copies on to Gilles. I'd always returned the original files to the office. I'd assumed my brother was up to some kind of money-making fiddle with the Customs down there, but only now did I link it with what Omar had told me about importing illegal artefacts from Egypt.

I drew a sharp breath. Mme Beaufort was quick.

'What is it?' she demanded.

I shook my head.

'Don't let me down, Malroux. I have put my faith in you.'

'It's not Hélène?'

'Who then?'

I took a long moment, as if debating within myself how much to say. 'It is Mlle Céline Allard.'

'Allard?' She uttered a huff of disdain. 'That girl is too stupid to put files back without botching it.'

I shrugged but remained silent.

'What makes you think it was Allard?'

'Twice I've seen her go in and out of your office when you were in a meeting upstairs.'

She frowned and her knuckles drummed on her desk. 'You chose not to report it?'

'I assumed she was just looking for you to ask more questions, as usual. It seems I was mistaken.'

Céline Allard was, as Mme Beaufort stated, a stupid girl. A stupid, lazy, sly girl who took every opportunity to blame her multiple mistakes on others. I was sure her days as a *fonctionnaire* were already numbered.

Mme Beaufort nodded. 'Thank you, Malroux.'

She sat very still, inspecting me. I desperately wanted to ask why she'd said she was losing me, but I said nothing.

'Malroux, I have been observing you and I believe you have the potential to progress well here at the Hôtel de la Marine, despite that business with the police the other day. But I warn you to steer clear of any more black marks on your record.' Abruptly she leaned forward and her voice softened. 'Are you all right? You don't look well. I know you were absent yesterday, so maybe you . . .'

'I am well, Madame. You need have no concern.'

She sat back, tapping her steepled fingertips together, satisfied. 'I expected no less of you.'

A silence crept into the room while I waited. She didn't hurry.

'Now, Malroux, I'm sorry to inform you that we are losing you.'

A thump inside my chest made me blink.

'Why is that, Madame? I like it here.'

'Someone has requested a transfer for you.' She picked up a manila folder on her desk and I saw the crest of the Ministry of Justice stamped on it. 'A personal request. One that I unfortunately cannot refuse.'

'To where?'

'The Ministry of Justice. I'm sure there will be excellent opportunities there for your advancement.'

'Who requested the transfer?'

She opened the folder and read out a name. 'Ministre Augustin Delamarche.'

CHAPTER TWENTY-SEVEN

◆ ◆ ◆

CAMILLE

I waited. I leaned against a wall in the patch of darkness where no streetlamp reached. And I waited.

A bulky wool scarf was wrapped around my head and over the lower part of my face. Even my own mother wouldn't know me. The snow had turned to a crinkly brown slush and spat up at me every time a car or bus rumbled past, but I stayed where I was. Watching.

On the opposite side of the road the shop lights were slowly extinguished one by one, as managers hurried to lock up and scurry home for the night to a hot meal, a swig or two of wine, and to curl up with warm willing flesh in bed before more snow swept in from the east. My eyes and my hopes had narrowed to mere slits when finally he emerged.

Even in the gloom I knew him. Oh yes, I knew him. Robespierre. He ducked his head against the freezing fingers of the wind and moved off fast.

I moved off with him.

He took the Métro to Belleville. That surprised me. I'd expected him to live somewhere more *confortable* than these run-down messy streets of north-east Paris.

I actually liked the grittiness of them, the lack of pretence, no Haussmann facades here, just cobbles and chaos. It was all rowdy cafés, broken windows, the cheapest of brothels, and pin-thin artists starving in attic ateliers. And after its colourful Friday markets on boulevard de

Belleville there was always the invasion of rats that savaged their way through the discarded piles of garbage.

But at its heart lay a hill. A long lung-pumping hill. And it was here that I had to watch my step even in the dark. The Métro had been crammed with tired Parisians eager to get home out of the cold, making it easy to vanish among the army of limbs and scarves and evening newspapers. Whereas here, I was exposed. The needlepoints of sleet had driven inhabitants off the streets and as he hurried up the hill, scurrying like an animal that knows its own territory, there was no cover for me to hide behind. If he looked back over his shoulder, he would see me. I kept close to the wall.

At a corner *épicerie* he dodged down a side street where the lamps had failed and I almost lost him. I quickened my pace and narrowed the gap. But an upstairs light flicked on at the crucial moment, throwing me a lifeline and revealing his dark shadow sliding into the narrow passage Julien Lacroix. Here the cobbles were pitted and broken, windows boarded and houses crumbling, the streetlamp long since having given up any attempt at functioning. But he moved like a cat moves at night, sure of its footing. Up the fifty or more wide stone steps that raised the passage to a higher level on rue Piat, and then . . . Nothing.

He'd gone.

I stood still. I listened. At first I heard only the moan of the wind and the quick intake of my own breath, but underneath it I caught the sound of a door opening, the metallic click of it closing. Off to my right. I didn't move from my spot glued tight to the wall. A minute passed. Two minutes. Three. Was he gazing out of a window searching the night for the faintest flutter of movement?

An upstairs light sprang into life, visible behind the broken shutters. I had him.

M. Sarrazin. Or M. Robespierre. Whichever you are. I know where you hide.

I needed to talk to Beau.

I headed south to the river, across the pont de Bercy and through the vast portals of Salpêtrière Hospital once more for my evening visit. Ever since hearing of M. Delamarche's request for my transfer to the Ministry of Justice, I was aware of a pain, like a blade of ice, deep under my skin, not from the snow or from the wind, but from the terrible knowledge I had gained today and I knew that if I didn't shift it, I would freeze to death. I wanted Beau to roll his amber eyes at me and say, 'Camille, look at you, you're wet through. Have you been swimming in the Seine?' I needed him to laugh his soft teasing laugh and to give me that smile of his that would melt the edges of the ice and let me untie the knots in my gut.

I burst through the double doors of the ward and hurried towards Beau's bed but came to an abrupt halt. Screens had been placed around it blocking him from my view. The knots in my gut tightened as I slid inside the enclosed space. His eyes were closed. The oxygen mask was back in place, his lips were blue behind it and two nurses were bending over him with faces trying in vain to hide their concern.

'M. Malroux,' one was saying to him in a voice that trod a fine line between panic and professional calm, 'can you hear me?'

There was no response.

I pushed past them, ignored their protests, and took his limp hand in mine, gripping it tighter than was kind.

'Come back,' I ordered.

Still no response.

I wrapped both my hands around Beau's and linked my fingers through his, like splicing a rope to stop him drifting out to sea. There was no way of telling where his fingers ended and mine started.

'Beau, don't go.' I breathed the words into his ear. 'Stay with me, Beau, I have brought something for you.'

It was the ankh, attached to a bootlace that was threaded through the upper loop. I reached with gentle movements behind his head and tied it loosely around his neck.

'Listen to me, Beau.' My voice dropped even lower. 'I could have been the one who died on the bus, but I didn't. I could have died in my room last night, but I didn't. Each time Gilles's ankh was with me. Now I am giving it to you. Stay with me, Beau.'

The older nurse, owner of a top-heavy bosom and a way of holding herself that said don't get in my way, stared at me and then stared at the ankh with disgust. 'Holy Mother of God, may the Lord forgive you, child. That is nothing but the devil's claptrap.' She stuck a needle in his arm.

I leaned closer and pressed my lips to Beau's unshaven cheek and held them there for a long moment, willing him to keep dragging air into his lungs.

'That,' the nurse said, 'is what will save him.'

I was gripped by fear for Beau. Sick with sorrow for what he was going through right now, and I imagined his soul clinging to the walls. To the white bed. To my hand.

'Talk to him,' the nurse had said. 'He needs a reason to fight his way back.'

So I talked. I combed my fingers rhythmically through his matted hair while I talked about M. Augustin Delamarche, minister attached to the Ministry of Justice.

Justice?

What price justice?

I described to Beau how I had made use of my position at the Hôtel de la Marine to dig into the leather-bound tomes that live in the library of the Ministry of the Merchant Navy and which include an up-to-date record of all the ministries within the French government. Augustin Delamarche was named in person. Disappointing though. His entry didn't give much away. He had been educated at the University of Paris, joined the military, become a junior minister in the Ministry of Finance under Raymond Poincaré, and since had risen fast within the ranks of the Ministry of Justice. He owned houses in Paris, Cannes and Chamonix and his principal interests were playing polo in the summer and in the winter *la chasse*. Of course they were. He was exactly the kind of man who'd get a kick out of blasting a wild boar off the face of the earth with a shotgun or caging a wild leopard. I wondered what other living creatures he had developed a taste for killing.

His wife, Geneviève Delamarche, a sculptor, died nine years ago in a skiing accident and he had one daughter, Dr Liliane Delamarche.

'An impressive family. Don't you agree, Beau?'

No answer.

'But it leaves me with three questions for you, Beau. Where did all Augustin Delamarche's money come from? Why does he own a toy-shop? And for what purpose did he go to the trouble of transferring me from Navy to Justice?'

I studied his closed eyelids. They were so thin and vulnerable to the lightest touch.

'Any ideas?'

I waited. But when the silence stretched to the point where tears were rolling down my cheeks, I added, 'Shall I tell you what I think?'

I looked for a sign. Any sign. A flutter of an eyelash. The flare of a nostril or jump of a nerve. The pressure of a finger on my palm.

'Please, Beau,' I whispered and kissed him again. This time I lifted the oxygen mask and kissed him on the mouth. To jolt him awake. His lips tasted of medicine. No response.

'What I think,' I continued, 'is this. Augustin Delamarche is involved in some way in this network that Omar told me about, the one importing illegal ancient artefacts from Egypt into France to sell abroad for huge prices. Why else would he employ Robespierre? Delamarche could well be the head of the network, for all I know. He's a man who likes to be top dog. He could be shipping them into his shop, the toys just a front for the real business that goes on in the back room. It's time for me to take a closer look.'

I uttered a small grunt of dismay.

'What? You're thinking I have no proof? Is that what's worrying you?' I prodded the tip of his chin in an attempt to set it moving. 'That may be true but honestly there's no reason for you to keep quiet.'

I felt for the pulse in his wrist. It was there but thready and uneven.

'You don't agree with me, do you, Beau? Tell me the truth.'

I paused.

'No, I tell you he's a nasty piece of work,' I continued as if he'd spoken. 'And he employs even nastier pieces of work to do the dangerous jobs.'

A one-sided conversation it might be, but I had the odd sense that we could hear each other's thoughts.

'You're saying I have absolutely no reason to believe this respectable government minister is involved in such dirty work. Really? Is that what you think?'

Of course it was what he thought. It was what any rational person would think.

'No, you're wrong. I am convinced that M. Delamarche is the kind of person who would use his daughter's expert knowledge, without her even realising it, to enrich himself and that he wouldn't hesitate to trample over anyone in his way. All right, yes, I admit you're correct in saying I have no proof. But there is something ruthless about this man that rings alarm bells in me.'

I lowered my cheek to his hand where it lay entwined with mine on the bed 'That's why I'm scared, Beau. Why does he want me in his own ministry? So that he can watch me like a hawk and tear me to bits if I step out of line.'

'Camille?'

He cried out my name.

My heartbeat stopped. I lifted my head. I had fallen asleep.

'Camille?'

His hands thrashed on the coverlet. In the gloom of our small space within the screens, I gathered his hands to me and held them tight.

'Hush, Beau, it's all right, I'm here, you're safe,' I soothed. 'You're having a nightmare.'

A nightmare so violent it had dragged him back from whichever black pit he had fallen into. He had yanked the mask from his face and was fighting for every breath.

'I'll call a nurse.'

'No.'

'You need—'

'I need you to listen. Please, Camille.'

I arranged the oxygen mask back on his face and wiped sweat from his forehead. 'Breathe, Beau, take a couple of minutes to breathe.'

He lay back on the pillows, eyes fixed on mine, and slowly his breathing returned to something like normal. Or what passed as normal in someone with broken ribs.

'I was back on the train,' he said. 'In the crash.'

'Oh Beau.'

'It was . . . bad. Screams and grinding metal and the roar of flames.'

I listened. Not just to what he was saying, but to what he was not saying. It came out in a scramble of pain and shock and images that had seared his mind. Gradually his voice calmed, his breathing eased.

'Rest now,' I whispered. 'I'll fetch a nurse.'

But his hand gripped mine. 'I love the way you listen,' he said. Behind the mask I could see his smile. 'So completely.'

I laughed. 'You're not bad at it yourself.'

For that one moment our smiles held, then slowly faded.

'What is it?' I asked.

'I remember.'

CHAPTER TWENTY-EIGHT

◆ ◆ ◆

CAMILLE

Amnesia is a thief. It steals who you are.
It robs you of hope and love and life. One day you love a person, a job, an activity. And the next day you don't even know they exist. And worse, when you are told that they exist, that they have been a crucial part of your life forever, you realise you've lost the emotions that were tied to those people, those places, those events. They mean nothing to you.

Your constant companions now are grief and anger and frustration. You are adrift.

You no longer know who you are.

It is a living hell.

Yet when I heard Beau say, 'I remember,' a splinter of terror slid under my nails.

'That is wonderful, Beau.'

That's what I said. And a huge part of me meant it. I wanted this man to be happy again and to see a future and a past for himself, I wanted him to regain his joy in life. Even if that life excluded me.

And yet . . .

'I get a stabbing pain in my head whenever I am going to sleep,' he told me, his voice quiet now. Such restraint. So little drama. 'It feels as if something is trying to break out. And just now it did so. A violent explosion seemed to blow my head wide apart, and I was back on that express train as it crashed into the stationary one.'

He released a rush of air, the only sign of his emotion.

'Then memories came hurtling back. Images ripping into me. Spinning me round and around. Everywhere I looked I saw red, the fields drowning in it, people losing rivers of it from their eyes and ears, the dark brick-red colour of blood in need of oxygen.'

I ran my thumb over his thumb, picturing the blood pumping beneath our skin.

'I'm so sorry, Beau.'

'Don't be. The memories have returned, swirling inside my head. Some are in bits and pieces, some have lost their order and I can't yet make them fit together properly, like a jumble of jigsaws. But others,' his eyes grew bright and intense, 'are sharp. As clear to me as your smile.'

I could sense the energy building in him. I leaned closer, my right leg tremoring with excitement. Suddenly Gilles was within reach.

'What are they, Beau? The memories that fit together? Do you remember your name and your job? Your family?'

'No. That is all still a blank. But I do know I was with another man on the train. I was following him for some reason. I knew who he was. He wore a tan coat and spectacles. Carried an umbrella and a large suitcase, brown with a strap.'

'His name?'

He knocked his knuckles hard against the side of his head with annoyance. 'Lafitte?'

I pulled a face.

'Wait. Lalonde? No, no. Let me think.' Angry with himself. 'I climbed into the carriage after him but no seats remained free.'

'Did that annoy you?'

'Very much. I would have to travel in the next carriage. I remember looking up at his heavy suitcase on the rack above his head and wondering who put it up there for him.' He frowned and narrowed his eyes, trying to peer through the mist within his damaged head.

Suddenly his face cleared. 'Laval. That was his name, Antoine Laval. Of course. Your curator.'

'Was he friend or foe?'

This was where his recollections stumbled. He was tiring fast. I thought about him standing there, looking at the Christmas travellers packed into the carriage, a sense of occasion making them all cheerful.

'Describe them, Beau. The other people in that carriage.'

He did so with remarkable recall of detail. A young woman and child, with a navy coat and a mouth turned down with worry. An older man quietly reading his Bible and another with a drinker's nose and a briefcase clutched tight on his lap. By the window sat a long-limbed man in black coat and hat, angular shoulders deliberately turned so that he could face the window and the darkness beyond. Next to him a younger man who had the appearance of a junior clerk was smoking a cigarette and opposite him a plump woman in a flimsy red hat was beaming at him in a Christmassy sort of way.

I considered all he'd said. 'Beau, do you do this for a living?'

'Do what?'

'Observe people. You're very good at it.'

He gave me a curious smile. 'Do you recognise any of them?'

'The man in the black hat, the one looking out of the window.'

'Yes?'

'He could be my brother.'

'Gilles?'

'Yes. It's possible.'

'If your brother was in fact tracking Laval, as Omar suggested to you on the bus before he was murdered, and if I was following Laval on the train too, it indicates your brother and I could have been working together.' He managed a grim nod. 'Now that's a thought.'

Stunned, I couldn't reply.

'Or it's possible,' he continued, 'that I was working with Laval in an attempt to steal Egyptian works of art from the museum and flee the country.' His amber eyes were solemn as they gazed at me. 'I could be a criminal.'

'Beau, I don't believe that for a second. Decency runs through you like a thread of silver.' I laughed softly. 'You're more likely to be a policeman.'

It was a joke. A joke. But a joke that went wrong. Our eyes locked on each other. A silence crept in between us.

I whispered it this time. 'You're more likely to be a policeman.'

CHAPTER TWENTY-NINE

◆ ◆ ◆

GILLES

She got him back into bed. Gilles didn't know how, but she did. He'd passed out where he lay at the top of the stairs. At one point he thought he heard the doctor's voice but that may have been a figment of his fevered dreams.

What he did know was that the pain receded, making him want to weep with relief. Twice he was aware of a needle in his arm. Twice he wanted to shout 'Don't!' but his jaws seemed to be welded shut. He knew he should worry but all he desired was sleep.

How long he was out, he had no idea, but the dreams that came had claws and teeth and left him bloodied. She woke him with a slap. It jolted his painful jaw and sent his thoughts crashing into each other, but his hand shot out instinctively and seized her wrist.

'Don't,' he warned.

'Or what?'

'Or I might report a certain stolen statue of the Pharaoh Hatshepsut. One with a hand snapped off.'

She laughed, the way you laugh at a pet cat's antics. 'Who are you going to report it to? The walls? The window? The mice under the floorboards?'

They both knew no mouse would dare enter this house.

The sweetness had vanished from her voice. It felt like glasspaper grating on his raw nerves. To his surprise the day had darkened and he could feel a night-time frost coating the air in the bedroom. How long had he slept? An hour? A day? Five days? What had they crammed into him this time?

Phenobarbital?

How much? The inside of his head felt like *bouillie* and when he tried to sit up, his leg seemed to rupture something. Had they stitched it?

'To the doctor,' he risked.

She laughed as if he'd made a bad joke and disentangled her wrist from his grasp. 'Let's be serious. A stolen statue of a pharaoh, even if it is a rare female pharaoh, is not what this is about, as you well know.'

'So what is it about?'

'The suitcase.'

Gilles let his eyes drift closed, as whatever drug was in his system was getting the upper hand again.

The suitcase.

Mahogany-brown with a strap and buckle to ensure it was firmly closed. Not even a violent leap from the carriage's luggage rack could burst it open despite the weight of its contents.

Its contents.

Powerful enough to kill a man. Not just any man, but specifically one who was breaking the law and stealing them from the Louvre to take them God knows where. Presumably to someone who had dangled a price so high it would buy a decent man's conscience for the rest of his life. Because until that point Dr Laval seemed to have been a decent hardworking honest employee of the museum who was passionate about Ancient Egypt and its works of art.

Laval had been making a run for it, that was clear. Not just from the museum's security people or from the police, but from Augustin Delamarche and Sarazzin as well. And it would cost him his life. He had double-crossed them and as a result they had hired Gilles as a hitman. Those two didn't play around. You cross them and you're finished. It was when Gilles's path crossed that of an Egyptian called Omar Youssef Ahmed when he was doing a job down in Marseille that he got involved.

An illegal network in Paris was smuggling what Omar claimed was his country's ancient heritage out of Egypt and Omar was wanting an inside man, someone to do his dirty work.

'I'm in,' Gilles had declared.

'Good. Sarazzin will be your contact because Delamarche always keeps hands clean.'

The infiltration of the network had been running smoothly until the train crash. Now the only way to get Delamarche to the guillotine was by finding that suitcase and by getting this Rosa Lagarde woman to release him. He still had no idea what the hell her part in all this was, but one thing was certain: he had to get himself back to Paris with that suitcase full of valuables.

The fact that Rosa had in her possession the statue of Hatshepsut worried him. Where on earth did she get her hands on it? The last time he'd seen it, it was in Sarazzin's possession. So what was the connection between the two of them? That worried him a lot.

Gilles closed his eyes and his mind started to spin around in what felt like a sandstorm inside his head. Camille was there too, he could hear his sister's voice calling to him, begging him to stay alive. Things weren't making sense. Before the train crash Gilles had broken off the statue's hand and appropriated it as his own when backs were turned inside the shop, much to Sarrazin's rage. They were both well aware that the statue's hand contained the hidden ankh.

Sarazzin would kill him, if Gilles didn't kill Sarazzin first.

CHAPTER THIRTY

◆ ◆ ◆

CAMILLE

'I've had a visitor.'

'Oh?' I waited for more.

'A woman,' Beau added.

I despised myself for the stab of jealousy that caught me just under my ribs. He wasn't mine, though he felt like mine. This strange bubble we lived in together had no door for visitors.

'Who was she? Some charity do-gooder doing the rounds of the wards?'

'No.'

'Who then?'

'I don't know. She said she was looking for her husband who had been on the express train that crashed and has since disappeared.'

'So she's checking the hospitals?'

'Yes.'

'Not your wife?'

Three words. They fell off my tongue unbidden. I could feel my throat lock up as though frightened what else might come out.

'It seems not.'

'Seems?'

'No, she's not. But . . .'

His words died in the air and for a split second I wanted to die with them.

'What did she look like?'

'Polite. Dark hair. Unusual eyes. Capable. She brought me bonbons.'

'Kind of her.'

'Yes.'

'Yet something about her has disturbed you.'

He nodded and I could see displeasure in the line of his mouth as he ran through the encounter in his mind. 'Sometimes it is hard to see the truth in another's eyes.'

'Do you think she is someone you knew before the accident?'

'Oh Camille, I don't know. There is something about her that jangles my nerves and I don't know why.' He wiped a hand across his forehead to banish the confusion in his mind. 'I just don't know. I can't remember.'

I imagined the blackness. The bleakness.

'If she knows you, surely she would have said so. Why would she hide it?'

'That's what I keep asking myself.'

'And your answer?'

'She's lying.'

'Why would she do that?'

But we both knew the answer to that. A wife who wants to be rid of her husband might leap at this chance.

'My story is gone,' he said. 'I may never learn who I am. All I'm left with are the ashes of a life.' But then he smiled at me, a genuine smile that reached right down inside him, not a feigned one. 'And you,' he added.

He reached over to his bedside locker and I saw the wince of pain he tried to hide.

'Here, take these.' He handed me a fancy box of chocolates that I wanted to hurl across the room. 'Give them to the nurses,' he said.

'We'll keep working at it,' I promised him. 'We'll build you a new story.'

The day dragged by as slowly as if it were built of lead. The huge typing office was chilly, the work was tedious and Mme Beaufort was tetchy. Or was my day slow because I couldn't get out of my head the expression on Beau's face when he said, 'I may never learn who I am'?

One of the advantages of working for a government ministry is that it is furnished with every one of the many telephone directories of the city. So instead of dashing across the river to Salpêtrière, I spent my lunch hour gathering together the telephone numbers of every single police station in Paris. I then stood with a bagful of coins in a telephone kiosk at the back of a bar and started to dial each of those numbers. You learn a lot about people when they don't know who you are and have no reason to be nice to you. Responses varied.

'Do not waste my time.'

'*Eh bien*, I'm far too busy, Mademoiselle.'

'Let me see what I can find out.'

'How distressing for your friend. Here's the telephone number of the Paris Police Prefecture which should have the information you require. *Bonne chance*.'

Like I said, you learn a lot about people.

My question was simple. 'Have any police officers in your district gone missing recently? I have a friend who was on the train that crashed at Pomponne and he is suffering from amnesia. He has no papers to say who he is, but believes it's possible he might have been a police officer. Can you help me, please?'

The *préfecture* is a large building located in the place Louis Lépine on the Île de la Cité and my telephone call was passed from pillar to post, but in the end the answer was delivered loud and clear: all present and correct. No police officers missing.

I didn't stop there.

In France the national police is a civil force; the gendarmerie in képi and cape is a military force. So next I set to work on the Directorate-General of the National Gendarmerie. It was a long and convoluted process but finally the answer came back the same. No officers missing.

A dead end.

I'm sorry, Beau, I'm sorry. I tried.

The windows were rattling in their frames. I'd hurried home that evening but despite the cold, a rowdy crowd had colonised the bar opposite and by the time I had my key in the door they had spilled on to the pavement. Somebody was blasting off with a riff of trumpet jazz while a couple who fancied themselves as comedians were belting out Louis Armstrong's "Ain't Misbehavin'". I was confident that Barnaby would be more than ready to abandon his paintbrushes.

I knocked on his door.

'Barnaby, my friend, I hope you've had a good day painting? Come on, show me what you're working on.'

As I entered the clutter of his room, he took one look at the bottle of rouge in my hand and burst out laughing.

'What is it you want, Camille?'

But he'd reached for the wine and extracted the cork before I'd even sat down in his comfy old armchair.

'First let me see what you've been slaving over today,' I urged and was surprised when he hesitated.

Normally Barnaby is eager to show me his latest work and I expected him to swing his easel round with a flourish to give me the full impact. He'd then point out the painting's strengths and weaknesses, what elements needed work and which parts he intended to leave alone. I'd learned a lot from Barnaby. I didn't like all his paintings because some were what I called too splashy for my uneducated taste, but I loved the life and energy he created time and again on canvas. Flowers would sway and rustle in a vivid burst of sunlight, figures would dance and I swear I could see their feet move.

But this time it was with a reluctant shrug that he flipped the easel around and the glass of wine in my hand froze halfway to my lips. It was Anne-Marie. Not Barnaby's usual luscious nude image of her, svelte limbs and abundant breasts tinted all the colours of the rainbow. This was just head and shoulders. She was staring out at me. Direct and arresting. It broke my heart. Straight across the pearly-white skin of her throat was a savage purple gash.

It felt like an accusation.

'Promise me, Barnaby.'

'I promise.'

He popped the shiny metal whistle between his lips and grinned around it. He was enjoying the adventure too much. It worried me.

'You remain right here,' I ordered.

Right here was a recessed doorway on boulevard Haussmann in the 9th *arrondissement*, only a kilometre's brisk walk north of the Louvre. Galeries Lafayette was just down the road and we had travelled by Métro to Opéra station which was a stone's throw around the corner. *Right here* was smart and stylish Paris. Chic Paris. Go-out-in-your-opera-cape Paris. An elegant boulevard where the nightlife glittered and sparkled, and where furs rubbed shoulders with white ties and tail-coats. Champagne laughter and heady perfume drifted indolently on the chill air.

This was a Paris where wary inhabitants kept a lookout at night for people like us.

'Stay hidden,' I urged. 'No moving from this spot.'

Barnaby nodded obediently. Too obediently.

'If you see anyone opening the door after me, you blow the whistle and immediately run like the clappers to the Métro. Understood?'

'Understood.'

Barnaby was my lookout man. Across the road from us lay Le Rêve, the huge toyshop owned by M. Delamarche, the place where Gilles had bought the tinplate car and where Robespierre worked. It was past ten o'clock at night now and the street was dark, but not as dark as I'd have liked. The clouds were thinning and at intervals the moon was casting down a silver mesh as though attempting to ensnare me. I'd have to be quick. I felt for the tools in my shoulder bag.

'Barnaby, this dark doorway will keep you safe. Do not venture out of it. Promise me.'

'Don't be silly, Camille, I'll be fine.'

'You saw what happened to Anne-Marie. Take no risks.'

'It was just a scratch on her throat, nothing worse. Not as bad as I painted it on canvas.'

'You painted what it was like on the inside. You painted what she felt. I know that.'

I pulled my friend to me, kissed both his cheeks, and then I was gone.

Let me tell you about locks.

There is the old kind and there is the new kind. The old kind is known as a warded lock. The more modern kind is a pin tumbler lock invented by Yale. The warded lock is my favourite. It uses a set of obstructions called *wards* to prevent the lock from opening except to the correct key. But – and this is what makes it my favourite – if you know what you're doing, it is easy to open. You see my point.

I was well wrapped up. A thick grey shawl covered my head and merged with the night. Haussmann is a beautiful wide boulevard, bearing the name of Baron Haussmann who carried out the modernisation and radical redesign of the city in the 1860s. The problem was that while it was lined with a mass of trees which offered cover, it was also well lit by Haussmann's frequent lampposts, which could pick me out like a torch.

I waited for a truck to rumble past, ducked my head and ran across the tramlines into the wide but recessed doorway opposite. A plume of my icy breath got there ahead of me.

In the dark I reached for the lock.

A Yale pin tumbler lock is a mechanism that uses pins of varying lengths to do the job of the wards. They prevent the lock from opening without the correct key but it is a more complicated set-up and therefore more secure. Immediately I knew I was in luck. The lock was a warded lock, probably the original one installed when the building was constructed. People are strange about locks. They seem to think they are all the same because they all do the same job.

I was here to demonstrate to M. Delamarche that they are not.

Even in the dark my fingers knew exactly what to do. From my bag I drew my set of skeleton keys. These have had the serrated edge carefully filed away so that they will open a range of different locks. Anyone in possession of a set of six of the basic skeleton-key designs can open any kind of warded lock thrown at him. Or her.

It took me less than half a minute. I was in.

CHAPTER THIRTY-ONE

◆ ◆ ◆

CAMILLE

L e Rêve toyshop did not feel so much like a dream at night. More like a vast cave of secrets where the darkness seemed to reverberate around me. It took me a moment to get my bearings as my eyes adjusted. I padded across the shop with care.

A faint light drifted in from the streetlamps, picking out the dark bulk of the display cabinets, and I was aware of the glass eyes of toys watching my every move, as well as a row of hobbyhorses lined up and ready to run. I made my way over to where I had spotted the Tutankhamen trinkets on my previous visit. Still there. The pyramid of colourful miniature tins was stacked neatly but one by one I proceeded to open them. Every single one.

Nothing. All empty. I had been hoping for too much.

I restacked them as best I could and moved on quickly. I was acutely aware of poor Barnaby waiting in the cold outside and when I heard footsteps on the pavement at the shop door, my heart leaped into my throat. I expected the whistle to shriek a warning but the footsteps hurried on past. I was jumpy. Breaking and entering was something I'd put behind me long ago. That was a part of my past that I chose not to think about any more. My life was respectable now, beyond reproach. I was a successful *fonctionnaire*. I'd worked so hard to turn a scabby street mongrel into a half-decent poodle, yet sometimes I looked at her in the mirror and I didn't know her.

'Who are you?' I'd whisper. And she'd look away.

Yet here I was tonight jeopardising everything. But Gilles had saved me. Now it was my turn to save him.

I risked a brief flick of my torch and tracked its pinpoint beam to the archway that I had noted before, which led to another even larger showroom. Here I was hidden from the street and I felt my heart rate drop a fraction as I examined the contents of this wonderland for children. Rocking horses and dolls' houses, bicycles and tricycles, kites, Meccano sets and fancy-dress costumes of princesses and pirates. And a whole wall of cuddly soft toys. The star was a giant teddy bear, all fluffy tubby body and floppy limbs, seated on a three-legged stool and resting back against a huge mirror as nonchalantly as a showgirl. I squeezed him all over.

No *shabtis* inside.

I headed quickly to the back of the showroom where my torch flashed on a door. I was searching for the stockroom, the one into which M. Sarrazin had vanished to fetch my tinplate car. Was that where they were hiding a store of *shabtis*? Ready to slip into an occasional toy?

Why? Why would they do that?

The door opened on to a short corridor with four more doors off it. The first was unlocked and proved to be a washroom. The second, a tiny kitchen. The third? Well, that was more interesting because it was locked.

Out came my tools once more and I soon found myself inside a large stockroom with shelves lining the walls, all jammed full of toys of every kind. The yellow finger of my torch skimmed over them, glinting on metal bumpers and tiny porcelain tea sets, but as there were no windows in the room I risked switching on the overhead lights and the wonderland leaped into life. I could feel something inside me start to ache but I wasn't sure what it was. Right in front of me was a brightly painted wooden farmyard and beside it stood boxes of small metal farm animals. Shire horses and pigs and sheep and turkeys and cockerels. My throat went ridiculously dry with desire. As a child among the stinking cobbles and passages of Paris I had dreamed of possessing even just one of these countryside animals that—

The whistle. Shrill and sharp. It rattled in my head.

I dropped a box of baby lambs and ran. I dodged out of the stockroom and back into the corridor, but the dark figure of a man was already standing there, gripping something in his hand. I leaped at him before he could even blink, trying to wrench the weapon from him.

'Hey, ease up, Camille. It's me.'

'Barnaby! You're supposed to be outside on guard.'

He was pushing me away, the metal whistle dangling from his fingers. I backed off

'Just testing.' He grinned.

'You idiot,' I yelled at him, 'I told you not to move. These are dangerous people we are up against and I don't want to see a knife at your throat while you're messing about in here.'

'I can look after myself, Camille.'

'Please, get back outside.'

'I thought that maybe you could do with a hand. I don't know what you're searching for but two of us can find it twice as fast as one.'

It was true. We went through that stockroom like a razor blade. Opening boxes, shifting cartons of board games, searching behind piles of roller skates and skipping ropes and train sets, squeezing every single teddy bear, every single doll, even those in boxes, scouring every last corner of that stockroom and we came up with exactly nothing. Nothing. Zero. I stood glaring around the place, frustration high. All my hopes had been pinned on finding hidden illegal imports of Ancient Egyptian statues and, even better, sparkling jewellery from that period. I was convinced of it. Certain that Augustin Delamarche and Robespierre had them stashed here somewhere.

'Where next?' Barnaby asked and I loved him for his loyalty.

'You get back outside with the whistle,' I told him, 'while I take a quick look at the last door in the corridor. 'I'll be fast.'

'Do you think they'll notice we've been?'

I would have laughed but I was all out of laughs. 'We've covered our tracks as best we can, but yes, anyone with a sharp eye will spot that things have been moved.'

'Does it matter?' He was peering into my face with concern. 'You said he knows where you live.'

'True. But I know where he lives too. Come on, let's not waste time here wondering what might or might not happen.'

I relocked the stockroom, pushed Barnaby out through the shop and hurried back to the fourth door. My guess was an office. I felt again for my keys. My guess was correct. A tiny office. It smelled heavily of Macassar oil. Everything neat and orderly. My torch jabbed into the darkness and found a filing cabinet and a desk with a smart tan leather desk set with clock and calendar. The desk drawers had been left unsecured but provided nothing of interest other than a half-empty bottle of yellow Chartreuse, too sweet for my taste, and a well-used shot glass.

The filing cabinet on the other hand was locked. More promising. Even a child can open most filing cabinet locks with a paper clip, it's so easy, and it yielded to my set of picks as readily as Anne-Marie to a john wearing gold cuff links. I felt my pulse rate ratchet up. The drawers were stuffed with paperwork and I was sorely tempted to scoop up an armful and make a run for it, but I resisted the urge. Paperwork was my business. So I took out bundles of files, ten at a time, and sat myself down at the desk with my torch. I flipped through them.

Excellent accountancy work. Records of suppliers, here and abroad. Buck Rogers pocket pistols and Kewpie dolls from America. Another file. Model cars from Schuco in Nuremberg, Germany. Wind-up monkeys and motorbikes from Japan. Another file. English manufacturers. Britain's lead soldiers and Bayko bricks to construct miniature houses. On and on. Rubber balls from India. More files. Jumeau Bébé dolls made here in France.

Nothing from Egypt.

The clock was ticking.

It *had* to be here. Evidence of some kind.

I started searching the furniture. Feeling for hidden drawers or secret compartments, acutely aware of the wretched clock ticking and Barnaby outside on watch, impatient and worried. It took me ten minutes to find it. It felt more like ten hours. I could feel sweat gathering.

It was inside the desk set.

The large rectangular leather pad was spread out on the desk alongside a pen holder and a glass inkwell. It was far too smart for the desk, which was the kind you'd stick in a back bedroom somewhere. The slit was well concealed. Thin as a knife blade. It ran along the bottom edge of the pad and was disguised by a decorative leather frieze, but not even that device kept it safe from my search. I eased in one of my lockpicks to lift the opening, slid in my fingers and touched unseen paper between the layers of leather. I paused. I could hear a pounding. At first I thought it was Barnaby pounding on the outer door. But no, it was in my ears.

I tweaked the paper and shifted its angle, so that I could catch enough of its edge to wriggle it out on to the desktop. I shone my torch full on it. A sheet of squared paper with a list of names on it lay in front of me and I snatched a notepad and pencil from my bag, scribbled them down and slid the paper back into its hiding place.

One final check round the room that everything was as I'd found it, the leather pad perfectly aligned with the edge of the desk, and I was gone.

Barnaby was on the pavement and he was not alone. Ten metres up from Le Rêve stood a lamppost and next to the lamppost stood a dog on three legs, the fourth one cocked to christen the iron post. A man was attached to the dog by a smart lead, rather than a piece of string like we used to use in Montparnasse, and it was this man who was engaged in conversation with Barnaby.I was just working out whether to walk towards them or away from them when the dog-man hailed me.

'*Bonsoir*,' he called out. 'Another of you lot working late again tonight. Your shop must be doing very good business indeed to need you working late so often.'

I walked casually up to the lamppost. 'Good evening,' I said politely. I assumed he couldn't hear the banging of my heart. 'A nasty night for walking your dog.'

The animal, a gingery concoction of numerous breeds by the look of it, regarded me with instant interest and started sniffing my feet. I didn't want its filthy nose on my meticulously polished shoes, but I didn't back off. There was a steady drizzle now that was making the dog smell like a dead goat.

Barnaby was looking pleased with himself. 'This gentleman was just telling me,' he said, 'that he walks his dog every evening around this hour and often sees people coming out of Le Rêve.'

'Oh yes,' the dog-man confirmed, eager to keep the conversation going despite the rain. I assumed he lived alone. 'Coco always likes to say hello to them.'

'Does Coco like to say hello to anyone in particular?' I kept it casual again.

'She does.'

A car swept past, splashing gutter water over my shoes and sending the dog into a frenzy of barking. It was time to leave.

'Can you describe him to us, so we can tell him tomorrow that Coco was waiting for him tonight?'

The dog-man's laugh was regretful. 'Unfortunately Coco's friend won't be working for a few days apparently. That's what they told me anyway.' He scrubbed his dog's shaggy head.

'Why's that?' Barnaby asked.

'Because the poor fellow has an injured leg,' the dog owner explained.

I was getting closer.

CHAPTER THIRTY-TWO

◆ ◆ ◆

CAMILLE

Sometimes you think you know someone, but sometimes you can be wrong.

When I informed Beau of my nighttime escapade into Le Rêve toyshop, I expected him to express dismay and concern at my recklessness. But he didn't. Quite the opposite.

'Expertly done,' he responded with a nod of respect. 'Show me the names you copied down.'

I placed the sheet of paper in Beau's hand and I could sense the ripple of pleasure it gave him. To examine clues. This was something he did, something he knew he was good at. It was obvious that this was part of who he was. He studied them for several minutes.

'Do you know what this is?' he asked.

I had read the list of names through a hundred times last night and a hundred times more, until they'd prowled through my dreams.

De Champlain M
De Lesseps M
Emeralda B
Victor P
Kagemni LH
Saturne M

'I looked up the names in the library, but I could only find anything on three of them,' I said. 'Apparently de Champlain was an explorer as well as a governor of New France in the seventeenth century.

The second one, de Lesseps, was a French diplomat and the developer of the Suez Canal in the 1860s.' I tapped the last but one name on the paper with my fingertip. 'This one is more interesting but still completely baffling. Kagemni was a vizier in Ancient Egypt married to a king's daughter. That's four thousand years ago.'

Beau beamed at me. 'Very thorough.'

I shook my head with frustration. 'Clearly *Saturne* is a planet. But *Victor* and *Emeralda* could be anything. And what is the significance of the letters down the side: M, B, P, LH?'

Beau was studying the names with a frown that carved a furrow between his brows. I'd noticed he seemed to be moving them more easily now.

'What on earth do an explorer and the Suez Canal have to do with a vizier and a planet?' I sighed with exasperation. 'It doesn't make sense. Do you think it could be a code?'

He drew a deep breath. He was half sitting up now, propped up with pillows, and I could hear that his lungs were less gravelly, functioning better.

'Maybe we should stop talking now,' I suggested. 'You must get some rest.'

'Camille! Don't.'

'Your nurses won't thank me for exhausting you.'

'I won't thank you for walking away with that name puzzle in your hand.'

We both laughed. Soft easy laughs that wound in and out of each other effortlessly.

'I mean it, Beau. You need your strength to recover, not to work on puzzles.'

'Listen to me, Camille.' His voice was low and intimate. I leaned my head closer to catch his words and he gently threaded a lock of my hair through his fingers. 'What you're doing is dangerous, you know that as well as I do.'

I hadn't told him about the night attack in my room.

'But,' he murmured, 'you are the only one who can find your brother, I realise that. The police have already failed. So I will tell you what I think these names are. I might be mistaken but if I'm right, I want you to promise me you'll be far more careful than you're being at the moment. You must not take any more risks that put you in danger because . . .'

His voice faltered. I heard it break. Tiny pieces of it stuttered and then fell silent. He swallowed hard as if something was hurting and I had no way of knowing if the hurt was in his body or in the words he'd left unsaid.

'I promise I'll be careful,' I whispered, 'but I will have to take risks, Beau. You and I both know that.' We sat in silence while I took his hand between mine and ran my palm over the back of it again and again. Whether I was soothing him or myself, I wasn't sure. Then I grasped it firmly and asked, 'Beau, tell me now, what do you think the names are?'

'You know I'm only guessing.'

'Yes.'

'I believe they are ships.'

I stared wide-eyed at him. Then at the names on the paper.

'Ships?'

'I believe so. Importing cargoes. It makes sense.'

Of course it made sense.

'How on earth did you work that out?'

'It was the letters down the side.' His eyes were alive with an intensity I hadn't seen in them before. He was as hungry for this as I was. 'LH is Le Havre. P is Paris. B is Brest. All major ports. And M is . . .'

'Marseille.'

'Exactly.'

I leaned right over him and kissed him hard, probably too hard, full on the lips. 'Beau, you are a genius.'

He removed the ankh from around his own neck and with a tender touch tied its leather thong around mine. 'That's to stop you getting yourself killed.'

CHAPTER THIRTY-THREE

◆ ◆ ◆

GILLES

Time passed. Gilles had no idea how long. But the piss bottle became his time-clock. When he did finally scrabble to the surface of his lurid dreams, he figured it must be many hours that he'd been out of it because he could recall using the bottle not once, but three times. His kidneys didn't lie. Not like Rosa Lagarde.

She had bent over him at one point, he could recall her floral scent that seemed to wrap itself around him, and she'd said in her usual gentle voice, 'Christophe, you are dying from your internal injuries. You must know that. It will be slow and crippling. If you tell me right now what you did with the suitcase contents, I will summon my doctor friend to come to offer a quick and peaceful end. He will give you an injection from which there is no waking.'

She was offering him a way out of this nightmare. Quick, painless and final. Part of him was tempted.

'Go to hell,' the other part of him yelled at her.

She slapped him so hard he felt a tooth crack.

Consciousness returned with a swoop and Gilles became aware that strong hands were gripping his arms and he was being propelled down a set of steps, half carried, half dragged. The pain in his leg was acute and he felt a strong urge to vomit, but a sudden rush of cold air cleared some of the fog from his brain. Were they taking him outdoors?

They? Who were *they*?

Not outdoors, but into a large gloomy room. Dimly lit and cold, unfurnished except for boxes and shelves. He was thrust on to the

201

solitary chair on the concrete floor and his arms dragged behind the chairback. They cuffed his wrists and stepped away

For the first time he got a good look at them. Two beefy men he'd never seen before, farmworkers by the look of them, both in denim work dungarees that smelled as if they'd been hauling pigs around. For a moment Gilles thought he was seeing double but no, they were identical twins. With no word to him they headed up the stairs he'd been dragged down and Gilles realised that he was in the basement. This was not a good start.

'Christophe, don't look so angry.'

Rosa's voice was soft and soothing. She was as good at soothing as she was at slapping.

She stepped out of the shadows below the stairs and stood before him, carrying the brown suitcase in her hand.

'What the hell is going on, Rosa? What are you planning now?'

She laughed. 'I need your help.'

'You have the suitcase, I see, so you have no need to hold me here longer.'

Rosa Lagarde sauntered over, swinging the case with exaggerated ease. Clearly it was empty.

'You cheated me, Christophe.'

'You're the one who has done the cheating, Rosa. That case was full the day I brought it here. When I dragged it off the train it was a dead weight, so I'm guessing you have emptied its contents into a safe hiding place somewhere. Correct?'

'Incorrect.'

She reached down, flicked open the two catches on the case and watched him closely as it fell open. Nothing inside. But he'd been expecting that. There was just a smattering of red grit inside it which caught his attention.

She moved closer but stayed well out of range of his feet. She was wrapped in a sleek fur against the cold and looked like some kind of animal in its dim winter lair. The only light source was an oil lamp standing on a barrel among an array of cartons and tea chests, but it was enough to illuminate her face. Gilles had seen faces of men on the brink of murdering him before, but never a woman's. Until now.

'What happened to them, Christophe? All those beautiful Egyptian artefacts that Dr Laval risked his life and reputation to steal from the vaults of the Louvre. I don't have them. Do you?'

If she did, he'd be dead by now.

'What happened?' he asked innocently.

'Who are you trying to fool, Christophe?' she demanded angrily.

His mind was clearer down here in the cold and he could sense a faint whiff of panic in her. He would bet the key to these wretched handcuffs on the fact that she was going to have to answer to somebody else for losing those valuable artefacts. The question was, who?

'Who do you think?' he said with a quiet smile.

She glared down at the open case but said nothing.

'So you were expecting to find valuable works of art inside, were you?' Gilles goaded her. 'But all you got was bricks.' It was a guess, judging by the weight that he remembered when dragging the case across the field and the red dust now, but it was a guess that hit home.

'Damn you! When did you make the swap? When I saw you turn up on my doorstep with this case, I recognised it immediately. It was the one I'd purchased myself for Dr Laval to use when he moved the items around. The Louvre has so much stuff gathering dust in its vaults, it wasn't going to miss whatever Laval was shifting out of there.'

'The man let you down, did he?'

'Exactly. He got greedy. Making a run for it. So when I opened the case and all it had inside was a pile of these . . .' She abandoned the case, marched across the cold basement and from behind a crate she seized a brick off the floor. 'I wanted to hurl them at you in that bed.'

'Rosa, listen to me, I'm just an innocent train passenger who took advantage of what was a moment of good fortune for some and a moment of tragedy for others. I stole a suitcase. That's all. I expect others did too. I had no idea what was in it. It felt heavy, so I hoped I would strike lucky with it. Whatever you're involved in, I know nothing about it.'

'And I'm Santa Claus,' she shouted at him and stormed up the steps, taking the lamp with her.

CHAPTER THIRTY-FOUR

◆ ◆ ◆

CAMILLE

Bills of lading had never been so interesting. Nor the office so enticing.

As I swept the long heavy carriage of the Royal typewriter across, I focused on every single item of cargo on the ship's manifest. This one was the SS *Gruffudd*, built at Harland & Wolff in Belfast and owned by the British & African Steamship Co. It was transporting 2,750 tonnes of sugar and rice from India. No toys listed. Destination Le Havre.

I worked fast, fingers flying at full speed because I needed to buy myself some time for when Mme Beaufort headed upstairs for her morning meeting. I kept my head down until at five minutes to eleven I saw her place her government-issue teacup, empty, on the side table. It was the job of Chloé, the most junior of our typists, to remove it, wash it meticulously and replace it in her office. I gave my supervisor ten minutes to get stuck into her meeting, then quickly headed over to the side records office where copies of documents were stored. I clutched a manifest in my hand as if needing to check something.

The records office was strictly utilitarian. Nothing but wooden cabinets. Not even a pot plant or a dull portrait of Eugène Frot, our current Ministre de la Marine marchande, on the wall. Nobody in the room. Just the smell of musty paper and ink. It took me no time at all to track them down in one of the many wide drawers that contained the registers of the ships that pass through French ports. A bill of lading is a document issued by a carrier to a shipper. It lists the type, quantity, and destination of the goods being carried. It should give me the answers I needed.

I started with the *de Champlain*. Interestingly it wasn't a cargo ship, as I was expecting. It was an ocean liner built two years ago by Chantiers et Ateliers de Saint-Nazaire. Owned by French Line. The fastest and most luxurious cabin class liner afloat, and it had moored in Marseille in September last year. Four months ago. I allowed myself to think about that and about how many illegal Egyptian artefacts you could cram into a cabin trunk.

The SS *de Lesseps*, *Emeralda* and *Victor* were easy. All cargo ships. Between 2,500 and 3,500 tonnes. Screw propeller, triple expansion steam engines, and in November they entered port in Marseille, Brest and the Port of Paris. Exactly as Beau had predicted. When I combed through their manifests and bills of lading, I had to fight my way past cargoes of timber, tinned pineapples, bolts of linen cloth and raw cotton, and much more besides to reach the cherry sitting there in plain sight. Three crates of children's toys listed on each ship. Loaded at Alexandria on the Nile Delta and destined for Le Rêve toyshop on boulevard Haussmann in Paris. I'd hit the jackpot!

The *Kagemni* was trickier to pin down. I had to switch drawers to another set of records and I could feel every single heartbeat tick by. If Mme Beaufort strode into the room and found me rummaging, I needn't bother to start concocting an excuse for being here because she would fire me on the spot. I flipped through page after page, and finally there it was, staring right back at me. The *Kagemni*. A larger and faster vessel. On board were six crates of toys for Le Rêve among a consignment of citrus fruits, spices and leather goods from Morocco, all unloaded at Le Havre in December. No doubt to boost sales at Christmas.

And the final name? *Saturne*. Alongside an M for Marseille.

Time was running out fast. Dare I stay longer to check it? It would most likely just show another consignment that arrived in Marseille

later in December for Christmas, confirming what we already know. I
heard voices outside. Rapidly I shut the drawers and glanced at the
door as I prepared an explanation for my presence. But the voices
moved away.

Leave now. Just go.

But something in me wouldn't let go.

I slid open another drawer. Rifled through more pages for December but no Saturne popped up in the lists of ships. I moaned under my
breath and was about to abandon the search. But I am stubborn. I
swung open the drawer containing this month's list of ships in
Marseille. *Et voilà!*

SS *Saturne*, I have you.

Large, fast and powerful. Built by Chantiers de l'Atlantique in
Saint-Nazaire. Four propeller screws, two four-cylinder compound
engines plus two low-pressure steam turbines. Speed seventeen knots.
So what was it shipping? My finger raced along the manifest list.
Tonnes of cotton from Egypt. Wine from Algeria. Animal hides from
Libya. And three crates of toys loaded on board at Tripoli. All bound
for Le Rêve in Paris. Who needs crates of toys *after* Christmas?

The date it docked? This sent my pulse spinning out of control. I
slammed the drawer shut, checked that everything looked undisturbed
and flew out of the room. Back at my desk I wiped the smile from my
face and made my fingers set to work, but I could barely read what
letters they were typing. All I could see was the word SS *Saturne*. Due
to dock in Marseille in four days' time.

Without turning my head, I was acutely aware that Mme Beaufort was
prowling the aisles between the rows of twenty-eight Royal typewriters and twenty-eight dogged typists. I sucked in a deep breath. I
couldn't hear the click of her heels on the floor, drowned out by the
incessant clatter of the keys, but I knew she was there because everyone's fingers suddenly flew faster, including my own.

Out of the corner of my eye I caught a glimpse of a black patent toe, gleaming like a mirror. She kept them that way, not a mark or smudge on her shoes all day, which meant she must be buffing them with a soft cloth every hour. I admired that. But not enough to want them to stop at my desk, which was exactly what they did, and my stomach chose that moment to swoop down into my own highly polished shoes.

'Malroux.'

'Yes, Madame?'

I rose to my feet.

'I have something for you. Here,' she said and placed an ivory envelope on my desk. The Ministry of Justice crest was hard to miss.

'Thank you.'

'He wishes to speak with you.'

I nodded, surprised.

'Malroux, take care.'

This woman, this strict supervisor who would tolerate no trace of slackness nor even the faintest infringement of her rules, on pain of instant dismissal, was staring at me with a concern that was completely out of character.

'Should I be worried?' I asked quietly.

'I have seen far too many young women like yourself, with promising careers ahead of them, have their heads turned and their livelihoods ruined by a deft web of flattery.'

'Oh Madame, it is nothing like that, I assure you.'

'I say again, Malroux. Take care. Men in positions of power can be dangerous.'

She turned on her heel to leave. In her usual sharp tone she added, 'Do not be late back.'

Walking into the hotel bar was like walking into a lion's den. I could hear the low roars of contentment and I breathed in that unique smell that is the strong musky scent of money. Men in tailored suits so crisp you could cut yourself on them and silk ties that boasted regiments and schools and societies too posh for me to have even heard of them. I thought about what Mme Beaufort had said. Was he trying to impress me or intimidate me? Or was he going to rip my throat open with his bloodied jaws because he knew I had invaded his office at the toyshop? Only one way to find out.

I marched across the long glossy room, the bar glittering with long-stemmed glasses on my right and men perched on stools, enjoying their lunchtime watering hole. Their heads turned to inspect me as I passed. On my left, armchairs and small round tables formed distinct enclaves. I could sense a pecking order here and deals being made. Down the far end lay the larger leather armchairs and shiny ebonised tables. I spotted Augustin Delamarche at one. Even among lions he stood out as the pride male. His mane might be trimmed but his claws weren't.

'Mlle Malroux, thank you for coming.'

He stood, shook my hand firmly but made no attempt to exert dominance through manhandling it. He waved me to a seat, ordered me a glass of wine and relaxed back in his chair. He treated me to a charming smile that set my teeth on edge.

'Relax, Camille – may I call you Camille? – you look nervous. I'm not going to bite.'

'Minister Delamarche, I am pleased to have the chance to speak to you. Mme Beaufort has informed me that you have requested a transfer for me to the Ministry of Justice at the end of this month. I would like to know why, please.'

'Because I see you for what you are.'

I sat straight. Shoulders back. Feet crossed. I took a long swig from my glass, looked him directly in the eye and asked, 'And what is that?'

'Someone who is ambitious. Someone who knows what she wants and will work hard to reach her goals.' He gave me a cold hard stare. 'Someone who is willing to step away from the straight and narrow if necessary to achieve those goals.' The charming smile was suddenly back in place. 'Let us talk frankly. I can see you are a bright young woman, Camille, one who could go far. A resourceful young woman who could be of use to me.'

'At the Ministry of Justice?'

'Among other things.'

'What other things?'

He flicked a hand at the barman and instantly two more glasses of red materialised. I was astonished to see my first one was empty. I don't know what wine it was that we were drinking, but it tasted of smoke and of mushrooms and dark rich berries on the tongue, earthy and delicious. It slid down my throat like silk. I had never met with any- thing like it.

He raised his glass to me. I returned the gesture and sipped my wine, but I didn't miss his small secret smile, as if he had won a point.

'What other things?' I repeated.

He leaned back into his chair, its wings seeming to wrap him in contentment, and he uttered a long sigh. 'With my daughter.'

'Liliane?'

'Yes, my dear Liliane. Another clever and ambitious young woman who is obsessed with only one thing. Over obsessed, in my opinion. Unlike you, she has grown into a foolish young woman who no longer has the sense she was born with, she is so blinkered. I believe she is being taken advantage of by others who make use of her expert know- ledge. She doesn't realise that it is not always good use. I want you to befriend her.'

I listened. Unbelieving. What exactly was going on here?

'Why me?'

'For some reason she has taken a shine to you. Maybe she sees in you all the things that she is not.'

He knocked back his wine in one hit and glared at me as if I were responsible for his daughter's failings. My mind was reeling. Liliane was the one with the brilliance. She was the one with the grace and the beauty, the success and the money. She shone bright as the pole star. She was everything I wanted to be.

The wine wove in and out of my thoughts as I struggled to make sense of this.

'Why would you want me to be her friend, Minister?'

'*Mon Dieu*, isn't it obvious. My daughter is naive. She spends all her days with her nose in research books or studying ancient pieces of rock and carvings. She has no idea about the real world and I want you to help her through it.'

'Why not one of her friends?'

'Her friends are all like her. Academics and rich idiots who live in a fantasy world that no longer exists. Look what is happening in Germany, look at the mess America is in, look how the Depression has ravaged Europe. The world is changing fast. One of these days she will get eaten alive by—' He stopped.

I waited. Held my breath. Here was the truth.

He snorted angrily. 'My daughter is an innocent. One day soon a shark will come to get her. And all her money.'

So. That was it. Money.

Ah, now it made sense. This man was all about the next franc, the next dollar, the next pound, the next Reichsmark. And if that meant exploiting his daughter's knowledge about Ancient Egypt to find crates of artefacts to import, he would do it. But woe betide any man who stepped up from the gutter to sneak in under the wire. That's what he wanted me for. To be shark bait.

We sat there in silence. Around us the place buzzed and a woman laughed high enough to crack the mirrors around the panelled walls. But for a long moment neither of us could find a word to say. More wine materialised on the table but this time I kept away from it.

Augustin Delamarche rubbed a hand across his moustache and it struck me that he was relieved. Had he been dreading the meeting as much as I had? But for totally different reasons. He thought he had me now. Job done.

He slid his hand into his inside pocket, slapped a buff envelope down on the table between us and announced, 'This will convince you.'

I didn't touch it. Thirty pieces of silver.

'M. Delamarche, I have a question to ask you. Do you know any-thing about the whereabouts of my brother, Gilles Malroux?'

'Who?'

'Gilles Malroux. He has disappeared.'

He scowled briefly, irritated by the change of direction. 'No, I don't know a damn thing about your brother. What's that got to do with the deal I am offering you? We're talking about my daughter.'

'I will happily be a friend to Liliane, a good friend, and will help in any way I can. But my friendship cannot be bought.'

He gave a low chuckle. 'Of course it can.'

I rose to my feet, picked up my glass and emptied its contents over his head. I walked out of there, claw marks on my back.

CHAPTER THIRTY-FIVE

◆ ◆ ◆

CAMILLE

Dusk was stealing like a grey thief across the river when I finally left the office. The city lights had started to shimmer in the gloom and the place de la Concorde, the largest public square in Paris, was lit up like a Christmas tree showing off its two vast monumental fountains and the towering Luxor obelisk.

For a full minute I stood in the cold and stared at that obelisk. I had looked at it many times before but now with new eyes, because now I had read about its history. Now I knew it was three thousand years old. That was almost impossible to comprehend. It stood twenty-three metres tall, carved from a single piece of red granite, and was covered in fabulous hieroglyphics. I could barely imagine how such a thing could possibly be accomplished.

Apparently it used to stand along with its twin outside the portals of the Luxor temple in Egypt. But in the early eighteen hundreds Egypt made use of its abundance of massive stone monuments as political sweetmeats to create bonds with the Western world. Come sign trade deals with us, they said, and supply us with armaments, and you too can have an ancient obelisk of your own. So this obelisk was shipped to Paris at crazy expense to be erected where the principal guillotine used to stand during the Revolution. Like a finger pointing up to the dead souls in the heavens.

I saw now what I had never seen before, how starkly beautiful it was.

'*Bonsoir*, Camille.'

I spun around. Behind me stood Liliane Delamarche. She was swathed in a stylish heavy cape against the wind, a practical hat and a colourful red scarf draped around her neck. But this was not the Dr Liliane Delamarche I knew, not the one with the easy smile and the confident flick of her head, the one who looked you straight in the eye as if you had something interesting to say. This Liliane looked lost and bemused.

'Camille, I need your help.'

I didn't hesitate. 'Come,' I said.

I led her to a small bar I knew on the other side of the river. We crossed over on the extravagant Alexandre III Bridge with its mass of glowing lamps and cherubs and winged horses that should have made us smile. I expected Liliane to comment on them, to tell me who this Alexandre III was, but she didn't. The dome of Les Invalides loomed ahead on the Left Bank as we walked in silence, then we ducked our heads against the north-easterly and turned into the narrow streets behind the quai d'Orsay. It was a relief to get out of the wind.

A group of grim-faced women trudged out of a nearby factory, clacking over the cobbles in sabots, and they threw a few rough remarks at us in our finery. Still no reaction from Liliane. I was concerned for her. The skin of her cheeks looked taut and brittle. In the bar I bought a dusty bottle of *vin rouge*, took two glasses and sat us down at a small round table in a corner.

'What is it, Liliane? Tell me what has happened.'

I filled our glasses and waited while she took a mouthful of hers.

She let out a long slow breath. I smelled cognac. 'It's Papa,' she whispered.

Something in the way she said it. The way it fell off her tongue. My leg started to tremor.

'What?'

'Papa is a decent honest man,' she said earnestly. 'I love my father dearly and I would never ever wish to hurt him. Everyone knows he is a fine and upright politician, much valued in the government.'

Not a word passed my lips.

'You know that, don't you, Camille? You've met him and seen that he's the kind of powerhouse that can get things done. He can help achieve progress for our country, he has already shaken up the old stick-in-the-muds at the Ministry of Justice.'

I tasted my wine. Hell, it was awful. 'You are very proud of him, Liliane.'

'I am. You're right. But . . .'

She stared down at her wine, so I couldn't see her eyes but I saw the grip of her manicured fingers, tight enough to snap the stem of her glass.

'I don't know who to turn to,' she murmured.

I leaned forward, my head close to her dusky blond one. 'I'm listening,' I said gently.

She didn't look up. 'I fear he may be doing something very bad, something criminal, and I don't know what to do about it.'

'I'm sorry, Liliane. What is it that you've discovered he's doing?'

Her head drooped miserably and I felt a wave of sorrow for her. We let a silence hang there at our table while she struggled to voice what she'd come to voice. The bar was filling up with the lively chatter of voices and the chink of bottles, while in the background the drumming of rain on the windows masked our words.

'I daren't tell anyone.'

'You can tell me,' I reassured her. 'I guarantee that I'll have heard and seen much worse where I come from.'

She scrubbed a hand through her hair and across her face. She couldn't look a mess even when she tried. I reached out and removed her hand from over her eyes.

'Tell me.'

She emptied her glass and her blue eyes stared straight into mine. 'He's stealing.'

That was it. Nothing more. But it was a start.

'Stealing what?'

'It doesn't matter what.'

'I think it does. If it's money from a hospital, yes, it matters. If it's crates of wine from one of his vineyard-owning mates, then not so much. There are degrees of theft. Some matter more than others. What rung of the ladder is his on?'

Her eyes had grown darker, to the vivid blue of the sapphire brooch on her jacket, and as she slowly shook her head they started to swim with tears. She brushed them away, embarrassed, and said flatly, 'A high rung. He is stealing from a country that has nothing. Its people are poor and need what little they have.'

'Which country?'

There was a long pause.

'From Egypt,' she whispered.

'How do you know?'

She placed her elbows firmly on the table to steady herself. 'He virtually told me. The other evening he questioned me in depth about what were the latest finds in the Valley of the Kings at Luxor, where they were being stored and who had access to them. He asked if anyone was touting them for sale around the museums of Europe and America. When I pointed out that it's not that easy to get an export licence for antiquities, he just laughed.'

I refilled her glass but her hand was shaking.

'I was horrified and told him so,' she continued.

'What was his reaction?'

'He said I was naive. Everyone was doing it.'

'Liliane, I know it must come as a terrible shock that your father is involved in an illegal trade. Especially when it's a country whose history you feel passionate about. But you must go to the police about this.'

'I have no proof.'

'Search his study. There's bound to be paperwork somewhere. Get your hands on it and—'

'No, Camille.'

I halted. This was suddenly difficult.

'Camille, do you have a father?'

'No.'

'Have you ever had a father?'

'No.'

Her face abruptly softened out of her own distress. 'You have no idea what it's like, do you?'

I remembered the way she looked at her father. 'I have a brother,' I said. 'So yes, I do know.'

'Would you turn him in to the police if you caught him in wrong-doing?'

'Of course not.'

Liliane gave a little grimace. 'There we have it. That's why I couldn't go to any of my friends, because they would have answered yes to that question.'

'Liliane, did you ask your father to promote me in the civil service?'

'I asked him to help you if he could.'

I exhaled to rid myself of irritation. 'I thought so, thank you. Now what are we going to do about your father? I think you have to start by having a talk with him. Confront him. See what he says. Tell him he is playing a very dangerous game that could end with him in prison. Or worse.'

'You're right, I'll warn him he has got to stop immediately. I think he'll do it for me.'

I stared at her. She meant it seriously. That's the kind of love she expected a father to have for a daughter.

Together we finished the bottle of wine.

The roads were wet and the sky was black as a tomb when we emerged, but on dark winter evenings Paris always looks festive in the rain. Its streetlamps set it aglow. A million reflections of light dance and shimmer on the wet thoroughfares throughout the city and even the sullen Seine comes alive with sheets of gold thrown on its surface by the lamps on the bridges.

Liliane and I made our way towards the nearest Métro sheltering from the downpour under her umbrella, our arms linked, and I thought about what I'd said to her father. *My friendship cannot be bought.* It was true. But it could be earned. The simple way that Liliane had drawn me under the protective canopy of her umbrella and slipped the warmth of her arm through mine was earning my trust. I do not give it lightly.

'Liliane, I have another question to ask about your father.'

'What's that?' She turned to look at me.

'Is your father a vengeful man?'

'Good Lord, no. What on earth makes you ask that?' Her gaze was intense even in the dark.

We were walking past a row of shops, all closed now, rain running in rivulets to the gutter.

'He has invited me to join his team at the Ministry of Justice,' I told her.

'Yes, I know.'

'If I turn him down, will he block my career where I am now at the Ministry of the Merchant Navy?'

'My father may be many things, Camille, but he is not a petty-minded man who—'

A male figure leaped out behind us from one of the shop doorways. The blur of movement in the darkness caught my eye and I swung round just in time to see him slam a policeman's white baton down on Liliane's back. She cried out and buckled at her knees. She would have fallen flat on her face on the wet cobbles had her arm not been laced through mine. I held her on her feet.

The man fled and the night swept his black shadow from sight. The umbrella lay in the road and the rain pelted down on us. What had I brought down on my friend's head?

'Why? Why would anyone want to attack me?' Liliane asked for what must have been the twentieth time. 'I don't understand.'

'It was probably just random. A thief.'

'But he didn't take anything. He didn't steal our purses. Just hit and ran.'

'I expect he intended to rob us but lost his nerve at the last minute. Probably because you didn't fall down and there were two of us. He knew we would protect each other.'

I hated the lies. I hated the smoothness of them. I hated my guilt. What I truly thought was that he mistook his target. It was meant to be me. A reminder from Robespierre's sidekick, but the fool got the wrong woman in the dark.

Neither of us wanted to involve the gendarmes and the endless hanging around in police stations that it would mean. All for no purpose as the attacker was long gone. So I had bundled Liliane into the back of a taxi and brought her to the safety of her apartment off the Champs-Élysées. I sat her down on her chaise longue, with her assuring me all the time that her injury wasn't bad, but when I raised the back of her blouse a bruise the colour of burst plums streaked at an angle down the delicate skin of her back. It sickened me.

'No ribs broken,' Liliane insisted. 'Just sore.'

I dosed her with painkillers and tipped ice cubes from her refrigerator into a tea towel to press on her back. She refused a brandy but I knocked one back myself. I offered to help her to bed, but she preferred to lie where she was on the chaise longue with a quilted Chinese rug draped over her, the lights lowered and Debussy's *Clair de Lune* playing softly on the record player.

I crept quietly out of the apartment once she'd slipped into a light sleep and I wondered which reality was more desirable. Hers or mine? No wonder her father wanted me to watch over her.

CHAPTER THIRTY-SIX

♦ ♦ ♦

CAMILLE

'Beau.'

He was browsing through a couple of books I'd brought him to read, *Le Blé en Herbe* by Colette and the latest Maigret detective novel. Neither of us knew his taste in reading.

'Beau,' I said again.

He looked up this time and smiled. It was the distracted smile that I was beginning to recognise, the one that meant he had found a new memory. 'I think I may have read about this Maigret character before.' His finger tapped the Simenon book. 'This tall, stolid, pipe-smoking commissaire of the Paris Brigade Criminelle.' Beau laughed as if his description summoned up someone he actually knew. 'I always preferred Maigret's instinctive methods to Sherlock Holmes's strictly rational process. Don't you agree? Maigret possesses infinite patience and compassion, and mistrusts hasty judgements.'

'Beau, that is brilliant.' I gave him a small round of applause and was rewarded by the look of pleasure that sprang into his job book.

I waved his thanks away with a flick of my hand but he was not allowing that.

'Don't, Camille. Don't diminish what you are doing. For me and for your brother.'

'It must be so hard,' I ventured softly, 'not knowing.'

'The truth is, Camille, it feels as if I've fallen off a cliff. My feet are scrabbling like mad to find a foothold in the rock as I plummet downwards and your Maigret book is one of those footholds. It has halted my fall for a moment.'

'Beau.'

This time he put the book aside, folded his arms and regarded me expectantly. 'What next?'

'I know you can't remember more than snatches of your life before the train crash, but do you remember your childhood? I thought it might be a good place to start building a more solid idea of who you are.'

His face changed, lost some of its seriousness and became somehow younger with a boy's bright eager eyes. 'I have unearthed one child-hood day from my memory,' he told me, 'one day when I was about eight or nine and I was on a beach.'

'On holiday?'

'I don't know. Maybe we lived by the sea. That's still vague. But I remember this summer's day when I was skipping over the waves. I can still feel the sand squeezing between my toes and the sun hot on my bare limbs.'

I could picture him. Young and golden, brimming with innocence and happiness. The image warmed my heart.

'I heard a voice call my name,' he continued, 'a female voice. Whether it was my mother or a sister or an aunt, I can't quite reach. But I turned and looked back up the beach to a small group of people settled on the sands and I remember waving to them.' The brightness dimmed and he frowned, shaking his head with impatience. 'I go back to that moment over and over again to find those people, to shift the blur that envelops them. I am convinced that they are my family but I cannot yet reach them. I make myself inspect the waves and gaze at the sunlight splitting into luminous splashes as if the sea were daubed with gold paint, and then I turn and look up to ...'

He drew in a breath abruptly, sharply. I feared he was in sudden pain. But no, a huge smile had transformed his face and I could see that he was truly happy.

'What is it?' I asked.

'It's Titou. My scruffy dog Titou, a black terrier. He was splashing through the waves with me and chasing seagulls that day, his pink tongue lolling out and covered in salt water. How could I possibly have forgotten my *cher* Titou?'

His face was flushed with delight and I felt my cheeks turn pink in sympathy. I was hoping that the more we talked about it, the more he would remember.

'Beau, if you could choose a childhood for yourself, what would it be?'

He closed his eyes for a full minute, considering the question. He possessed a mind that was always thinking things through. When he opened them he was calm and controlled, but I could sense the yearning in him.

'I would have an older brother to show me exciting ideas and activities, and a younger sister for me to look after and take fishing. My father would be a keen sportsman, whisking us off to go camping at weekends, and he'd work as an architect. Building things.' He nodded, satisfied.

'And your mother?'

'She'd be a pianist. And she'd love breeding pedigree cats that would chase Titou around the house.'

I gazed at this man who had such specific dreams. 'I think that sounds the perfect family. Is that what you had?'

'I don't know. Yes, parts of it feel real. The cats and the camping. I can't tell whether the rest is real or conjured up by my brain to fill the black hole.' He smiled at me. 'And you? What would your perfect family be?'

'I've never thought of it in those terms. Just having enough to eat and a mother who worked in a bakery instead of on the streets would do me.' I paused and almost didn't say my next words but they tumbled out of my mouth before I could stop them. 'And no beatings.'

His face darkened and he gripped my arm as if to drag me away from that vile place. 'And what kind of father?'

'A father who was kind. Who would kiss my forehead and teach me things like tying strong knots and reading good books and maybe we'd have a garden and I'd learn about plants from him.' I was getting the hang of this. 'Gilles would still be my brother and our house would be near a wood where I could build dens and construct forts and have adventures with cap guns.'

He let out a laugh. Such a laugh. 'Oh yes, Camille, I'm certain you'd have adventures. Can I come and join you in them?'

'Yes.'

We grinned at each other so hard our faces ached.

The hospital would be throwing me out soon at the end of evening visiting hours and Beau was looking at me with blatant disapproval. I wanted to place my lips on his again to kiss away their downturn.

'Stay away from him, Camille, this Delamarche. I don't like the sound of him. And if he is employing the man you call Robespierre, you can be certain he means you harm. Look what happened to Omar on the bus.' He squeezed my fingers. 'Don't get involved with him.'

'Beau, I am already involved with Delamarche because he has arranged my secondment to the Ministry of Justice. He claimed to know nothing of where Gilles is, but I wouldn't take his word as gospel on anything.'

'No.'

There was a tension between us now and I didn't know why. I could feel a kind of anger in him, a current below the surface that baffled me, and not for the first time I wondered if I was bad for Beau. Like I was bad for Liliane.

He lay back against his pillows and closed his eyes. He'd said he was feeling stronger today but he didn't look it. There were bruised shadows under his eyes and a whiteness around his lips that frightened me. Was I slowly killing him?

'Beau,' I said, breaking the silence, 'would you prefer my visits to stop?'

He gave a single shake of his head but his eyes didn't open.

'Camille, every morning it takes everything I have to open my eyes and look at a world that is a stranger to me, to look in a mirror and see a stranger looking back.' He spoke in a quiet voice, a matter-of-fact voice, no trace of self-pity, his eyes still closed. 'So no, I wouldn't prefer that your visits stop. You are the reason I open my eyes, the reason I take my first breath, the reason I have spent all my waking hours trying to visualise your brother that night when he drew me back from eternal night.'

I placed my head on the edge of his pillow. He smiled and continued, 'I have dragged some images out of the chaos of that night. I remember a dark coat. And blood. And a moustache. I can see him now, leaning over me, a gash on his forehead dripping down on me, and determined chestnut eyes pinning me to this earth.'

I didn't breathe. I didn't want him to stop.

'A bright light pierced the darkness. Honestly I thought I was dead. Screams of demons all around me. The roar of flames. This was the end. The bright light that people talk of when death comes for you.' He opened his eyes and turned on the pillow towards me, our faces almost touching. 'The light was your brother's torch. I remember the yellow force of it, like a portal to another world that I was no longer a part of.'

We lay there, inhaling each other's breath, and I could smell a medication on his.

'Help is coming,' Beau murmured. 'That's what Gilles said to me. Hold on. *Hold on.* So I held on to him and he held on to me.'

'I'm glad,' I whispered.

'I was barely conscious, I realise now, but I felt his hand dig around in my jacket. Searching for my wallet. The pain it caused was excruciating but the strange thing was I wanted him to have it. I wanted him to be me. Somehow I knew that if he became me, I'd still be alive.'

'Oh Beau.'

I felt him turn his head and brush my forehead with his lips, a light tender touch.

'So now I want you to find your brother because I need to see this man with the white blaze in his hair. The man who kept me in this life.'

'I'm trying, Beau. I am going out there tomorrow.'

'Where?'

'To the field.'

'To the crash site?'

'Yes. I know it's probably pointless because of course he won't be there, but I'll hunt around and see if I can dig up anything.'

'Find him, Camille. Find Gilles.'

That night I sat at the desk in my room – all right, it was a small table that served for everything, if I'm being honest – and I studied the ankh in greater detail. I wished I had one of those jeweller's eyeglasses that Liliane possessed to examine it even more closely, but I didn't. So I made do with a scratched magnifying glass I scrounged from old Émile in the room below me. He used it to read his newspaper.

Faïence. That's what Liliane said it was made of. I have looked it up more thoroughly in the library. It's a kind of non-clay ceramic made from crushed quartz and processed to give it a bright blue or green lustre. This one was blue. A beautiful heart-stopping blue. It meant something, I was sure of that, but what? And why was Gilles carrying it so closely in his wallet? Oh Gilles, give me a sign. I'm coming in search of your trail tomorrow and I'll need all the help I can get.

A thought slid unbidden into my mind. It was the day in our child-hood when Gilles had taken out his knife and shown me how to slit open an oyster, gnarled and grizzled as rock on the outside but hiding a tasty treasure inside. I'd stared in total amazement. It was the memory of that day that clung to me mind and made me look at the ankh with fresh eyes. I drew my skinning knife from my bag. Don't ask me why. I don't know why. But as I held the ankh in the palm of my hand I felt that this small blue object was lying to me. I wanted the truth from it, its tasty treasure. I laid it on a sheet of paper, pressed the knife blade against its surface and started to scratch.

A piece chipped off. It flew across the room. Another piece. My heart catapulted against my ribs, it was knocking so hard. Piece by piece, chip by chip, I scratched the faïence away. When I'd finished I found I was holding another ankh, a completely different one that had lain hidden under the blue covering.

It was gold. Pure gold. Gleaming and shimmering in my hand, the ancient symbol of eternal life. Thank you, Gilles.

CHAPTER THIRTY-SEVEN

◆ ◆ ◆

CAMILLE

I'd arrived at the hospital early.
'Beau, let's talk about your job.'

Beau had just had a bed-wash and his dressings changed, a relentlessly painful procedure, but as always his welcome to me was warm and courteous. His skin was shiny from the ointments but he was a better colour and the whites of his eyes were much clearer, less bloodshot, more ... I searched for the right word ... more aware. I could imagine them being an investigator's eyes. When they looked at me, I wondered what they saw.

'My job?' He gave a little snort of disgust. 'I have no job. Look at the state of me.'

'Beau, I think we should write down all that you remember about your job before the train crash.' I pulled out a notepad from my bag and rummaged for the pencil and pencil sharpener. 'Gathering all the strands together might help you remember more.'

I sat beside his bed, pencil poised over a blank page. He didn't look keen. I suspected that he had been pummelling his brain day and night until it was now on its knees with exhaustion.

'Let's start with the train,' I suggested. 'You were on it with my brother Gilles and Dr Antoine Laval, curator from the Louvre Museum. And a brown suitcase.' I was as businesslike as if I were at the office. 'Correct?'

'Correct.'

'Anyone else you knew?'

'No. Not that I recall.'

I jotted it down. 'Why were you on the train with them?'

A long pause. 'I believe I was following them, but I am not sure. I remember that the suitcase was important.'

'Did you know what was in the suitcase?'

'Yes.' No hesitation. 'Items from Ancient Egypt.'

'Why was it on the train?'

That slow considered smiled of his surfaced. 'That's the wrong question, Camille.'

I flushed but remained focused. 'So tell me, Beau, what is the right question?'

'Why was I following Laval?'

I jotted it down in handwriting that Mme Beaufort would have been proud of. 'Why were you following Dr Laval?'

'That, Camille, is the big question. Either I was tracking his movements to prove he was stealing the contents of the case or,' he released a great gust of air, 'or I was planning on stealing it myself.'

'Which?'

'I don't want to be a thief.' He shrugged uneasily.

I didn't rush in to reassure him this time. I pushed further. 'If you were tracking him, who were you working for?'

'I want to say the police, but you have already checked with them and discovered that none of their officers is missing.'

'True.'

'Therefore the options are that I was an intelligence agent of some kind or a private detective.' He paused while I wrote the options down and I heard a sharp click of his back teeth. 'Or I was a member of the criminal network that was stealing the illegal goods and I was after him to snatch them back. Maybe even to kill him in the process.'

I added Option Three to my list.

'There's one more option that you haven't mentioned.'

'What's that?' he asked.

'That you might have been tracking Gilles. Not Laval.'

'It's possible.'

'And how did you know what was inside the case?'

His eyes locked on mine. 'Tell me.'

'Because you'd seen inside it before you got on the train.'

Slowly, reluctantly, he nodded. In a flat voice he said, 'Exactly. And that makes me complicit.'

'No. Not necessarily.' I was quick to throw out that option.

'I'm afraid it does, Camille. For me to have seen inside that case means I must have been working either with the thief, Laval, or with Gilles and the criminal gang. There's no other way I could know the contents of the case.'

I drew a heavy black line through my option list, almost tearing the paper. 'No. Don't say that.'

We stared at each other and I could feel a quick pulse of air between us. My stare became a glare. 'There must be another way.'

His stare softened. 'How? How else could I know?'

The silence between us stretched. Around us sounded the murmurs of other patients and the irrepressible chirp of the young nurses, as the light from the tall windows created patterns on the floor. My mind was in turmoil.

'You could be wrong,' I pointed out. 'You could be fantasising. It's possible that there were no ancient artefacts in the suitcase, but ...' I thought quickly, 'bars of soap.'

He laughed and I loved him for it. It was just as I was about to tell him my plan for tomorrow when footsteps stopped at the end of the bed. I turned my head and saw Dr Arquette with his troop of white coats massing around him.

'Good day, M. Malroux,' he said, ignoring me and picking up Beau's medical chart. 'How are you feeling today?'

'Better than yesterday.'

Of course he'd say that. I stood and asked, 'How is he doing on the chart?'

'Improving,' was all Arquette offered before one of his white coats, a young man with acne and a nose that had once been badly broken, swept me aside while the curtains were drawn around Beau for privacy. I was about to object to being bundled out with so little courtesy, when the houseman put a finger to his lips, slid a piece of paper between my fingers and disappeared back behind the curtain. In my hand lay a sheet of cream notepaper folded into a small square with a dab of scarlet sealing wax holding it closed from prying eyes. On the outside the name M. Malroux was written in neat feminine handwriting.

For five minutes I waited impatiently while Dr Arquette examined Beau, pronounced him a fine fellow and strode away without a glance in my direction when a nurse whisked the curtains open. I scurried after the acne houseman who hung at the back of the pack, as if expecting me.

'Who gave it to you?' I whispered.

'A woman outside the ward door.'

'Did she say anything?'

'Just "Please give this to Gilles Malroux."'

'What did she look like?'

'Hard to say. She was wearing a hooded cape that covered her up.'

'Young? Old?'

He glanced anxiously after the white coats vanishing behind another curtain. 'Somewhere between,' he said and scuttled away.

I sat down on the chair. Beau looked as if the examination had been an ordeal, though he made no complaint. I handed him the unopened note.

'What's this?' he asked.

'A woman gave it to one of the junior doctors to give to you.'

He studied the handwriting. 'Who?' he murmured.

'She didn't say.'

He snapped it open and started reading its contents aloud. 'Tell that guttersnipe at your elbow that if she keeps sticking her nose into other people's business, she will end up with it …' He ceased reading.

'Don't stop.'

Beau shook his head. He glanced up at me, his eyes dark with alarm. 'You don't need to hear more.' He screwed up the note and crushed it into a tight ball. I removed it from him, unravelled it and read aloud the final words.

'She will end up with it sliced off and a knife stuck in her throat.'

Beau snatched the note back from me and tore it into pieces, again and again. Every movement was taut with fury.

'Don't worry, Beau. Idle threats. She didn't even dare to say it to my face.'

But my leg started to tremor.

Later that morning I was sitting on the train, and the flat winter fields trundled past outside the window, denuded and lifeless except for the occasional drift of a sooty-winged crow, and I found I couldn't bear to look at them.

I was not expecting to feel this, this stiffness of my fingers, this churning in my stomach, and the cold sweat trickling between my breasts. It was as though my brother's fear was alive inside me. That tragic moment when the express train slammed into the rear of the local train between Lagny and Pomponne had somehow seeped from Gilles's blood into my own blood. With each turn of the wheels my heart shuddered at the thought of so many killed.

Yet I couldn't help thinking about Beau too. He was on the same train on that dark night two days before Christmas. Were they both in pursuit of Dr Antoine Laval and his suitcase? Had Beau and Gilles been working together? Surely Beau would have remembered. I had taken a photograph of Gilles into the hospital to show him but it rang no bells. So was Gilles really working with Omar Youssef Ahmed, who was dedicated to retrieving some of his country's artefacts for the Cairo Museum? Unlikely. But that's what Omar had claimed. Gilles did not make a habit of working alongside government security officials, of that I was one hundred per cent certain, so what was going on?

I closed my eyes and in the back of my mind I could hear screams.

I had taken a taxi from the local station to the crash site or as near as I could get to it by road. I could ill afford the cost of the ride, yet when I pictured the nice fat envelope of franc notes that Augustin Delamarche had offered for my cooperation, I didn't regret my decision to decline it.

The driver was obviously doing a nice little bit of business on the side by ferrying gawpers out to view where the worst train accident in the history of peacetime France had occurred. People will always stare. Disasters are like catnip. Thank God, they think, it's them and not me. The taxi driver dropped me in a country lane in what looked like the middle of nowhere with clear instructions how to reach the site.

'Just across that field, you can't miss it.'

He was right. I couldn't.

I just followed the noise. I trudged through ankle-deep mud and along a scattering of wooden planks laid down as walkways until it all seemed to leap up in front of me. It was like a scene from hell. There was an army of workmen, shouting and digging and banging and sawing, chains crackling and metal sheets shrieking. Everyone labouring to clear the site of a mountain of crash debris. In places they'd started the reconstruction of the stretch of railway track that had been destroyed, but mostly it looked like dismantling the buckled lines was still the main task.

In the centre of all this noise and chaos stood the remains of the battered express locomotive. Black and bloodied, it brooded over the scene like a gigantic monster that had emerged from the dark earth. The other locomotive had already been removed, as well as many of the broken carriages, and a gigantic crane stood nearby, towering over the scene. A wide area was crawling with workmen, yelling instructions, hammering bolts into new wooden sleepers, shovelling ballast and grinding through iron bars. Fires burned here and there. Smashed-up lengths of wood were being fed into them, snapping and spitting, and the smoke hung in the air like net curtains to hide the worst of the destruction from sight.

'You can't go any closer, Mademoiselle.'

A police uniform barred my way. Startled, I stepped back. Only then did I realise there was a cordon around the crash site, manned by a detail of policemen who looked very bored and very cold. Several were hovering near one of the bonfires for warmth. The day was bright and the sky a flat wintry blue, but that easterly wind cut any exposed flesh like a razor. For a moment we both stood gazing at the aftermath of brutal violence in what should have been a quiet rural scene, transfixed by mental images of the carnage of that night. Hundreds killed. Hundreds injured.

Gilles and Beau among them. Our sorrow was overwhelming.

'Move along now,' the policeman said gently.

'Have all the personal belongings, like suitcases and bags, been collected and kept somewhere safe?'

'Oh yes. We are trying to reunite them with as many owners as we can.' He looked at me keenly. 'Did you have anyone on the trains?'

'Yes. My brother.'

His face crumpled. He must have been about fifty and maybe had a son himself. 'Is he all right?'

'No.'

'I'm sorry.' He meant it.

'He has disappeared.'

'What? That's terrible. What's his name?'

'Gilles.'

'Have you reported it at the police station dealing with the missing persons?'

'Yes. They have no record of him.'

How could I tell him that his colleagues believed Gilles was dying in a hospital bed in Salpêtrière?

'Do you know,' I asked, 'what happened after the crash occurred? I read that the police and ambulances were slow to get here.'

'No, that's the newspapers blowing it up to make us look bad. It's not true.'

'Did local people help?'

'Oh yes, many of them flocked to help. Getting the injured out of the carriages, risking their own safety. They were heroes. Doctors and priests too.'

'Priests?'

'Yes. They came to give the last rites to the poor souls dying.'

'Of course.' I felt an unexpected glimmer of hope. 'Thank you for your help.'

'I wish I could help all the ones killed and injured,' he murmured under his breath.

I touched his arm. For a moment we stood there in the bitter cold, grieving.

Seven churches later, my hope turned into expectation.

I tramped from village to village, hamlet to hamlet, along muddy roads with only ducks and ghostly pale cows for company. Wherever I glimpsed a church spire or a tower I aimed directly for it and as it was a Sunday I was in luck. Most of the priests were hovering somewhere near their altars, doing whatever priests do, when I opened the heavy oak doors. I hadn't been inside a church since I left school where church attendance was as compulsory as eating stale cabbage, and a lot of old memories that I thought I had done with came flooding back.

The first few priests weren't much help.

'Yes, my dear, I did rush over to the terrible crash that tragic night. I think we all did. To offer words of comfort and hold a hand that needed to cling to life.'

I thought of poor wounded Beau lying there in the field in the darkness clinging to Gilles's hand, saying it saved him. Oh Gilles, where are you? But the priest could remember nothing of a man with a white streak in his hair.

Nor the next priest.

Nor the next.

The fourth one scared me. A small compact man with a wide girth that even his soutane couldn't hide.

'It is the hand of the Devil,' he intoned with eyes blazing and both hands raised to the vaulted roof. 'The eternal fight of Good versus Evil. Lucifer walks among us and End Times are nigh.'

I got out of there fast.

My hope was dwindling. Had I come all the way out here for nothing? When I could have been at the hospital with Beau. I missed him. I missed his clever mind and his way of looking at me while I described my meetings with the Delamarches, father and daughter. I wanted him to be here with me. He'd know what questions to ask. Was Gilles somewhere nearby? Or did he take off for the other side of the world? But as I continued my tramping along the lanes, I felt the tug of Gilles's hand on mine, I swear I did.

The fifth priest was 'unavailable'. No reason given.

The sixth church was tiny, with a tiny priest to match. He wanted to be helpful and told me of survivors being borne away in donkey carts or on motorcycles, any form of transport that could carry them to safety.

Were you one of those, Gilles? Spirited away to God-knows-where by some kind-hearted soul? Is that it? But if so, why have you not contacted me? Why am I here in the middle of nowhere struggling to pick up the scent of your trail? Because there must be a scent, I keep telling myself that.

I was chilled to the bone by the time I reached my seventh church and hope was no more than a small fluttering thing in my chest. The priest had a kind face with gigantic eyebrows and took one look at me and my mud-caked shoes, sat me down on a pew and offered me an aperitif to warm me.

He perched beside me, cradling his own glass of something dark and sweet in his hand. 'Now what can our Lord do for you, child?'

'I am searching for my brother.'

'Is he lost?'

So I went through it again. The train. The crash. The silence from him at Christmas. My need to care for him if he's hurt. My hope that someone locally has taken him in and given him shelter.

He smiled, a warm caring smile, and I thought how many million miles away he was from the hawklike priest who used to come to our school to teach catechism with a switch and the back of his hand. I sipped my drink, lowering my gaze to the rich blackberry concoction, so that he wouldn't see the dismay in my eyes when he told me he knew nothing of use.

'What is your name?'

'Camille.'

'Camille, our dear Lord tells us, "Whoever loves his brother abides in the light".'

'Does that mean you can help me?'

'No.'

I sat. Still as stone.

'But,' he added, 'I know someone who can.'

CHAPTER THIRTY-EIGHT

◆ ◆ ◆

GILLES

Blackness is a strange beast. It alters your perception. The basement no longer felt large. It seemed to Gilles that it had shrunk like a shroud around him and his world was reduced to no more than the chair that he was handcuffed on. He could see and feel nothing else.

But darkness had never been a problem for him, always more of a friend than a threat. As a kid he would dodge through alleyways black as pitch fleeing from someone who was trying to knock seven bells out of him for snatching an apple or stealing a pocket-watch. The shadows were his shelter. His protection. What he needed to do now was get himself up the steps before Rosa returned with her twin bullocks.

First he had to detach himself from the chair. It should have been a simple task but proved otherwise. The problem was his injured leg. Each time he attempted to lift his cuffed hands over the backrest as he stood up, the manoeuvre threatened to tip him off his feet, so while still seated on the chair he shuffled it backwards towards a wall. When he could feel it solid behind him, he turned the chair sideways so that his shoulder could lean against its cold surface to steady his balance. In a rush of energy he forced himself upright, twisting to raise his arms over the wooden chair-back. With a clatter the chair skidded to the floor but Gilles stayed on his feet.

He was now free but his hands were behind him. He crouched down with his hands close to the floor and eased them forward so he could step backwards over them, not exactly easy with a bad leg but Gilles worked at it till he managed it. When you are in a fire pit, you face down the flames because you have no option.

With his wrists cuffed together in front of him, he set off into the blackness. Over the next hour, according to the luminous dial on his watch, he established one crucial fact. Rosa Lagarde had had the good sense to remove any object that bore the slightest resemblance to a tool or a weapon before she'd had him thrown down here in the basement. He'd been through every cardboard box, every tea chest but he was out of luck.

Gilles didn't like to hold a losing hand. He was good at conjuring a straight flush out of nowhere,

First. He'd stumbled on to a broom. Literally fallen over it. Not many bristles on it, but he wasn't interested in its sweeping abilities. He flipped it upside down and by doing so, turned it into a very passable crutch. He was now more stable and could venture away from the wall.

Second. One of the tea chests held what felt to his groping fingers like a mix of old paint pots. He tested the weight of each in his hand and selected the heaviest.

Third. He discovered a bicycle dumped on its side under the stairs. He ran his hands over its frame blindly. The rear wheel and saddle were missing, but it was otherwise intact. With painstaking care in the darkness he detached the loose chain.

Four. He raised the paint tin and crashed it down on to the bicycle's spokes. He lost count of how many times but by the end of it he had in his hand a long thin metal spike.

Five. He tore off a flap from one of the cardboard cartons.

He now had a five-card straight flush. He was ready to play.

Hours passed and no spoon arrived with its sticky liquid, no needle came with its nasty little bite. It was obvious that Rosa Lagarde no longer trusted him not to escape now that she knew he was more mobile than she'd realised, hence the basement captivity. Hence the handcuffs. The more he thought about it the more it surprised him that she'd used handcuffs instead of rope to tie him up. What kind of woman has handcuffs lying around the house? Unless for use in the bedroom, like Camille's friend Anne-Marie, but Rosa didn't strike him as the type.

But now it seemed she thought it was time for some rough treatment. Sledgehammers he could deal with as long as he could see straight and stand on his feet without falling over, but as the hours passed and the fire in his leg turned into a roiling furnace, he had his doubts. He sat on the chair wrapped in one of the old blankets he'd found in a cardboard box because his body was shivering. He was tempted to pile on more coverings but he knew he was burning up and needed fluids, so he sat in the total blackness and waited for her to come.

She didn't come.

The door at the top of the steps remained resolutely closed and the pain advanced with unwavering force like one of Napoleon's armies. Unstoppable. Trampling on everything.

Gilles was prepared. If she didn't come to him, he'd have to go to her, but this time he wouldn't be sitting in a chair and he wouldn't be defenceless. Around the knuckles of his right hand the bicycle chain was wound like a bandage, a black metal bandage with teeth.

He felt his way across the basement to the bottom of the wooden stairs, leaning heavily on his makeshift crutch. He dragged himself up step by step and at the top he put his ear to the door and listened. No sound. Just his own pulse pumping. No voices. He had to assume that her fancy hall was empty.

He leaned down to the thin crack of light at the bottom, slid the sheet of cardboard under the door and inserted the bicycle spoke into the lock, his fingertips acting as his eyes. Immediately he felt the key leap out on the other side and heard it land on the cardboard. His heart gave a small jolt of triumph. He'd be out of here with or without Rosa Lagarde's permission. Smoothly and slowly he drew the cardboard towards him back under the door and picked up the key. It was a big old iron one.

He slid it with care into the lock and turned. There was a quiet click. He pushed the door and it swung open. He was free.

'I think not, M. Malroux.'

Rosa Lagarde stood right in front of him, flanked by the dungareed bullocks.

'*Bordel de merde!*' was as far as Gilles got before the twins hurled themselves at him, one coming in low and throwing his massive shoulder into Gilles's groin. The force of it smacked Gilles over backwards and both of them went crashing down the stairs. Gilles twisted his body as he fell, so that he hit the basement's cement floor on top of the slab of muscle that was his attacker. The moment they landed, he slammed his fist with its bicycle-chain bandage into the side of the bullock's head. The man's eyes rolled like marbles up into his head and he was out cold.

The second one came at him.

But it was obvious these men were not fighters. Gilles was still crouched down on the ground and the new attacker assumed he was an easy target. This twin approached too close. Gilles struck upwards and sank the bicycle spike deep into his thigh. With a low grunt the bullock buckled on to the bottom stair where it would have been the work of a moment to finish him off had Gilles chosen to.

'Stop right there!' Rosa Lagarde's voice rang out down the steps.

Gilles looked up. She was standing on the top step, eyes blazing with anger, but whether it was anger at himself or anger at the muscular twins, he didn't know or care. What was causing him concern was the pistol in her hand pointed directly at him.

'If you move a muscle, Malroux, I will put a bullet in your other leg and let you bleed to death.'

Gilles didn't move. But he noted the use of his name. Like he noted the kind of gun she was holding, a Model D semiautomatic pistol, the new police weapon.

'Maurice,' she called to the man hunched on the bottom step, 'get yourself and your useless brother up these stairs and out of my house at once. You incompetent fools.'

The twin ripped the large cotton scarf from his neck, looped it around his thigh and fixed it tight. Then, in a display that indicated how he hauled pigs around, he seized his brother, who was just beginning to stir, under the armpits and dragged him up the stairs. The noise of the effort it took wasn't pleasant.

'Rosa,' Gilles said calmly. 'There's no need for this. Let's talk things through.'

'I'm finished talking with you.' The eye of the gun was still fixed firmly on him.

'Rosa, have you considered whether it is Sarrazin who has double-crossed you. Not Laval.'

It was a shot in the dark. He had nothing to lose now and nothing to gain by playing innocent any more. He needed to raise questions in her mind.

'You and your interfering little sister are finished,' she shouted down at him. 'This door will not open again until you are long dead.'

She seized the key from the lock, stepped back into the hall and slammed the door shut, taking the pool of light with her. *Your interfering little sister.* Oh Camille, what are you doing? He stood there in the darkness, feeling the silence and the pain sink their teeth into him. He was in his tomb.

CHAPTER THIRTY-NINE

◆ ◆ ◆

CAMILLE

The daylight was almost gone and I was riding behind a mule. The animal was shuffling along between the shafts of a battered old two-wheeled cart and clearly wasn't happy about being asked to venture out on the lanes at this hour, exchanging his warm stable for a chill evening on the road. He kept flicking his long ears whenever he heard my voice as if he knew who was responsible.

'Not far now,' my companion assured me – or maybe he was assuring the mule – as he rippled the reins along the animal's back.

The man's name was Pascale and he worked on an arable farm but his passion was chickens. Faverolles, to be exact. I liked a man with a passion. The priest I'd spoken with in the seventh church, the one with the kind face and the eyebrows, had marched me down a lane and along a muddy farm track out to an old stone barn which echoed to the squawking of a large flock of chickens long before we came anywhere near its threshold.

'Pascale,' the priest had bellowed above the noise, 'the Lord has a mission for you.'

Out of the barn had trundled a middle-aged man with a cockerel tucked comfortably under one arm, a wide smile on his freckled face and a belly that was two paces ahead of him.

'What can I do for you, Father?' He touched his cap to me and introduced the chicken. 'This is Louis.'

Louis was a colourful creature, all scarlets and blacks and creams with big fluffy feet. I'd never been comfortable around chickens. Jerky unpredictable things. Its red eyes regarded me as if I might be a welcome addition to its menu but Pascale beamed with besotted pride at the bird. 'The gentlest nature in Christendom,' he declared.

'Pascale, this young lady is looking for her brother who was on the train that crashed.'

The farmworker's face crumpled into lines of distress. 'A terrible night, that were.'

'Father Bastien tells me that you drove an injured man out to a village not too far from here,' I said. 'Is that right?'

'Ah yes, I did that. The young man was in a right state. He needed a doctor's attention.'

'But you didn't take him to one.'

'No, the doctors would be rushing to the trains, so we took him home to his wife.' He gave me a concerned smile. 'Your brother, you say?'

'My brother is missing. I'm hoping the man you helped might be him. Can you recall his name?'

He scratched the cockerel's head instead of his own while he tried to remember. 'Christophe something, I think. Does that help? I could drive you out there if it would help.'

'You are very kind.'

I stroked Louis in return.

By the time we reached the village I had learned more about the breed of Faverolles chickens than I thought it was possible to know. Their dietary preferences. The fact that they have five toes instead of four and are the main producers of eggs for Paris. It seems they are so gentle-natured that they get bullied in a mixed flock. And then there was Josephine, the Faverolles hen that roosted each night on the end of Pascale's bed. I told him how lucky his chickens were to have him look after them so well but he laughed and said, 'Oh no, Mademoiselle, they are the ones who look after me. We all need looking after.'

I didn't argue with that.

The evening was chill but the clouds had cleared and the sky was splashed with a bold flamingo pink on the horizon. It turned the mule's ears the colour of watermelon slices as the little cart rattled along past fields that looked brown and desolate in their winter coats. I wasn't used to such unending space and it unsettled me.

Even the village was eerily quiet except for a dog barking and the rumble of our wheels on the dirt road. Oddly I felt more exposed out here than I did in the busy streets of Paris, and I could feel a hard knot of tension under my ribs as we pulled up outside a house on the far side of the group of dwellings. It was set well back from the road, apart from the others, smarter and more private. Green shutters and a neat gravel path. A metal boot-scraper was set into the ground beside the step up to the large oak front door.

Gilles? Are you here?

I tried to *feel* him here but I wasn't my mother. All I got was an odour of damp plaster and a bitter taste in my mouth. Plus a kick of excitement at the thought that he *could* be here. But I couldn't trust any of them.

I thumped on the door with the knocker, a brass lion's head. I was impressed and I hadn't put a foot over the doorstep yet. I was glad Pascale was at my side because he was so reassuringly decent and honest. I was going to say normal, but I'm not sure a passion for feathered Faverolles counts as normal.

The door opened and a smart dark-haired woman not far off forty eyed me up and down with interest. She barely glanced at Pascale.

I came straight to the point. 'I apologise for disturbing you, but I'm looking for my missing brother, Gilles Malroux, and think he might be here.'

'I'm afraid you are mistaken, Mademoiselle.' She gave a soft, sympathetic smile. 'There's no one here but me.'

She was not the kind of woman I expected to find tucked away in the back of beyond. Too alert, too sharp around the edges despite the charm of the smile. Her sausage-curl hairstyle and shapely woollen dress had a whiff of outdated about them, but both were worn with confidence. I was looking at a woman who knew exactly what she wanted. And what she didn't want. Right now she didn't want me on her doorstep.

'Remember?' Pascale said at my elbow. 'I came over the night of the terrible train crash with Father Matthieu and we brought your husband home to you. He was injured.'

'Of course I remember that. It's not the kind of thing you forget.'

'How is he now?' I asked.

'He's gone.'

'Gone?'

Did she mean dead?

'He left me.'

Her eyes were an unusual silver-grey and their brightness was suddenly obscured by unshed tears. The three of us stood there in the darkening light, uncertain what to say.

'I'm sorry,' I mumbled. 'Do you know where he went?'

'No.'

'Were his injuries serious?'

'They were bad but not what you'd call serious. Mainly a damaged leg.'

'Yet he was able to leave? On his own?'

'He wasn't alone.' She removed a spotlessly white handkerchief from her pocket and dabbed the tears away. 'He had a *friend* who picked him up in a car.'

'Male or female?'

'Female. But I don't see that it's any of your business.'

'If it's your husband, you're right, it's none of my business. But if it's my missing brother, I need to know.'

I flashed a photograph of Gilles in front of her. He was in a fisherman's sweater on a boat on the Seine, laughing at me behind his camera. One of our happy days. I had shown it to Pascale earlier but he said it might be the man he helped or it might not be. It had been dark and the injured man was covered in blood from his head wound, so . . . hard to say.

But this woman didn't even look at it. 'Do you think I wouldn't know my own husband?'

'Of course you would.'

'He's not here.'

The disappointment was a bitter pill to swallow but I had no reason to disbelieve this woman. Why would she lie to me, a total stranger?

Sometimes it is hard to see the truth in another's eyes.

Beau's words came to me from nowhere, the words he said the day he had an unknown female visitor who jangled his nerves. How did he describe her?

Polite. Dark hair. Unusual eyes. Capable. She brought me bonbons.

Unusual eyes.

'May I ask your name?' I said politely to this dark-haired woman with unusual eyes and a manner that hid a steeliness behind the kid gloves.

'I am Mme Lagarde.'

'And your husband?'

'M. Lagarde. Christophe.'

'M. Christophe Lagarde?'

'Correct.'

I felt the tingle then. Like needles pricking the tips of my fingers.

'Mme Lagarde, may I see inside your house?'

'*Mon Dieu!* Why on earth would I allow such a thing?'

The sky was darkening. Pascale and his mule needed to get back to his chickens. Yet still I could not let go.

'My brother is missing and I am worried sick. Please.'

'What? Don't be absurd. Are you going to search every house in the village?'

'I will search until I find him, yes.'

What did she hear in my voice? In an abrupt change the silver eyes smiled kindly, as Mme Lagarde stepped back into the hall and invited, 'Do come inside if it will make you feel better.'

I stepped inside.

Luxurious, that's the only word for it. The furnishings were far grander than I expected. Beautiful cupboards and tables with fancy scrollwork and inlays and carvings. I don't know anything about wood but these pieces glowed from within, as if the years of growing in woodland sunshine were seeping out through the grain.

We didn't linger. We marched swiftly through the rooms while Pascale remained stolidly beside the front door. Rosa Lagarde opened every cupboard and drawer for me with polite courtesy and I couldn't help but stare with respect at her gilt-edged bone-china crockery and her gleaming rows of silver cutlery. Everything matched. Cups and saucers and plates. No cracked bowls or thick chipped enamelware. I tried to imagine myself eating off it, but that would be a different me.

In the hall, before heading up to the next floor, she opened the cupboard under the stairs but nothing struck me as helpful in there. I did take more care in examining a tall dark-brown wardrobe that stood in the hall against the wall. It was the only piece out of place. Inside hung her coats, very nice coats too, a sensible but boring cupboard for them. Unlike her crockery, it didn't match. It was plain. Nothing else in the hall was plain, so it stood out as a piece that didn't fit in. I wondered why she had chosen it to go here. She watched me examine it with a perfectly calm set of her mouth but I was feeling her desire to be rid of me.

Upstairs we moved quickly through the spare bedrooms, the bathroom and then into what was clearly her own bedroom. Classy and modern. Glass and chrome and geometric shapes. For a moment I forgot about my search. I wanted to linger here, to touch things, to smell the perfumes on her curved dressing table, to trail fingers along the gossamer negligée laid out on the bed and run a hand over the bold black-and-white design of her bedcover. But I left the room quickly before I made a fool of myself.

'Satisfied?' she asked as we stood on the landing.

I could have said yes. I could have thanked her and walked away. This woman had been more than accommodating and had put herself out to reassure me.

But I didn't.

'May I just take another look at the green bedroom, please?'

I didn't wait for a yes or a no, but headed back along the corridor to what was clearly one of the guest bedrooms. I opened the door to it once more and stood still, letting my eyes rove over its pale-green furnishings and its pretty pink chair. Something was clawing at my mind but I didn't know what.

'Is something the matter?' Rosa Lagarde asked, her tone less patient.

It was the smell. So faint it was barely there but I knew that smell from my childhood. It used to permeate my mother's room, sweet and spicy, as she lay comatose across her bed and I was always terrified she was dead. It was Gilles who used to clear up her vomit and remove the bottle of laudanum from her bedside.

Laudanum is addictive. Violently addictive. It is concocted from opium combined with alcohol. Opium is so bitter to taste that it is mixed with many things to make it palatable, including honey and all kinds of spices like saffron, bergamot, nutmeg and many more. It was used to ease many ailments, but especially as a painkiller. Just the faint smell of it broke my heart all over again.

How much pain are you in, Gilles? Has this woman been helping you or hindering?

Fear for my brother crawled up into my words.

'Has someone been ill in this room?'

'Yes, I told you, my husband was injured in the crash. I nursed him in here.'

It was plausible.

I turned to her. She was standing in the doorway watching me closely. Could I blame her? No. A crazy stranger comes and demands to search your house for a mythical brother. Of course she'd be wary.

'Thank you,' I said.

'Now leave my house and never come back.'

I took a last look around the room. Gilles and I had guarded each other's backs all our lives. I knew that if he'd been here he'd have been certain I'd be on his trail and he'd have left me a sign. But what? And where?

I walked over to the bed. Its pale-green cover lay undisturbed and its headboard was gleaming with polish. I crouched down on the floor and examined its wooden legs. Right at the bottom I spotted a scratch, one that had been made with something hard, rather than something sharp. I glanced over at the dressing table. Maybe the mark was made by the tip of a hairbrush or a comb. I leaned closer, just as I heard Rosa Lagarde's footsteps approaching behind me. I could make out the scratch more clearly now, its arms, its loop. An ankh.

I leaped to my feet as the woman placed a hand on my shoulder and shook her off.

'You liar,' I screamed in her face. 'You liar.'

I took off for the door, shouting my brother's name. 'Gilles! Gilles! Gilles!' I raced down the stairs. 'Where are you, Gilles?'

I startled Pascale, who was dozing in a chair in the hall, as I came to a stop and looked around me. My eyes were drawn again to that plain wardrobe that had no right to be in this elegant hall and I hurried over to it. Nothing but coats inside, but on the floor at its feet were what looked like recent scuff marks. It had been moved. I seized a corner of it and tried to shift it, but whatever wood it was made of, it was very heavy.

Pascale lurched over to help. 'Should we be doing this?' he muttered but I could see he was enjoying the unexpected adventure.

He gave it one almighty tug and half of it swung away from the wall with a screech across the floor. Behind it lay a door.

'Gilles!' I cried out.

'How dare you?' Rosa Lagarde came striding across the hall and grabbed my arm. 'Get out of my house.'

I yanked myself free and helped Pascale shoulder the wardrobe clear of the hidden door. I tried the knob but it was locked.

'The key?' I demanded.

'Go to hell.' She raised a hand as though to slap me.

'Don't even start that because you'll lose,' I snapped.

It hung in the balance for a split second, then she thought better of it and turned away fast. She scooped up her handbag that lay on a small table and rushed to the front door, extracting what looked like car keys as she went. I let her go.

My only concern was Gilles.

It took Pascale six massive kicks with his hobnail boots against the lock to spring it open. A black pit opened in front of us.

'Gilles!' I bellowed.

A sound. Was it a voice? Or an animal? Impossible to say.

I snatched a candle in its ornate silver candlestick from the dining-room table, lit it with Pascale's lighter and hurried down the steps into a basement.

'Gilles?'

Again the sound. A groan.

I found him. Shivering on the ground, burning up with fever and streaked with blood. A metal spike was gripped in his hand though he was barely conscious. I wrapped my arms around my brother and held him close, rocking him gently back and forth, my tears mingling with his blood.

'Camille,' he whispered through clenched teeth, 'you took your bloody time.'

I laughed and held him tighter. Gilles was alive.

CHAPTER FORTY

◆ ◆ ◆

GILLES

G illes was roused from a nightmare of flames and crashing build-ings by a needle bite in his arm. He lashed out and caught the culprit full in the face.

'Hey, steady on, old chap.'

The voice penetrated the smoke that was blanking out his mind and Gilles blinked himself fully awake. He was in his sister's bed. Her English artist friend Barnaby was leaning over him, rubbing his sore cheek with one hand, a syringe in the other, and a smile of welcome on his face.

'Back in the land of the living, I see,' Barnaby said cheerfully. 'Good. Camille will be pleased.'

'Where is she?'

'She's popped out to the market. Getting you some food, wine, coffee and cigarettes, I gather. She knows you well.'

'She does.' Gilles struggled to sit up with Barnaby's help. 'How is Camille?'

'I've seen her better.'

'How did she manage to find me?'

'You know what she's like. She doesn't let something go when she has her teeth in it.'

'What have you been shooting into my arm?'

'You don't want to know, *mon ami*. I have a contact in one of the hospitals. She is a student doctor and—'

'Tell me no more.' Gilles grimaced. 'Whatever it is, it's helping with the pain. Thank you.'

Barnaby placed the syringe on the tiny table beside the bed. Everything in Camille's room was tiny because of lack of space. He said with typically English nonchalance, 'She's not going to let this go, you know. She can't. She's in too deep. Now she's found you, she should stop, but she says these people you are involved with won't let her just walk away. I worry that it is dangerous but she won't be told.'

Guilt is a dead weight. It can crush you if you let it. Gilles stretched out a hand to Barnaby. 'Get me out of this bed and stick whatever is left in that syringe into me. I'll leave her in peace and deal with these men who are a threat to her.'

'Oh no, Gilles, I don't think you should be . . .'

'What, Barnaby? You want her dead?'

Barnaby didn't hesitate. He picked up the syringe.

CHAPTER FORTY-ONE

◆ ◆ ◆

CAMILLE

'Hello, Christophe.'
I whispered the name in Beau's ear. He was dozing when I arrived at the hospital but at the touch of my breath on his cheek his beautiful honey-coloured eyes slid open and a smile spread like sunshine across his face.

'Shouldn't you be at work, Mlle Fonctionnaire?'

'I did report in this morning but went straight to Mme Beaufort. I told her I needed leave for a couple of days because of a family emergency. She wasn't happy.'

'What kind of emergency?'

'My brother was dying.'

'Did she believe you?'

'I don't know. It was true yesterday, if not today. She wants a doctor's note from me to validate it, but I'm not worrying about that now.'

'So what are you worrying about now?'

'You.'

He reached out and threaded his fingers through a lock of my dark hair as if to stitch us together. 'Why call me Christophe? Are you changing my name yet again?'

I cradled his hand between both of mine. 'Does the name mean anything to you?'

Slowly he shook his head, but I could see that he was aware that something had changed. Not just his name.

His fingers curled tight inside mine. 'Tell me, Camille. Tell me what happened at the crash site yesterday.'

So I told him. All of it. The policeman grieving beside the huge express train that looked like a dead dragon, trekking to the priests and finding kind Pascale among his beloved Faverolles chickens. The next part was hard. I related it flatly. No tremors, no tears. Our approach to the smart house. Our meeting with Mme Rosa Lagarde.

I paused there. Expecting something. Anything. A reaction of some kind, but there was none, just his eyes fixed intently on mine, waiting for me to resume my tale. I described the inside of the house in detail, but still no dawning of remembrance, not even when I told him about the lavish black-and-white bedroom. He passed no comment, gave no sign of recognition. The end I kept short. Our finding Gilles half-dead in the basement and Rosa Lagarde's escape in her car. That was it.

Beau closed his eyes and exhaled heavily, as though he had been holding on to something inside and could now let it go. He opened his eyes.

'It was the woman who came here and gave me the bonbons, wasn't it?'

'I believe so, yes. Silvery eyes and her hair in tight sausage curls. A core of steel deep inside her that she tries to hide.'

A silence came between us, eased its way into the minuscule gaps between our fingers, as solid as if the woman were standing there, tearing them apart.

'Rosa Lagarde,' he whispered.

Neither of us spoke the four words that tolled in our heads.

Rosa Lagarde, *wife of Christophe Lagarde.*

Instead I told him all that had happened to Gilles.

'Had I known it when I stood next to her in her house,' I said, unable to hide my anger, 'I'd have thrown her down the basement stairs.'

It had been hard getting Gilles home. Pascale and his tough little mule had generously taken us to the station in the dark, Pascale urging us in vain to go to the police. He'd even provided a coverall raincoat to hide Gilles's bloodstained clothes and a wooden strut that worked as a makeshift crutch for him. There are a few rare people on this earth who are so kind that they make even me believe in angels. I gave him every last sou I possessed for his chickens, but of more value was the embrace from us both for dear Pascale.

Once in Paris I bundled my semiconscious brother into a taxi from Gare de l'Est all the way over the river to Montparnasse where Anne-Marie coughed up the fare. Another sweet angel. It took us twenty minutes to haul Gilles up to my room on the fourth floor where he slept for twelve hours straight after Barnaby's medical student friend had stuck a needle in him. I sat by the bed all night. Counting the ways I would bring the wrath of Osiris down on that Lagarde woman's head.

I heard a tap-tap-tap on the floor behind me. I saw Beau look up and break into a smile, so that even before I turned I knew exactly who the visitor was.

'Gilles,' I said and carefully hugged my brother, steering clear of the worst injuries. He looked better than yesterday. Almost human again. 'What are you doing here? You should be in bed, resting that leg.'

When the student doctor had re-dressed Gilles's wound, I saw for myself how bad it was and it turned my stomach. The whole leg was infected, discoloured and swollen, with trails spreading out like a crimson spider's web. At the door as she left, the student had muttered, 'It might have to come off, you know.'

'The dressing?'

She looked at me as if I were a simpleton. 'No, the leg.'

I'd gazed in horror at my brother on the bed. His eyes were open and concentrated on her, he'd heard every word. Neither of us mentioned it again.

I acquired a good strong pair of crutches for him from one of Anne-Marie's clients who had no more need of them, and I'd left Gilles asleep when I slipped out to come to the hospital. But I knew that keeping him in bed would be an uphill task.

I stepped aside for Gilles to approach the bed to meet Beau for the first time since the night of the train crash, but Beau held up his hand as a signal to stop.

'Wait,' he said.

Gilles halted, surprised, and we both watched as Beau grabbed a deep breath, gritted his teeth and pulled himself fully upright in the bed. He threw back the covers with a dramatic flourish and slid his legs, clothed in hospital pyjamas, over the edge and on to the floor. I held my breath, but couldn't hold back my grin. With an effort that nearly floored him, he stood up, swayed alarmingly, then got his balance. I stayed exactly where I was despite an overwhelming urge to step forward to steady him.

'I've been practising for this moment,' Beau said. 'I can't greet the man who saved my life lying flat on my back in a hospital bed.' He held out both hands to my brother, a wide-open gesture of gratitude, and Gilles grasped them. 'Thank you, my friend,' Beau said in a voice brimming with emotion.

'Come here,' Gilles responded and, abandoning his crutches, drew Beau to him in an embrace.

The two men stood like that together for a long time.

The thing about Gilles is that he believes he can move mountains. He has always believed that. So once he decides which path to take and there's a mountain in the way, he shoulders that mountain aside. It's why he is so good at achieving whatever he undertakes, whether it's getting a doctor to treat our mother though we had no money to pay him, or driving me to the coast for me to see the sea for the first time though he owned neither a car nor a driving licence. Or infiltrating an illegal network of criminals. He will not be deterred. I have always loved that courage in him.

The drawback is that it's tough to persuade him to change course. That evening we stood in the dark on boulevard Haussmann and I made one last-ditch effort to make my stubborn brother stay safely inside the shelter of the same doorway I'd stood in with Barnaby.

'You can't run,' I pointed out for the tenth time. 'What good are you if you can't run? I don't want you to get caught.'

'I won't get caught.'

'Stay here and keep watch for me. You've told me what to look for.'

'We're in this together, Camille.'

'You're in no fit state.'

'If I fall, I've got you to pick me up,' he laughed softly.

'Always,' I sighed and set off across the road.

The lock of the toyshop had been altered. Le Rêve was now more secure since my previous break-in. No longer a warded lock. A modern tumbler one had been installed but it presented no problem to my tools and skills, though it took a fraction longer to lift the levers and for us to slip inside the toyshop with Gilles manoeuvring on crutches. I drew out my torch but didn't switch it on yet. Too visible from outside.

'Are you sure about this, Gilles?'

He didn't reply, just gave me a look.

We headed through the archway into the rear showroom where the level of darkness deepened and my pulse quickened. Behind me came the tap-tap-tap of the crutches, sounding like a hound dog on my trail. I flicked on my torch for all of ten seconds.

'Here?'

'Yes.' Gilles rested his shoulder against the wall. He didn't look good.

We'd reached the giant floppy teddy bear, the one almost as big as myself and seated on a stool in front of a mirror. Still there. Nothing had changed. The rocking horses and the rows of fluffy toys watched with unblinking eyes as I removed the bear and its stool from their position and knelt down. The mirror was taller than Gilles. With my fingertips I started to examine the bottom of its frame at floor level.

'On the right-hand side,' Gilles reminded me.

As if I needed reminding.

Outside, the headlights of a car passed and we both froze, though we couldn't be seen and the torch was off. When it faded into the distance we breathed again and I continued to search for the small lever Gilles had told me was hidden in the carvings of the frame. I could sense Gilles's impatience with himself that he wasn't able to reach down and trigger the mechanism himself.

'Further along,' he whispered.

I ran my hand nearer to the end of the frame and it caught on a raised section within the carving. I flicked my fingernail under it and pulled.

A click.

'Good work,' Gilles murmured.

The bottom of the mirror had edged a fraction away from the wall. I tucked my finger under it and pulled harder this time and on the right it swung away from the wall like a door. I flashed the torch for a moment and saw a thin plywood screen in front of me. I pushed. It opened to reveal a treasure trove. Was this thundering excitement the same as Howard Carter felt when he looked into the famous tomb that first time?

'It's magical,' I whispered.

'I don't know about magical, but it is certainly fabulous,' Gilles said. 'The stuff of fables.'

Neither of us could keep the sense of awe off our faces. We had stepped inside the hidden room, closing the screen firmly behind us, and only then did we risk the torch on full beam to illuminate the treasures in all their glory. We were surrounded by artefacts of all kinds, thousands of years old, all beautiful, all skilfully made, all mesmerising. I was seated on a square block of blood-red stone carved on all sides with what I knew from Liliane to be hieroglyphics and at the same time I was running my hand over the smooth head of a bronze leopard. I wished Liliane was here to see it all. She would have loved this collection. I knew she would covet them to take under her wing at the Louvre.

There is a difference between seeing objects carefully curated in a museum and seeing them here where they nudged up against our shins and rubbed against our shoulders like living beings. Here they had more power. I could feel it. And I could see in Gilles's eyes that he felt it too.

The room was small, more of a large walk-in cupboard really, and the objects were all neatly arranged.

'Look at those canopic jars,' I said, not able to curb my enthusiasm. I was pointing at four exquisite alabaster jars with lids depicting the sons of Horus. 'Made to preserve their organs for the afterlife.'

They were standing on shelves alongside gorgeously decorated bowls and vases and statuettes of gods and pharaohs all stacked and labelled. On the floor I also spotted a large stone hippopotamus and a magnificent bronze falcon side by side.

'I knew they were stored behind the mirror,' Gilles said, 'but I've never seen inside before. Delamarche is on to a fortune here. The American market is crying out for this.' He lifted one of the labels attached to a strange green figure that looked half-human half-animal. 'Dated 1550 BC, Sekhmet, it says.'

'That's the lioness goddess,' I said. 'Goddess of healing and war.' I smiled at him. 'Appropriate.'

He studied me thoughtfully for a moment. 'You've changed, Camille. How do you know about Ancient Egyptian goddesses and canopic jars.'

I looked around me. 'I've been reading up on it. I can understand Liliane's passion for it. Oh Gilles, the whole culture is fascinating. This hoard of objects should be shipped straight back to Egypt where they belong.'

'Yet you wear the ankh I brought back from Egypt.'

That caught me by surprise. 'You? In Egypt?'

He turned towards the door and swung himself into position to leave. 'Now, Camille, you go to the police.'

The police were surprisingly courteous. Maybe Gilles was right, maybe I am changing. On the outside anyway. I was learning that other people value you as much – or as little – as you value yourself.

'What can I do for you, Mademoiselle?'

'I wish to report a crime.'

'What kind of crime?'

'Stolen ancient artefacts from Egypt.'

The officer didn't laugh. He didn't tell me to stop wasting his valuable time and to go away. I had been dreading walking into the police station because in my mind all police were bad police. Without exception. It was that simple. The voice of experience. But when I walked into this police station at ten o'clock on a windswept night wearing my smartest grey work costume, they listened.

It sounded fanciful even to my own ears.

'I was walking along boulevard Haussmann after window-shopping at Galeries Lafayette, and I heard a door burst open in a shop a bit further down. A man raced off down the road leaving the door wide open and a light still on.'

'Did you investigate?'

'As a good *parisienne*, Officer, I was concerned. So I called out into the shop to see if anyone needed help, but received no answer. I ventured inside. That's where I found a mirrored door hanging open. And a large number of what looked to me like Ancient Egyptian objects inside the room behind it.'

The police officer sat there open-mouthed. I didn't blame him,

'What makes you think they were stolen?'

That was the tricky question. But I came prepared.

'Because there were an awful lot of them, all piled in there together. And,' I added just a touch of Mme Beaufort's scorn to my voice, 'who keeps beautiful Egyptian works of art in a silly toyshop?'

'The name of the shop?'

'Le Rêve.'

'On Haussmann, you say?'

'Yes.' I gave a little nudge. 'You need to be quick. I closed the shop door but anyone could walk in at any time.'

'Thank you, Mlle Malroux. If you remain here, I will speak to my superior.'

There, Minister Augustin Delamarche, owner of Le Rêve. Let's see you get out of that one.

CHAPTER FORTY-TWO

◆ ◆ ◆

GILLES

'What the hell have you been doing to it?'

The student doctor was back. She took one look at his injured leg and exploded because Gilles had undone all her good work.

'You need to be in hospital,' she informed him in an impatient tone, 'or you will do irreparable damage to it and to yourself.'

'Thank you for your concern, but I just need it patched up again and a shot of something to knock the edge off the pain.'

She scowled at him. Scowled at Barnaby across the room for getting her into this. But because she was being well paid by Gilles, she shut her mouth and did as he asked. When she'd left, Barnaby handed Gilles a glass of wine.

'Cat's piss, I'm afraid, but it's all I've got.'

'Thanks. Even cat's piss is better medicine than the muck your doc hands out.' He drank down half the glass. 'I'm worried that Camille is not back from the police station yet.' Gilles swung his legs to the floor and stood but his bad leg buckled.

Barnaby grabbed his shoulder. 'Why didn't you get your leg fixed in hospital before?'

'There's a certain woman I intend to visit when we're back from Marseille to ask that very question.'

'Marseille? When are you travelling there? It's a long way, you know. Are you up to it?'

'Tomorrow.'

'Camille too?'

'Yes.'

'Look, Gilles, I don't know what's going on here but it seems seri-ously dangerous. People are getting hurt. Do you think you should be taking her with you?'

Gilles gave him a grim smile. 'Have you ever tried stopping Camille from doing something she is intent on doing?'

Barnaby refilled Gilles's glass. 'I take your point, *mon ami.*'

'Camille has an essential piece of paper that I need in Marseille and she won't give it up to me until we both arrive there.'

The two men looked at each other and raised their glasses. 'To Camille!' they laughed.

It was gone midnight before Camille burst through the door. Her hair was wind-blown and her limbs heavy and she brought with her the distinct odour of defeat that Gilles could smell at fifty paces. He was so relieved to see her safely home that he took off her coat, kissed her forehead and sat her down on the bed before he asked a single word about what had happened.

'All for nothing,' she groaned.

He felt a dull ache settle behind his eyes. 'Didn't the police believe you?'

'Oh yes, they checked out my story. Like we wanted them to.'

'And?'

She hesitated. The words wouldn't come. He could see clearly in the tautness of her face that the last two days had drained the strength from her, his courageous sister, and he accepted the blame for that. It clambered on his back and stayed there.

'There was nothing there,' she said.

'What do you mean? Nothing where?'

'In the secret storeroom behind the mirror.'

'You mean that all those stolen Egyptian objects were gone?'

'Yes. The storeroom was empty when the police arrived there.' She let her head drop in her hands. 'Delamarche has moved everything. He must have had people watching the place.' She looked up at Gilles, her green eyes glittering with anger. 'He outwitted us.'

Gilles wrapped an arm around her as they sat shoulder to shoulder. 'Tomorrow,' he said, 'we'll travel down to Marseille, go to the port, collect the three crates earmarked for Le Rêve, and take them un-opened to the police as proof that Delamarche is smuggling in illegal artefacts from Egypt along with his toys. It's not over yet. Don't give up hope.'

It sounded easy. But nothing was ever easy.

CHAPTER FORTY-THREE

♦ ♦ ♦

GILLES

The train loomed alongside the platform, panting heavily. It was the 9.03 to Marseille. Smoke billowed grey as storm clouds through the station, the bustling Gare de Lyon, where Le Train Bleu restaurant flaunted its frescoed ceilings and its gilded chandeliers in the faces of the street beggars. The odour of hot engine oil clung to the back of Gilles's nostrils.

Swing, follow through, step.

It was all about the rhythm. Gilles was concentrating hard on walking with the wretched crutches, so that he didn't have to concentrate on the train. But it breathed its sooty specks over his cheeks. It soiled his clean white shirt. It demanded his attention. So Gilles stopped walking and stared at it, a long unforgiving stare. Deep in his gut burned an anger so fierce that he almost vomited it up on the concrete platform under his feet.

'You all right?' Camille was at his side and turned her head to him with concern as he hobbled past the rear luggage van.

'I'm fine.'

She didn't argue, but clearly neither did she believe him. A different doctor had materialised at her door at six o'clock that morning with a whole case full of ointments and potions. 'These will sort you out,' he'd announced and already Gilles was moving easier.

'This train won't crash,' she assured him.

'Sure?'

'I'm sure.'

'Promise me?'

'I promise. I have a secret weapon.'

'What's that?' he asked.

She reached behind her scarf and pulled out the gold ankh on its thong. It shone brightly even in the gloom. 'It will keep us safe.'

He wasn't sure if she was saying it for herself or for him.

The distance from Paris to Marseille is 777 kilometres. The journey would take around ten hours, more if they hit ice on the line. Gilles seated himself by the window again, didn't remove his replacement black fedora, and prepared himself to look out on to a dismal winter's landscape for the next ten hours. Ten hours. Of screams in his head.

It was a journey that would carry them down through the flatlands of the north of France, south-east to the vineyards and the hills of Burgundy before skirting the towering granite cliffs of the Massif Central. On to Lyon. Here the skiing crowd would leap off the train with their gear on their backs and head for Grenoble and the gleaming peaks of the French Alps.

The train would then growl its way down along the cleft that is the Rhône Valley and finally rumble into the hectic port city of Marseille. In Marseille, perched on the Mediterranean coast, the two worlds of Europe and Africa merge in an ever-shifting blend that Gilles found entrancing.

He could feel the vibrations with every turn of the wheels.

CHAPTER FORTY-FOUR

◆ ◆ ◆

CAMILLE

Giles was quiet, too quiet. How many of the passengers who survived the terrifying crash had climbed up the steps on to a train once more, I wondered, and sat trembling in their seat? Judging each jolt and jump of the wheels, the fear rattling around inside them? It would be hard to let go of it. Like the stabbing on the bus. It came with me everywhere I went.

I was acutely aware that beside me Gilles had his head turned away, gazing steadfastly out of the window, only the back of his black coat and hat visible to me and our fellow travellers. But I knew Gilles, so I knew exactly what he was doing. While each town and each kilometre swept past, he was studying the reflection in his window of the inner door to our compartment and of the corridor running behind it.

A corridor train made us more vulnerable than a train with compartments that only opened on to the platform. At any moment the inside door could slide open and anyone could step inside. The compartment wasn't full, only six of us facing each other and trying to avoid eye contact. Opposite me sat a woman smartly dressed, flat brown brogues, a brown felt hat with a narrow brim and hazel hatband, and on her lap a wicker basket that contained a cat. A not very happy cat judging by the unholy yowls issuing from it at intervals. The woman bent her head over the animal and whispered endearments which seemed to calm the creature momentarily, but their little battle of wills went on hour after hour.

I recalled what Beau had told me about the bus, the one on which I had travelled across the bridge with Omar. Visualise the passengers, he'd said. Well, I was visualising my fellow passengers today. A middle-aged couple by the door, both reading books, both wearing glasses. He was holding an unlit pipe between his teeth. Contented faces. Opposite them was a lone young man bundled up in a heavy grey overcoat. Bushy black hair. Dark eyes that I caught looking at me whenever he thought I wouldn't notice. A couple of smiles. A faint blush when I smiled back.

That was it. The conductor popped in, swaying easily with the movement of the train, and we all proffered our tickets to be punched. A few clicks, a few thank-yous and it was done. All reassuringly boring. Yet I wanted to put the flat of my hand on Gilles's chest to see if his heart was beating as hard as mine. Instead I kept watch on the small section of train corridor visible outside our compartment in what I hoped was an unobtrusive manner, with lazy glances as if I had nothing better to do. When anyone walked past, I noted their appearance and watched for a reappearance, but no one roused suspicion.

My mind was turning over the question of why Augustin Delamarche would try to involve me more deeply with his daughter. To watch over her? But it worried me, and I could think of only one explanation. Delamarche realised now that the net was closing in on him and he was planning on making a run for it before the police or his enemies came to break down his door. That's why the secret stash of illegal artefacts in the stockroom had vanished. He intended them to fund his future lifestyle in New York or London no doubt, but I still didn't understand why he had chosen me.

It didn't make sense.

And what would Liliane's reaction be when she finds out that her father was arrested because of me? An aching sadness welled up inside me. For a moment I gazed through the train windows on the far side of the corridor to the rows of black stumps in the vineyards beyond and the image of Omar lying dead on my lap rose unbidden in my mind. I felt something harden within me. His killer must pay.

It was at that moment that everything changed. The train was crossing the swirling river where it loops round at Migennes and a young man in the corridor crossed my line of vision. Tall, long legs, an impression of ungainly movement, and wearing a navy-blue coat with a double row of brass buttons like a sailor's. I'd seen him before. Like a punch in the gut, I felt the air leave my lungs.

'What?' Gilles whispered the word in my ear.

'That man.'

But he was gone.

'What man?' His gaze followed mine to the now empty corridor. 'Describe him.'

We were speaking in low tones. 'Nondescript. Tall. Dark coat. Brass buttons. Last time I saw him he was wearing a balaclava and holding an axe to Anne-Marie's throat. But his eyes are unmistakable. Dark and deep-set.'

My brother was already on his feet and grabbing his crutches.

'Gilles, I remember him now. He was one of the passengers on the bus.'

'The bus with Omar?'

I nodded and gripped his arm. 'Sit down, Gilles. You can't go chasing down the train on crutches.'

I leaped to my feet and in two strides I was out of the compartment.

The difference was this. I could run, my quarry could not.

He could only hobble. Because only a matter of days ago he'd had a knife sticking through his calf. I recalled the terror on Anne-Marie's face, the purple gash across her throat in Barnaby's painting, the scarlet flood spewing out around the dagger in Omar's neck, and fury ripped through me. I raced after him down the narrow swaying train corridor, sweeping aside any passenger who got in my way. I was no longer the polite and biddable *fonctionnaire* of Mme Beaufort's typing pool. No, I was the avenging whore's brat raised among the rats and the flick-knives of Montparnasse.

I spotted him pulling open the door that led to the next train carriage and disappearing from sight. For an injured man, he moved fast, but he didn't glance over his shoulder, so I dared hope he hadn't realised I was coming for him. Had he recognised me in my compartment earlier? Why was he on this train? For the same reason as Gilles and myself, I assumed. To collect the illegal cargo arriving in Marseille.

I grabbed for the door at the end of the corridor but a steward walked through it from the opposite direction carrying a tray bearing a coffee jug and barring my way. I seized the jug and flattened myself against the wall of the carriage to squeeze past. The steward yelled after me, outraged, but too late. I was in the next carriage.

CHAPTER FORTY-FIVE

◆ ◆ ◆

GILLES

G illes stepped into the corridor, cursing the crutches. They were cumbersome and the heavy pads under his armpits still felt awkward. He manoeuvred himself into a stable position, braced against the shuddering of the train, and checked the corridor in both directions. Two men were standing by one of the windows, smoking and talking in loud voices about Hitler taking over power in Germany.

'That's what we need here in France,' one stated. 'A strong leader who will . . .'

Gilles pushed past them. He'd seen Camille head in the direction of the front of the train, tracking down her man. A phantom of her anxious mind? Could be. But Gilles thought not. Camille was not someone prone to imaginings, though he'd noticed a change in her. She carried herself differently, walked with a firmer step and seemed to trust herself more. He was inclined to believe that if this man was real, the danger was also real.

Up ahead he heard a steward shouting, making a fuss about something, and he quickened his pace. Swing, follow through, step. Keep the rhythm going; but the rocking of the train constantly knocked him off balance. At one point his crutch caught a man on the shin and the man responded with a shove that sent Gilles slamming into the wall of the train. Any other time and he would have taught the man in his smug pinstriped suit some manners, but right now he had to reach his sister.

Instinctively he took in the faces inside each compartment as he swung past, seeking out any that might be a threat. Mainly men. Some couples. A few solitary women. All wrapped up against the cold. A smattering of furs and hard wealthy eyes. Most compartments were at least half-occupied and one was full to the gunnels with a rowdy pack of skiers anticipating keen competition up in the snow on the Alps.

But two carriages down, one compartment was surprisingly empty. A man was standing alone in the doorway, as though guarding entry, but his back was turned towards the corridor while he scanned the hilly landscape beyond the outer window of the compartment. Gilles knew the back of that head instantly. It was one of thousands in the file within his mind. Broad and domed, above a bull neck with the tip of a tattoo peeking up from the back of his collar. Indifferent hair that was oiled back.

'Sarrazin.'

The man jerked round to face him and a look of pleasure dawned on his face. It was the bastard Henri Sarrazin, the one Camille called Robespierre.

'What the hell are you doing here, Sarrazin?'

Giles had halted, placing himself between Sarrazin and wherever his sister was now, his crutches blocking the corridor. But he hadn't allowed for the fact that Sarrazin might not be after his sister. The big-chested man burst out of the compartment and started barging like a buffalo back down the way Gilles had just come, towards the rear of the train.

Camille, kill your man. Or keep him talking. Either way, I will come.

Gilles took off after Sarrazin. Swing, follow through, step.

CHAPTER FORTY-SIX

◆ ◆ ◆

CAMILLE

I was gaining on the injured man, step by step. We ploughed through more carriages and the pleasure it gave me to see him limping and in obvious pain was immense. He plunged onward, aware of me now. Scared of me, I liked to think. He knew what I was capable of.

And I knew what he was capable of.

I drew closer, five metres, four metres behind him. Closer. Three metres. I could hear the smothered grunt of pain each time his right foot hit the ground. Passengers saw us coming and flattened themselves against the side wall.

'Stop that at once!' a man in a military uniform shouted after us.

We ignored him and entered another carriage. Less busy but nearer the engine and a window was open, allowing black specks of soot to dart through the air, stinging our eyes, soiling our nostrils. I blinked to rid myself of them and in that half-second the limping man was gone. I pulled up short. He couldn't be gone. We were on a dirty rattling train, not on boulevard Haussmann where you could duck down into a Métro station or vanish into the crowds in Galeries Lafayette. You can't disappear on a train.

Unless you jump off.

I was about to run on to the end of the carriage to check the outer door, but I noticed that one of the compartments further along had its privacy blinds pulled down. The inside was blanked off. Without hesitation I stepped forward, slid its door wide open and came face to face with the young man who had broken into my room at night to kill me.

He was staring at the knife in my hand.

'Welcome,' he said unpleasantly and pointed his gun at me.

I hurled the coffee jug at him and the hot liquid spewed in his face.

To look into the eyes of a person and see that he intends to kill you is a soul-shaking moment. My life balanced on the tip of a bullet.

A thousand things careered through my mind, crashing into each other, and a thousand emotions cracked my heart wide open. I wanted to shout: Wait, wait, let me say goodbye to Gilles first, to enfold Beau's hand in mine for one last time, to embrace Barnaby and Anne-Marie and to breathe in the air that stinks of Paris streets, not of juddering steam locomotives, and to read one final Victor Hugo book that I know I should have finished by now and drink one final bottle of Simone's finest red. Wait, wait: I need time so badly to become the person I want to be.

I long to tell Beau I love him. But the realisation has come too late.

My leg started to tremble.

'Sit,' he shouted.

I stepped into the compartment and sat down on the first seat. All the others were empty. My quarry was standing, dripping coffee on to the floor. I laid the knife, a serrated skinning blade, across my knees and looked up at him. I knew a hundred like him. He was the kind of male I had grown up with on the streets, sharp-eyed, angry, their nerves so raw that if you touch them they will rip your arm off. Acne faces and greedy fingers. Young men who have nothing and want everything. This one was all legs and cheekbones and eyes that hated me.

'Leg hurting?' I asked.

'Bitch.'

He took out a handkerchief and scrubbed at his face, keeping the gun levelled on me.

'I take that as a yes then.'

'Take it how you like, *putain*. Toss your knife on the floor.'

I didn't move a muscle. 'Come and get it yourself.'

Despite drying himself with the handkerchief, he was sweating. I saw a sheen above his top lip and I wondered why. Was he in so much pain from the knife wound in his calf? Or from the dousing in coffee? No, he would have grown up with pain and beatings as daily companions. No, not that. I was guessing that this was the first time he was about to kill a woman. The attempt in my bedroom had ended in failure, but this time he knew there was nothing standing in his way.

A gun. Against a knife.

The outcome was not in doubt.

CHAPTER FORTY-SEVEN

♦ ♦ ♦

GILLES

Sarrazin was fast, compact and coordinated. He ran like a runner. Gilles was cumbersome and slow. He set his sights firmly on the man's broad back but drifted further and further behind, as passengers sidestepped him in the tight confines of the corridor. His leg had improved slightly with whatever the doctor had slathered over it this morning, but racing down a train's shaking corridor wasn't exactly helping.

Navigating the short interconnecting gangways between carriages was a devil. The steel plates bucked underfoot and kicked like a mule, nearly upending him, while all the time he was acutely aware that Camille could be needing him. But she had her knife. She had her speed. The question was, did she have the nerve? The first was always the hardest.

At the far end of the carriage ahead of him Sarrazin had come to an abrupt halt. He'd reached the end of the train with only the rear luggage van remaining and he opened its door. It should have been locked, so either Sarrazin had unlocked it in advance or he had paid someone to do it for him. No guard in sight. Conveniently absent.

Gilles drew breath and jerked the crutches into motion, all rhythm lost as he bounced off the wall of the speeding train. He saw Sarrazin turn, pause and stare down the corridor directly at him. The bastard smiled, an I-dare-you-to-come-and-get-me smile. Then he vanished into the *fourgon à bagages*.

Start saying your prayers, Sarrazin.

Gilles entered the luggage van and kicked the door closed behind him. The first thing that hit him was the smell, a strong pungent animal smell. The lighting was dim but he could see well enough that the van was piled high with hefty luggage trunks and wooden crates of God knows what. Off to one side stood a bicycle, on the other side a crate of chickens. Right in front of him sat Sarrazin on a pink Lloyd Loom blanket box, looking for all the world as if he was about to crack open a bottle of something to welcome Gilles inside. Except there was a gun in his fist.

'Where are they, Sarrazin?' Gilles spoke first.

'Where are what?'

'All the ancient objects amassed from Egypt?'

'That's exactly why I got you here. To talk about that. I have questions I want answers to. Your wretched interfering sister has been a pain in the arse for us and now we want rid of her before she—'

A low-throated snarl ripped through the van, making Gilles's skin crawl.

'*Merde!* What the hell is that?'

Sarrazin grimaced. 'It's Delamarche's leopard.'

'What?'

'Crazy rich son of a bitch. He sent for the beast from Cairo as a fancy toy for his birthday to show off like that dancing *putain* Josephine Baker does, flaunting her cheetah Chiquita in the streets of Paris. But he's shipping it back. It mauled one of its keepers, too fucking dangerous. Like your whore sister.'

'Sarrazin, I will slice out your tongue for that when the time comes.'

'Not before I blast yours through the back of your head.' He raised the muzzle of the gun to aim at Gilles's head.

Another long nerve-scraping rumble came from the back of the van where the shadows lay thickest and Gilles could make out the shape of a large cage with a tarpaulin draped over it.

'What I want from you first before I pull this trigger, Malroux, is the key that was hidden in the statue.'

'I don't have it.'

'So where the hell is it?'

At that moment the train lurched. It took a curve with too much speed, setting the van rattling and rocking on the rails. Gilles reacted fast. He faked a stumble and half-dropped his right crutch. He bent, seized the lower end of the crutch as though rescuing it from the floor and before Sarrazin could straighten himself on his seat, Gilles swung the crutch with all his strength in a vicious wide arc. Before the seated man could even think of raising his gun again, the solid wood underarm-end of the crutch slammed into Sarrazin's temple like a mallet.

He dropped off the blanket box like a log.

CHAPTER FORTY-EIGHT

◆ ◆ ◆

CAMILLE

The gun had a silencer. Silencers are a device invented to kill cattle more quietly. Was that all I was to this dangerous young man? A piece of raw meat to dispose of? *Phut.* Gone. But how to dispose of a body on a train? It would be a hard job to chuck the dead-weight of a person out of a train window, even one as skinny as me.

My eyes were fixed on his, dark deep-set slits. That's where I'll see it, the moment when he decides to pull the trigger. It was all planned, of course it was, the walking past the compartment where I was sitting with Gilles, knowing one of us would give chase. Knowing it had to be me because of the crutches, luring me straight into this trap. Now all the bastard had to do was pull the trigger and jump off the train at the next stop, Auxerre, which was coming up in just a few minutes. He'd probably stretch me out on the seat as if I were fast asleep. Dead tired. It could be hours before I'd be found.

'Do you work for Delamarche or Sarrazin?' I asked mildly.

I was struggling to keep my limbs under control. I didn't want him to see me shaking, but at the base of my throat a pulse was jumping like a firecracker.

'What's it to you who I work for?'

'I want to know before I die who to come back to haunt.'

'Shut your mouth, *putain.*' He waved his gun closer to my face. 'You won't be haunting nobody. You'll be burning in hell.'

'I'm not the murderer who stabbed my companion on the bus. You are.'

'That's because the Egyptian was making a shitload of trouble for them.'

'I hope they're paying you more than enough to make it worth your while to burn in hell for eternity.'

He was getting twitchy, plucking at his brass buttons and shifting from one foot to the other, but the muzzle of the gun remained steady as a rock.

'Fuck off. You and that murdering brother of yours are about to join him.'

Gilles? Where are you?

I couldn't stop my head turning towards the door. Gilles would have followed me, even if he'd had to crawl. My captor saw the movement and laughed, a shrill squeal of enjoyment.

'Don't you bother looking for your brother, you stupid whore. M. Sarrazin will have him screaming for mercy by now.' Again that piercing laugh.

Something broke inside me. I felt it, like the snap of an artery. Sorrow and anger tore through me and it took every scrap of willpower to prevent myself leaping at him and ramming my blade down his lanky throat.

'You're lying,' I whispered.

His squeal became a screech.

'Sarrazin knows that your brother was passing on information about our network. He wants to know names. He's going to cut your brother's fucking balls off.'

I flew at him.

CHAPTER FORTY-NINE

◆ ◆ ◆

GILLES

T he moment Gilles flicked back the tarpaulin, the animal hurled itself at the bars. A wild scalding hiss and a flash of fangs made Gilles step back smartly. The force of the attack shook the whole cage. A metal mesh ran around outside the bars which prevented any claws from sneaking through to rake Gilles's flesh, but the force of the leopard's rage was like a hammer blow. Enough to strike terror in the heart of any who approached.

Gilles examined the animal. He'd never seen one this close. The fur and muscles beneath were rippling with beauty and power and its amber eyes burned with a copper sheen of fury. How could anyone think to cage such a glorious creature? For a split second he imagined himself in a cage. In a prison cell. His fury would tear the walls down.

Around the animal's neck lay a heavy metal chain, the end of which was threaded through a special iron fixing at the rear of the cage. It meant the leopard could be pulled to the back of it if necessary, presumably for feeding or injecting with sedative. Attached to the top of the cage was a leather strap with a label tied to it. *Cleopatra*, it read, and an address in Cairo.

'Well, Cleo,' Gilles purred, 'you and I have work to do.'

When Sarrazin crawled his way back to consciousness, Gilles was seated on the blanket box, now located just outside the cage, his crutches propped against it. He was smoking a cigarette and held the end of a chain in his other hand.

'Now,' Gilles said calmly, 'let's talk.'

Sarrazin started to scream.

'Hush now,' Gilles said in the same calm voice, 'you're annoying her.'

At one end of the cage the chain was pulled so tight and wound so securely around one of the metal poles that formed the structure of the van that the leopard's head was wedged hard against the cage's metal bars. If it had been fierce before, it was now a frenzied killing machine. Only the noise of the train's clang of metal on metal, the rumble of its engines and the screech of its huge wheels as they rattled their way through France covered the anguished howls of the animal.

Inside the other end of the cage, only ten centimetres beyond hell's reach, lay Sarrazin.

CHAPTER FIFTY

◆ ◆ ◆

CAMILLE

My quarry was quick but not quick enough. Sometimes there is only the width of an eyelash between life and death. My knife slashed down. He would have died. The blade would have opened up the artery in his neck, he would have bled out on my skirt the way Omar did. Had he not blinked.

When Gilles and I were children he used to teach me how to watch for that vital moment just before the attack came. Not *when* the attack came. But *before* the attack came. That's what could save your life. I learned to look for the small tells that shouted loud and clear 'I am coming for you'. The widening of the eyes to expand the range of vision, the dilation of the pupils to draw in more light, the muscle in the jaw tightening as the decision is made, a fist bunching, a wider stance from which to launch an attack, one foot forward and one foot back like a boxer. And always the eyes focusing for a split second on where on your body they intend to inflict pain.

'Keep watching their eyes.'

Just when my quarry should have been focusing his eyes on the violence and where to aim the bullet, he blinked. I don't know why. To blank me out of his sight? Maybe. Or perhaps because he could pull a trigger more easily on a girl if he wasn't looking at her. Who knows? But suddenly, with that blink, he seemed so young. Seventeen? Eighteen at most. But the blink of his dark eyes, the glimpse of his pale greasy eyelids, caught me off guard and knocked off my aim.

My blade struck his shoulder bone instead of into the soft flesh of his neck. He screamed and pulled the trigger. Far too late.

The bullet tore into the sleeve of my coat and slammed into the wall behind. It took no more than a scoop of skin off my forearm with it, but even with the silencer, the gunshot sounded loud in the confined space. It would be being reported as we stood there.

He panicked. Cornered with no escape, bleeding and enraged. This was the second time I'd stuck a knife in him and he'd failed to kill me, but he had just enough sense not to risk a second shot which would bring the guard running. He did what all cornered animals do, he bolted.

Out the door with a curse and a '*Va au diable!*' for me. But I stood frozen there, my eyes fixed on the knife in my hand, waves of shock pulsing through me. Runnels of scarlet were slithering down the serrated blade and dripping on to my shoe but I couldn't move it away. I almost killed a man.

I almost killed a man.

The shock of it drove deep into my mind.

Who was I? What kind of person lived under my neat blouses and woollen winter skirts? Had I learned nothing from all the books I'd read, from seeing Liliane's grace and kindness, from holding Beau's hand hour after hour and feeling the goodness of his heart leak into mine? Was I still the child in the schoolyard who broke a boy's finger because he pointed it at me and jeered?

Gilles. What have I become?

With a jolt, I came back to life, dragged in a huge breath and raced after the young killer.

I found him. He was at the end of the carriage by the entry steps and was repeatedly wiping the blood from his shoulder that ran down on his hand on to his sailor jacket. More to the point, he had opened the carriage door and the icy ground outside was hurtling past at a frightening speed with nothing but billows of smoke between us and it.

He backed away from the opening the moment he saw me.

'You took your time,' he sneered.

The wind whipped at our clothes and hair and snatched away his words, as the racket of the iron wheels roared through the small space. I was expecting to find the gun still in his hand, but it wasn't anywhere to be seen and it dawned on me what he was planning. This time no bullet. No knife. No murder inquiry or manhunt. This time it would be a young woman's suicide because of losing her brother and changing her job. Unsound mind. Cut and dried.

'Time for you to jump,' he hissed at me and let out one of his screeching laughs.

I still had my knife. The cramped spot where we were standing at the top of the steps allowed little room for movement; we were no more than a couple of metres apart, and he was closer to the gaping hole where the door should be than I was, so I couldn't see how he intended to manage it. I kept my eyes fixed on his. He flattened himself against the side wall and spat down on to the iron plate at my feet.

'You won't be needing that knife where you're going.' He grinned and his eyes flicked to something over my shoulder.

I started to turn, fear gripping my throat. I was fast, but not fast enough. A hand thrust against the centre of my back and sent me flying through the open door.

CHAPTER FIFTY-ONE

◆ ◆ ◆

GILLES

'Right. Now that we understand each other, let's have some answers.'

Gilles wanted this over quickly. He needed to locate Camille. She was well able to get herself out of trouble, but this wasn't just trouble, this was a cliff edge.

'Let me out of here,' sobbed Sarrazin, crouched on his knees inside the cage.

'Answers first.'

The snarls of the frightened leopard were savage as it lashed out towards Sarrazin with massive paws. Its claws, mottled and brutally sharp, raked the bottom of the cage only a hand's width away from human flesh, great curved scimitars creating a rasping sound that stilled the heart in terror. A wild predator changes things, even the air you breathe. It smells of death. The creature was still clamped by its neck-chain to the rear bars but it didn't for a second abandon its fight to reach the prey trapped within its cage.

Sarrazin grew smaller with each snarl. He sank deeper into himself. His broad chest seemed to collapse into an ever-narrower space and his body flattened.

'So where were the Egyptian objects shifted to? The ones that were in your secret stockroom.'

'I don't know, I swear.'

Gilles exhaled his annoyance. 'Let's establish the ground rules here. Every time I think you are lying to me, I will loosen the leopard's chain by one link. Those lethal claws will—'

'No, Malroux, no!' the man screamed. 'Let me out and I will tell you everything.'

'No, I prefer it this way. So I'm asking you once more, where are the illegal Egyptian objects now?'

'I tell you I don't know.' His hands were clinging to the bars, knuckles bone-white. 'It's the truth,' he screamed as Gilles hobbled over to where the chain was wound around the pole and he wriggled it looser.

The leopard sensed the fractional easing of its bonds and uttered a blood-chilling growl as it threw itself forward yet again but still came up short. The choke on its throat made it cough, a harsh rasp that set Sarrazin shaking uncontrollably.

'Where?' Gilles demanded.

'Everything was crated and packed into a van.'

'On whose orders?'

'Delamarche's.'

'Where did the van go?'

'I wasn't told. A secret hideout somewhere in Paris. But I have no idea where. It's the truth.' His voice was rising.

'Who was driving?'

'Delamarche.'

'What kind of van?'

'One with the toyshop's name on it, Le Rêve.'

'Where did it go?'

'I told you.' He was shaking so badly his teeth were stumbling over his words. 'I don't know. I'd tell you if I did.'

Gilles stood silent. The sound of the train's great wheels grinding under them relentlessly merged with the animal's wild hissing and Sarrazin's sobs. Gilles unwound the chain by one more link.

'Nooooo,' his captive screamed as the leopard came at him again.

'Try harder,' Gilles said coldly.

Sarrazin's cheek was pressed in desperation against the outer mesh as if he could squeeze out of there in a thousand tiny pieces. 'Somewhere in the Louvre.'

'Inside the museum?' Hidden in plain sight. He hadn't expected that.

Gilles slid another link through. This time the lethal talons reached to only a finger's width from Sarrazin's coat collar. His scream was hoarse, and Gilles could tell that parts of him were breaking but this time he didn't change his story.

The Louvre Museum. Was it true?

'Sarrazin, tell me this. Did you give the order to kill my sister? In her room at night? And now again here on the train?'

'No, I . . .'

'One more link is all it will take.' He reached for the chain.

'It was Delamarche,' Sarrazin screamed. 'Delamarche made me. Ordered me to get young Manuche to do it. The kid had done work for us before.'

'Killing work?'

The captive tried to nod but his head was trembling too much.

'But she tells me that you personally threatened to cut off her hand if she didn't find the ankh that was hidden in the statue. Isn't that so, Sarrazin?'

'No, no, no, no, I didn't. She's lying.'

'I warned you.'

'Malroux, listen to me, listen. We can work together, you and I.' Clinging to the bars. Tears on his cheeks. 'We'll split, fifty-fifty. No, sixty-forty, you get the sixty. We can—'

'Sarrazin, I do not work with a murdering piece of scum who tries to kill my sister.'

Gilles unwound the chain from the pole and headed out of the baggage van. He closed the door on the screams.

CHAPTER FIFTY-TWO

♦ ♦ ♦

CAMILLE

The killer's hand seized mine. When you are falling out of a train with nothing but cold air to hold on to, you take what you can get. He yanked me back towards the open doorway of the train as the ice-hard ground roared past beneath me.

My feet fought wildly to find purchase on the solid metal of the carriage steps. Noise and wind and fear robbed me of all sense, everything blurred. Harsh fingers were scrabbling at my neck and my mind was questioning why my attacker was trying to throttle me when he had just saved my life.

'Bitch!' he yelled in my face. I tasted his spittle.

Awareness came back with a jolt. I was standing on the tiny platform above the steps where the door hung wide open and was crashing back and forth. His hand on my throat had me jammed up against the wall while his other hand was trying to yank the thong from around my neck, nearly ripping my head off.

'What?' I screamed at him.

'I'm having that ankh, *putain.*'

That's why he'd grabbed my hand. Not to save me. To steal the ankh which he must have seen flap loose as I'd started to fall. I looked down. No knife in my hand now, probably out on the rail track back there somewhere, but he released his hold on me and I saw a small blade in his grip heading for my neck. My fist shot out. My knuckles slammed into his windpipe. He jerked back with a cry but I was too close to him for the blow to have real force.

His knife sliced through the thong and instantly I became redundant. It flashed into my mind to wonder who had pushed me off the train the first time, but it was obvious that this time the young killer would be doing the pushing at the point of his gun, which had replaced the knife. I crashed a vicious kick on to his kneecap, but again I was too close. He stumbled and rammed his gun against the side of my head.

'Jump,' he hissed in my ear.

'If I jump, I'm taking you with me to hell, you bastard.'

Two strong hands suddenly grasped my attacker from behind by the shoulders, hoisted him off his feet and hurled him out through the open doorway. His scream stopped abruptly.

In front of me stood Gilles.

CHAPTER FIFTY-THREE

◆ ◆ ◆

GILLES

G illes and Camille stepped off the train only minutes later at Auxerre. They watched it steam out of the station, then bought tickets for the next one bound for Marseille. They stood side by side on the station platform in silence, more crows drifting overhead like undertakers looking for their next client.

Gilles took off his scarf and wrapped it around his sister's neck. Partly because the wind was bitter on exposed flesh and partly because her throat was seeping a trickle of blood where the skin had been torn by the thong. He looked at her hands and scrubbed them with his handkerchief to rid them of the scarlet stains, then he removed his leather gloves and tucked her hands into them. Her face was calm, her gaze steady; no other passengers would have seen cause for alarm, but Gilles saw it. The tumult deep inside her and the small smear of blood on her teeth where she had bitten the inside of her lip.

'It had to be done, Camille,' he murmured. From his pocket he drew the gold ankh that he'd scooped off the floor of the train, and slid it unobtrusively into hers. '*It will keep us safe*, you told me, you and your secret weapon. You were right.'

'Thank you, Gilles,' she said quietly. 'Thank you for saving my life.'

'You saved mine in that basement.'

They continued to stand on the cold platform, shoulder to shoulder, drawing warmth from each other.

CHAPTER FIFTY-FOUR

◆ ◆ ◆

GILLES

Marseille was a different world from Paris. Both were large cities and both were major ports but the air in Marseille tasted of warm spices and smelled of the spices of Maghreb. The Mediterranean breathed on its narrow streets and terracotta roofs day and night, and the busy commerce of ships and trade were its lifeblood.

Men with swarthy skin sat around sipping mint tea in thimble-sized glasses and the smell of Arab cooking and Turkish coffee wafted on the soft breezes. Marseille sat at the mouth of the Rhône and was the gateway into France from Africa, the first step into a greener world. It linked the French North African colonies of Algeria, Morocco and Tunisia to France itself and the mix of cultures opened up a wealth of uncharted opportunities. Gilles felt the usual kick of heat and scent of adventure the moment he stepped off the train.

It was dark. Late evening. The Customs Office would be long closed for the day. At his side Camille was silent. He hauled himself and his crutches down the monstrous flight of stone steps that led from the station into the city and at a cripplingly slow pace trekked through the laundry-strewn alleyways to a bar he knew.

'Gilles, *mon ami. Ça va?*'

'*Oui, ça va.*'

A man with a big gut and a grin to match threw his arms around Gilles, planted a kiss on each cheek and sat him on the best chair in the bar. It was the bar-owner's own seat, upholstered in purple velvet and endowed with armrests. Then he pulled up a wooden stool and gently positioned Gilles's injured leg on it.

'What you been doing to yourself, my friend?'

'I fell over the cat,' Gilles replied.

'You don't look so good.'

'Whereas you, Timéo, look like you've found yourself a new woman to keep your bed warm.'

Timéo bellowed with laughter. Others in the bar joined in. It was that kind of warm-hearted place and Gilles felt some of the knots in his muscles loosen.

'This is my sister, Camille.'

Timéo swept her up in a bear hug, seated her alongside Gilles and before either of them had even shed their coats two glasses of rich red wine had materialised on their table. These were swiftly followed by a full bottles and a couple of plates of tagine and rice.

'Thank you, Timéo.' Camille smiled. She looked exhausted but tucked in readily to the wine and aromatic stew.

Gilles had no appetite. He'd had enough of today and he wanted to take a hacksaw to his leg.

'You got a couple of beds going spare for tonight, Timéo?'

'*Bien sûr*. My bed is your bed. And Mlle Camille shall have the best bed in the house.'

'Thank you. But first you and I have some business to discuss.'

Timéo showed his teeth in readiness, but paused and stared pointedly at Camille. She took the hint, downed a last mouthful of stew, scooped up the bottle and stood up.

'Show me to my room,' she said.

'The bill of lading, please?' Gilles held out his hand. Without the duplicate bill of lading she'd created for the imported crates, things could get tricky.

She dug into her bag and handed it over. 'Don't get yourself knifed in one of those alleys tonight,' she murmured and trailed after Timéo.

Gilles drank his glass of excellent wine, closed his eyes and thought about Rosa Lagarde.

By day Marseille revealed how impressive a port it was, bustling with energy and echoing to the sound of abundant activity and traffic and languages. Gilles stuck a needle in his leg. Something he'd obtained last night. God knows what was in it but it was quick to act. He managed to get down the narrow stairs without help.

He and Camille headed down to the port under a sky so blue and so taut it looked as if might snap. Not the Old Port flanked by its two large forts, the Saint-Nicolas and the Saint-Jean, but the newer and larger Port de la Joliette. It took him five hours to get to see the right people and to negotiate the right fees. Some were greedier than others, but when he waved the bill of lading that Camille had conjured up under the nose of a customs officer, the price went down. Camille was a silent presence, hour after hour. She watched and listened and learned. When necessary she would produce a good-quality cognac from her shoulder bag, place it on an appropriate desk and give a smile that was as good as a handshake.

Deals were done. Arrangements made. Times agreed. Crates transferred.

'We've earned a drink,' Gilles announced and his sister didn't argue.

So by mid-afternoon Gilles hobbled past the market, where women in colourful dresses sold almonds from Morocco and watermelons from Egypt, to a sheltered table out of the sunshine and ordered them both a pastis. They gazed up at the dramatic Notre-Dame de la Garde basilica that overlooked the city from its vantage point high up on a nearby hill.

'Gilles,' Camille said – she had barely stitched two words together all day – 'when we get back to Paris, we are turning the crates over to the police, aren't we?'

'Instead of me running off with them into the wide blue yonder, you mean?'

'Yes.'

He shook his head. He studied her tense pale face and the purple bruises on her neck, not completely hidden by the scarf. She'd been through too much. He knew that. Far too much. He and she didn't often voice their affection for each other, it was something that was left as understood between them, but right now he felt a great wave of love for his sister.

'No, Camille, don't worry, I'll not run off with what should by right be returned to Egypt. I intend it to be the means of putting Delamarche in jail.'

She regarded him solemnly. 'Why this passionate hatred of Delamarche? Besides the fact he ordered his people to kill both you and me, I mean.'

He finished off his pastis and smiled at her. 'You don't think that's enough?'

Slowly she returned his smile. 'There's something else, isn't there?'

Giles felt the old familiar anger stir into life. He looked away from her, up at the basilica's bell tower with its statue of Madonna and child. An image of pure love. But not all mothers love their children.

'Camille, you remember the john who used to come and beat you in the cellar before he'd have sex with Maman?'

It was as though he'd slapped her. She jerked back on her chair. It was something they never discussed.

'That man,' Gilles continued, 'wore a suit. A smart expensive suit. He was a government minister who enjoyed slumming it with whores, and when I hear about Delamarche I see him as that man, even if he's not him. All those men in government who treat ordinary people as subhuman and expendable. Like they did in the war. Cannon fodder. I want Delamarche to pay for all those people, as well as for trying to kill us.'

Camille pushed her chair back and came to him with arms open and wrapped them around him. So tight he could feel the energy rising in her, suddenly hot and intense.

'Let's get on that train to Paris,' she said in his ear, 'and show him that if you take on one Malroux, you take on both.'

CHAPTER FIFTY-FIVE

◆ ◆ ◆

CAMILLE

The overnight train pulled into Paris's Gare de Lyon station. The sky was shifting into the soft pre-dawn greyness that blurred the city's edges and the pigeons abandoned the station's extravagant clock tower to search the platforms for last night's leftovers. I jumped off the train and ran to the baggage van at the rear.

All through the night I'd checked on the van every single time the train rolled to a halt. At each scheduled station, while the engine stood there puffing black smoke at me on the deserted platforms, I watched what went into that baggage van and what came out of it and sighed with relief when our crates remained blithely undisturbed at the back.

Gilles clambered off the train and swung his crutches into action. He went in search of the vehicle he'd arranged to meet our train. It was there, ready and waiting on the forecourt of the station, a dark-green Citroën C4 van with a side-mount spare wheel and plenty of raw power in its six-cylinder engine. Gilles always came prepared.

I was relieved. I felt safer here in Paris, less exposed. And Beau was here. Fear does strange things to you. It makes your senses more alert but it also expands time. Everything seemed to take so long. The unloading of the valuable crates. The porters. The trolley. The loading into the C4. The slowness. It all seemed to stretch. When the rear doors finally closed on their cargo, I jumped behind the wheel and we eased past the flower-seller, down the hill on to boulevard Diderot in the direction of the river.

Gilles had taught me to drive as soon as I was old enough. 'An essential life skill' he'd called it. But I'd had little need of it. Paris had more public transport than anyone could need in a lifetime of living here, but without fail every couple of months Gilles would roll up in a car and get me to drive him around Paris for the day. I'd never seen the point. Until now. He was unable to drive because of his leg.

'I'll take the river route across town,' I informed Gilles.

The traffic was heavy, the usual rush to work each morning; the city was on the move. I was headed in the direction of Austerlitz when Gilles said suddenly, 'Take a right here.'

I turned right, no arguing. I heard something in his voice. I glanced in my rear-view mirror.

'Right again,' he said two blocks later.

I turned right into a smaller emptier street and in my mirror I watched a grey van turn with me, hanging back as though in no hurry. I put my foot down. After a pause in which I thought I might be mistaken, so did the grey van.

My heart lurched and I made an instant decision to make a run for it across avenue Daumesnil.

'I'm making for the maze of narrower streets in the Bastille district,' I said.

Gilles nodded. He said nothing. He was trusting me.

'Up there,' I told him, 'I can lose the van.'

I was wrong.

The van was an ordinary Renault KZ but it stuck to my tail like glue, despite our extra power. I dodged in and out of side roads, I shot around sudden corners and ducked down any alleyway that looked like a wide-enough escape route. The amount of traffic didn't help; it boxed me in and slowed me down.

At one point the van had forced its way past the two cars behind me, so that its tall sloping radiator was hanging right over my rear bumper.

Delamarche's men weren't giving up. Without hesitation I braked, threw my van into reverse and slammed it into the Renault. There was a screech of metal. I saw Gilles grinning. I didn't hang around. I fought my way through streams of cars in the vast place de la République with its beloved nine-metre bronze statue of Marianne, and raced north and westward into Montmartre and Pigalle.

'You treat this van like a motorbike,' Gilles laughed.

I slowed its pace as we rolled down the hill past the Moulin Rouge with its gaudy saucy posters. 'Gilles, I was thinking overnight on the train that you obviously can't enter a police station with me to hand over the smuggled goods in the crates. You'd be arrested.'

He grimaced. 'It's true. I'm sorry, Camille. I don't like to put you through it alone.'

'I am worried that they won't believe my story, even though the crates are still sealed by Customs.'

Gilles tilted his head and studied me. He smiled. 'What's your plan?'

'I would have more chance of being believed if I had a respected expert with me who could vouch for the value and authenticity of the smuggled Egyptian artefacts.'

As I dropped down through the streets of Pigalle district I could feel his stare.

'You mean Liliane? Delamarche's daughter?'

'Yes.'

He gasped, astonished. 'You think she would do that? Incriminate her own father?'

'I want her to be there. I want her there when the crates are opened, Gilles, so that she will see with her own eyes what her father is doing.'

He turned the idea over in his mind for what felt like an eternity, but I knew he was considering all options and outcomes. It was what he did.

'It could work,' he said at last.

I turned my head to nod agreement with him, to say I was sure she would still be at home today, taking time off after the street attack. My eyes were off the road for one half-second but that was all it took. The grey Renault hurtled out of a side road and rammed into the side of our van at speed, smashing us up over the kerb and against a wall.

The noise was deafening. We were stunned. Bruised and shaken but not injured. I watched in disbelief as I saw the Renault back up fast into the side road and gun the engine to come at us again to finish us off.

'Go!' Gilles yelled.

But I held us there, such a tempting target. They couldn't resist. They charged forward once more and only at the last second did I throw our battered Citroën into first which sent it leaping forward in a mighty kangaroo hop as the engine power surged. The Renault crashed straight into the wall. As I drove away, in my rear-view mirror I saw steam pouring out of the Renault van's broken radiator.

The door to the apartment on the top floor was beautiful, its surface alive with honeyed sunlight. But it was an illusion. The light came from a spotlight placed skilfully above it and it occurred to me that Dr Liliane Delamarche was good at bringing out the best in things, new or old.

'Ready?' Gilles murmured at my side. 'This won't be easy.'

I rang the doorbell. The door opened and Liliane stood there on the threshold in a stylish royal-blue wool dress. Her mouth dropped open at the sight of me.

'Camille, I thought you were dead,' she gasped and drew me to her. 'Come in, come in and let me tell you how grateful I am for the way you looked after me the other night. Are you going to introduce me to your friend?'

'Why did you think I was dead?'

Her cheeks flushed a soft pink and she shook her head with a wry smile. 'Take no notice. It's just me being foolish.'

'How?'

'Forget it. It's nothing.'

She drew me into the elegant reception hall once again and I had the unsettling impression that her Ancient Egyptian statues were listening to our conversation.

'Foolish in what way?' I persisted. 'Why would you think I was dead?'

'You'll laugh.'

'I assure you I won't.'

She gave a long sad sigh. 'All right, last night I dreamed that you were dead. I saw you with Anubis. He had come for you and was leading you away, holding your hand. It felt so real.'

'Who is Anubis?'

'The Egyptian jackal god, often depicted with the body of a man and the head of a black jackal with a long snout. Anubis is the god of death. He's the one who guides souls to the afterlife.'

'You saw him holding my hand?' I felt cold, as an icy finger nudged the back of my neck.

'Yes. And then . . .' She paused, unwilling to describe what she had seen.

'Go on.'

'Then Anubis was weighing your heart against a feather.'

It was so intense, this talk of death and of jackals. As though they were in the room, stalking us, leading us away from our accustomed paths.

'Was my heart heavy on the scales?'

Liliane broke free of the grip of the gods with a shake of her head and she laughed her easy laugh. 'I don't know, I woke up. But let's leave all that. And talking of leaving, I have left my manners behind.' She smiled at Gilles engagingly. 'Please do introduce your friend.'

Gilles held out a hand. 'I am Camille's brother.'

Her eyes widened, examining him with interest. 'The missing brother.' She shook his hand firmly. 'Missing no longer, it seems.'

'No.'

She moved towards one of the doors off the hall. 'Shall we go into the study, it's cosier?' She led us past the closed door of her drawing room where her father's birthday party had been held and into her study with all her books. She was right, it was much cosier but I recalled with a shudder the leopard that had been in the room beyond. Telling Liliane the reason for my visit was not going to be easy when I had to go into the details of her father's involvement. She seated herself behind her desk and we sat facing her, the way I had the first time I met her, but now her expression grew solemn and she took her time looking from me to Gilles and back again. It felt like being stripped naked, her gaze sharper and more probing than before.

'What is it I can do for you, Camille?'

'I need your help.'

'Tell me how.'

But before I could say anything, Gilles leaned forward on the desk and asked in a low voice, 'Are we alone here?'

'Yes, don't worry. We have total privacy.'

But Gilles didn't sit back in his chair. He remained upright and alert.

'Go on, Camille,' Liliane prompted. 'Tell me why you have come here.'

'It's a long story. In recent days we learned that stolen artefacts from Egypt were being smuggled into Marseille. They've been hidden inside crates alongside imports to a shop in Paris.' I avoided naming the shop at this point. 'Gilles and I travelled down there two days ago and we have returned with three crates still unopened. Sealed by Customs. We want the police to open them and to hold the owner of the shop responsible. So the Egyptian objects can then either go to the Louvre or back to Egypt. People have been murdered by this network, Liliane. It is extremely dangerous. They are probably the ones who attacked you in the street, and Gilles and I were almost killed on the train.'

I'd expected an outburst of anger from Liliane in response, some level of rage at the criminals, but she sat very still.

'It makes sense,' she said quietly, 'for the artefacts to be returned.'

'I'm here because I need you to give authority to the importance of these Ancient Egyptian artefacts that are being smuggled in illegally. As you represent the Louvre Museum, your word would have influence. So I'm asking if you'll accompany me, please, Liliane?'

I had yet to mention her father's role in all of this.

She rose to her feet and paced back and forth behind her desk, considering what I had said and what I had asked of her. I glanced at Gilles and found him staring fixedly at the door at the back of the room. Had he heard something?

Liliane stopped pacing, her energy suddenly focused. 'Of course I'll help you, Camille. It's an abomination.'

An abomination. I liked that. A perfect word for it.

'You're good at finding things, aren't you, Camille. First the ankh, then your brother, now these crates containing smuggled goods.' She smiled at me. 'I congratulate you.'

Something wasn't right, I could sense it, but what exactly? Did she guess what I was about to say next about who owned the shop?

'She's good at finding the truth too,' Gilles said.

Liliane looked at him and nodded. 'Sometimes the truth hurts.'

So she knew.

Gilles rose to his feet and leaning heavily on his crutches he swung over to stand near the far door to what I thought of as the leopard room and he leaned casually against the wall, as if to stretch his leg. Yet he looked anything but relaxed.

'Liliane,' I said, 'I want to talk to you about your father.'

'Papa?'

'Yes.'

Immediately she sat again at her desk. 'What about him?'

'I'm sorry to tell you he owns the shop that is smuggling these artefacts into France illegally. It's Le Rêve.'

Gilles and I both watched her. We saw a shudder ripple right through her body like an aftershock and her head collapse into her hands. 'No,' she whispered. 'Papa would never do such a thing.'

The odd thing was that it was as if her mention of her father had the power to conjure him up from whatever black pit he was filling with dead bodies. We heard the front door of the apartment open and close with a solid bang and heavy footsteps cross the hall to the study door. It swung open with a flourish and Minister Augustin Delamarche filled the doorway.

'Papa,' Liliane said in obvious distress, 'I wasn't expecting you today.' She hurried over to him and kissed both cheeks.

He ran a hand along her arm in a gesture of concern. 'What's the problem, *chérie?*'

'*They* are the problem.'

She was standing side by side with her tall father, both staring at us.

'*They* are the problem,' she repeated.

'No, Liliane,' I said firmly. 'Your father is the problem.'

'How is that?' he demanded.

His daughter looked up him and let some of her anger seep out. 'They are accusing you of illegally importing artefacts from Egypt into Le Rêve. Tell them they're wrong.'

'Of course the fools are wrong.' His fist thumped his own chest. 'I've never done anything illegal in my life. If you start spreading these malicious lies, I will have you in court before you can say guillotine.'

Gilles moved forward on his crutches, away from the wall. 'My sister and I were attacked on the train to Marseille by two men; one was your employee Sarrazin.' He took a step closer. 'Both said they were ordered to do so by you, Delamarche.'

'They were lying turds,' Delamarche exploded.

It came to me then with awful clarity. It was in the way his daughter looked at her father, the flicker of pity not quite able to cover the faintest gleam of triumph. We had the wrong Delamarche.

I stood up and faced her. 'Liliane, it was you, wasn't it? All the time it was you importing artefacts and hiding them in your father's shop, no doubt paying Sarrazin well to keep his mouth shut.' My lungs suddenly tightened, stopping my breath, as the full significance of what that meant hit me. 'You were the one who gave the orders to kill us. To murder Omar. To attack me in my bed at night.' I gasped. 'You probably set up the attack on yourself too to fool me.'

She didn't deny it. Not any of it. I wanted her to shout 'No!' To reject the accusation. I wanted so much to be wrong.

'Don't be ridiculous, girl,' Augustin Delamarche roared at me. 'You are delusional.'

He stared at his daughter. 'Tell them, Liliane. Tell them they are wrong and that we will go to the police immediately about this to have them had up for slander. Tell them that . . .' His words faded. As did the colour in his face. 'Tell them, Liliane.' His face was aghast. He seized her arm and shook her. 'For God's sake, tell them.'

'Papa,' she said gently to him, 'I think you should leave now.'

He looked as if she'd just put a gun to his head.

She was going to kill Gilles and then me. We all knew it. I felt a sickening wave of sadness at the thought of not seeing Beau again, and I looked across at Gilles. He nodded. Even injured, my brother could take down the father and I was more than a match for the daughter. The question was, where was her gun?

I took two steps towards her. 'Liliane, listen to me. There is no need for this. Maybe Omar's death cannot be traced to you, but there are a number of people who know of my connection with you recently.' Another step. 'Police will come asking questions and—'

The door at the back of the room burst open and I realised that was what Gilles had been waiting for all this time. He'd heard something and positioned himself. He seized the person who charged into the room and clamped his arm around the throat from behind. A shriek ripped through the study.

It was Rosa Lagarde and in her hand was a gun.

CHAPTER FIFTY-SIX

◆ ◆ ◆

GILLES

The woman's neck was like a bird's under Gilles's arm. One more squeeze of his muscle and it would snap.

'Put down the gun.'

She should have shot him, there and then. She should have put a bullet into any part of him she could reach if she'd had any sense, but she was too terrified to think straight and did as she was told. She threw the gun on to a nearby chair. Instantly he released her and picked up the gun.

'You bastard,' she screamed and poured out a stream of curses on him.

'Rosa!' Augustin Delamarche shouted. 'What the hell are you doing here?'

'This woman was in on it all with your daughter,' Gilles informed him. 'You know her?'

'She is my aunt on my mother's side,' Liliane answered and darted forward to her. 'Are you all right, Rosa?'

'No. I meant to shoot that oaf.'

'Dear God,' Augustin Delamarche moaned, 'what have you two women done?'

'Oh Papa, I've been collecting objects of breathtaking beauty from Egypt. Objects far too beautiful to lie in a museum's vaults gathering dust, never to be seen. I love them with a passion.'

Her father looked aghast. 'You've been stealing works of art? No, Liliane, no, tell me it's not true. I always knew you were obsessive about Egyptian treasures, but I never thought you'd take it this far. It will ruin my career, you realise that, don't you? How could you do such a thing when . . .?' Suddenly he gasped and his eyes grew sharp. 'Are you selling them? Is that it? Making a fortune for yourself?'

'Papa, you always think of money,' Liliane scolded. 'I only sell the ones I no longer have room for. Yes, it brings in money for me to buy more.' She smiled at the thought. 'Rosa was helping me.'

'I'd been taking information from my husband's reports.' Rosa Lagarde gave a bitter laugh. 'He's an undercover government security agent who was tracking the network of smugglers. Ironic, isn't it? He thought he was working against them when all the time he was unknowingly helping them because I was passing on information about the investigation from his files.'

Gilles saw Camille flinch. Something snapped in her. She pushed past Augustin Delamarche. 'I'm calling the police,' she declared and reached for the door.

Liliane threw herself at Camille, seizing her wrist, but Camille wrenched it free with a quick twist. Gilles watched it play out, ready to intervene, and in that brief second of inattention Rosa Lagarde made a bid for the gun in his hand. She barged him with her shoulder to knock him off his crutches and was unexpectedly strong as they wrestled for the weapon, before crashing together to the floor.

The gun discharged. Gilles felt blood hit his face.

CHAPTER FIFTY-SEVEN

◆ ◆ ◆

CAMILLE

By the time the police arrived, Gilles was gone. No one tried to stop him. He kissed my cheek as he passed me at the door and this time letting him go was harder because I didn't know if he would be coming back. I gave the chief officer the keys to the van parked outside with the four crates inside and I watched Augustin Delamarche break down in tears as his daughter was led away in handcuffs to the police car. Rosa Lagarde's body was removed to the morgue and it fell to me to inform Beau of his wife's death.

The weight of sorrow for everything caused by one woman's insane greed for Egypt's historical beauty was lodged forever within me, yet when I entered the hospital ward and for the first time saw Beau sitting in the chair in his striped hospital robe, hair brushed and a smile of welcome on his face at the sight of me, I felt the healing power of love. I'd tied a scarf to hide the bruising on my neck but I couldn't hide the shock on my face or the horror of discovering that Liliane was the ruthless person she was under all that finery.

I pulled up a spare chair beside Beau and let him hold me in his arms, while I told him the full story. Including the fatal accident with the gun and his wife, Rosa Lagarde.

'Camille,' he murmured softly against my hair, 'how can I grieve for someone I don't know? I feel sorry for this woman because you tell me she was my wife, so she must have meant something to me, but I feel more sorry for Gilles, who has to be on the run now to stay out of prison.'

'He always told me that if things go wrong, he will take ship to Canada and make a new start. They speak French over there.'

'You'll miss him.'

'Yes.'

I'd miss him like I'd miss a limb, but I had already decided that I would save up. I'd sail across the ocean to visit my brother in a wide-open new country where they have bears and moose roaming loose. Just the thought made me smile, at a time when I thought all smiles were dead inside me.

'While we were waiting for the police to arrive, Liliane led us to a locked room behind a sliding partition wall in her apartment,' I told Beau. 'It was packed with so much beauty, just like she said. It's where she stored all the Egyptian artefacts she'd brought over, plus the ones she had stolen from the vaults of the Louvre. Statues and pharaohs' heads and exquisite brightly coloured jewellery. You should have seen her eyes, Beau, they glowed with happiness.'

He stroked my hand. He didn't mention the terrible sorrow with which others had paid for that happiness.

'I have something to tell you too.' He tweaked my chin towards him, then leaned forward and kissed it. 'I've remembered what happened to the brown suitcase that I was following on the train.'

'That's wonderful, Beau.' I tucked an arm through his and drew closer. 'But Gilles told me that Laval's suitcase contained nothing but bricks, it seems.'

'That was my doing, I'm afraid. The memory of it came back to me in bits today, piece by piece, and slowly I've fitted them together. I followed Laval from his house that morning and saw him take the heavy case to the left-luggage lockers at Gare de l'Est early in the morning. He went to work as usual at the Louvre and was obviously going to make a run for it in the evening with the case. So I opened his locker at the station. Illegal, I know,' he admitted. Beau was so relieved to have found another memory and I was pleased for him. 'I emptied its contents into another case that I put into the next locker, and I replaced them with bricks in the brown case.' He chafed my knee. 'You'll have to get the police on to it.'

'For someone who has avoided the police like the plague all my life, I'm spending an awful lot of time in their company these days.'

He didn't laugh. I'd expected him to laugh. Instead he said in a voice that wrapped itself around my heart, 'You're changing, Camille. You're not who you were.'

I laid my hand in his. He was feeling stronger each day now. We both had a long way to go, but we'd walk it side by side. There was still so much for us both to learn about each other and about ourselves, but we would take it step by step together.

I learned something new about myself that night after I arrived home. I learned that I don't clean under my bed often enough. There was a note under my door when I walked in from Gilles. Delivered by a guttersnipe kid, Anne-Marie told me.

Nothing can be done, except little by little.

That was it, the message. No time. No place. But I knew.

The words were Gilles's favourite quotation from the work of the poet Baudelaire and there was a bar we used to hang out in on the corner of rue de Plaisance called Le Baudelaire. That's where he'd be waiting for me.

I was in such a hurry to turn around and head back out on to the streets that I dropped my glove. A thick woolly one that I wouldn't want to leave without, so I ducked down to pick it up and happened to glance under my bed while I was down there in the shadows. I frowned. There was something there. I pulled it out and sat back on my heels to examine the object. It was a small piece of wood about the size of a paperback book. I'd never seen it before.

I stood up and took it over to the window for better light. The wood was dark with a tight grain and looked very old. There was no indication as to what it might be. Just a lump of wood. But more to the point, how did it get under my bed?

The longer I examined it, the more I became convinced it was part of one of the shipments from Egypt. Had someone slipped it under my bed at some point to incriminate me in the smuggling? Maybe when they emptied the secret storeroom at the toyshop and I was at the police station. I suspected so. I used the old magnifying glass to study it in greater detail and almost immediately I found one solitary hole in it. A misshapen tiny hole at one end. I studied it for several minutes, then more on a whim than expectation of success, I unhooked the thong around my neck, the one that held the gold ankh.

I inserted the lower end of the ankh into the hole and it fitted perfectly. I turned it. A mechanism clicked inside and the bottom of the piece of wood separated from the body of it. The inside was hollow. It was a secret box. I was ridiculously excited to think that maybe no human had opened this box for two thousand years. My mind couldn't take it in. I slipped the top off and inside lay a folded piece of linen, aged to the colour of oak. I was growing hotter just thinking about it. Clearly whoever put it here in my room had no idea what it was.

With great care I lifted the linen out of the shallow box and un-wound it delicately. I gasped. A necklace lay in front of me, so dazzlingly beautiful it was hard to believe this wasn't one of Gilles's drug-induced dreams. A necklace fit for Cleopatra. Exquisite emeralds and fiery diamonds shimmered on a strip of gold. I ran my finger over them respectfully and sat on my bed for half an hour gazing at it on my lap. There are moments that can change your life, and I recognised this as one of them.

I pulled on my green coat and woollen gloves, eased the box and its contents into my pocket and set off for the Baudelaire bar. As I walked under chilly blue Parisian skies I contemplated my options. I could take it to the Louvre. I could hand it over to the police. I could take it to the Egyptian Embassy. Or I could let it live in my pocket for a while.

I'll go to meet Gilles and I'll talk to him about his new start in Canada. A new start costs money. I patted my shabby pocket. It's not what's on the outside that's important, it's what's hiding on the inside that counts.

Nothing can be done, except little by little.

ACKNOWLEDGEMENTS

◆ ◆ ◆

Paris is the City of Light. A beautiful city that draws me to it again and again, and brings me joy the moment I step off Eurostar in the Gare du Nord and smell the coffee. I cannot keep away from the Musée d'Orsay with its fabulous Impressionist art or the compelling Egyptian Antiquities in the Louvre. So to research this book was a pleasure and a privilege.

My first attempt to explore the *quartiers* of Paris that I didn't know already was doomed to failure. I arrived full of expectation but within twenty-four hours I was struck down by Covid, so only managed in that brief time to scurry around the edgy multicultural district of Belleville. Up on its hill, it is a fascinating amalgam of old and new with striking Street Art and a wonderful street market that scents the air with its exotic spices.

My second attempt to explore parts of Paris for my book was more successful. My twin sister accompanied me and we had a blast, roaming around the lively Montparnasse *quartier* and ending up inside a French police station - but that's a story for another time!

It takes a large team to bring a book into the world in hard copy, digital and audio formats, so I am grateful to many people for their input throughout that process.

I want to say a passionate thank you to my editor Jo Dickinson for her support, encouragement and insight into the heart of the book. I value her every word. And my grateful thanks go to the whole fantastic team at Hodder for turning this story into an actual hold-in-your-hand book with a beautiful cover. My thanks to you all. Especially to the eagle-eye of Jake Carr for his tight copyedit and for making me laugh through a time of sporting thrills and spills.

I am eternally grateful to my agent Teresa Chris for her unswerving belief in me and my book. She is my champion and my guide. Thank you, Teresa, for being you.

My thanks also to my twin sister Carole Furnivall for all the fun and laughter we had in Paris and for trekking miles with me as we explored the city's streets and gazed at its wonders. Unforgettable.

There are many dear people who have encouraged me along the way. I particularly want to express my gratitude to my son Edward Sharam for our late night discussions on creativity, to Brixham Writers Group for their relentless supplies of encouragement, laughter and cake, and to author David Gilman for letting me moan when the days are dark and the words elusive.

Also my thanks to Marie Laval for her generous assistance in my research into the French Civil Service. It was a tough workplace for women in 1933.

Above all I thank Norman with all my heart for his irrepressible belief in my books and for his enthusiasm for my writing. It means the world. As always he is a fund of clever ideas to get me out of sticky corners that I've written myself into. We are about to visit Paris again to say a huge thank you to it.

My gratitude also goes to the brilliant reviewers, bloggers and shops who help *The Crash* spread its wings. And to you, my readers, I will be forever grateful and give each one of you a virtual hug.

Salut!